DEAD REMNANTS

ARMARNA FORBES

Sun Disc Publishing

The author would like to thank the following sensitivity readers:

Fatima Masud Franklin
Nathan Gervais
Adam Coles
Hilary Butterfly Woman

Your combined contributions for those scenes where the author had no personal experience is greatly appreciated.

The author would also like to thank Helen Bleck for her superb editorial expertise.

First published 2019
001
Copyright © 2019 by Armarna Forbes

A CIP catalogue record for this title is available from the British Library.

ISBN 978 1 9161736 1 3

Sun Disc Publishing

To my husband, Chris

CONTENTS

The question, O me! so sad, recurring—What good amid these, O me, O life?

Answer.
That you are here—that life exists and identity,
That the powerful play goes on, and you may contribute a verse.

— Walt Whitman
"O Me! O Life!" — *Leaves of Grass* (1892)

PART ONE:
DENIAL

1

PEOPLE IN HATS CAN'T BE TRUSTED

It's just your imagination.
It's just your imagination.
It's just your imagination.

Ashen Deming gulped down her dread and glanced behind her. Nope; not her imagination. In the last seat of the bus, some guy—some creepy guy—leered at her. It was clear he hadn't showered in weeks. Black and gray tangles sprouted from his scalp. His pallid tinge coupled with his paper-white lips reminded her of an old, mangled mannequin.

She took a deep, even breath. At least she wasn't riding alone.

An elbow nudged her side. "Earth to Ashen?"

"Huh?"

"I said, 'What do you think of them?'" Her best friend, Jacob, pointed at her neck. From a pair of dangling headphones, Bon Jovi blared about giving love a bad name.

"Rad, aren't they?"

"I guess they're not awful."

Jacob's features clouded. "Ungrateful. Last time I share my tapes with you."

"Dude!"

"Kidding, kidding. But you gotta listen to my new favorite song." With a cocky grin, he snatched the Walkman from her. "I'll drag you into the modern era even if it kills me."

Guitar riffs filtered from the headphones as Jacob messed with the fast-forward button, each belted ballad interrupted by a screech whenever the cassette started, stopped, then started again. Ashen wiggled her leg up and down, jostling the plastic container on her lap. Through the perforated clear lid she could see her box turtle poke his head out from the shredded newspaper covering him. He looked up at her and blinked.

"Sorry, Langhorne." She clasped her knee to quell her nervousness, but the act did nothing to ease the queasy sensation in her stomach. "Didn't make you motion sick, did I?"

Blink.

"Good. Not too much longer, okay? Twenty minutes, tops."

Her turtle's low-key response made her smile. She hated making him travel like this. Her options, however, were limited. Although the kids at the Children's Home loved Langhorne and could certainly use a pet to brighten their days, Ashen hadn't been able to convince herself to abandon him there. He had become her unwitting security blanket, and ever since that cowboy hat-wearing shadow had attacked her when she was little, she could use all the calming she could get.

"Jacob, I uh," she shivered at the memory before clearing her throat. "I didn't get to say thanks earlier. For coming to get me. And Langhorne."

"Of course! Couldn't make you two wait till the weekend to get out of that place. Must've been terrible."

"It wasn't so bad. Better than living with Mom, mostly. Just…" She shrugged. "Sad. The Home is all those kids have."

"Yeah, I guess. Too bad my parents couldn't pick you up, though. Would've been a lot faster." He crinkled his nose. "Less grody smelling, too."

"Honestly, I'm just glad they're gonna foster me for the last few months of senior year. You know, before I have to go get a job and become a legitimate adult. It'll be nice to get back to some kind of normal."

"Boring, you mean?" Jacob laughed. "Anyway, you deserve a little more normal in your life, Ash."

She smoothed the mess of tight, chestnut coils piled on top of her head as she studied Jacob, her emotions alternating between annoyance and fondness. Jacob was a good guy. Though only an inch or two taller than she was, what he lacked in height, he made up for with a handsome face and athletic build. He was responsible. He was dependable. And after her mother's abused liver had finally given out more than a year ago, when Ashen's father hadn't bothered to save her from becoming a ward of the Children's Home, Jacob had done the one thing no one else had managed. Been there for her.

Other than Langhorne, he was the closest thing to family that she had left.

A thin smile played on Ashen's lips as she shifted her focus to the dingy bus window. Beyond the passing traffic, she could make out the distant Denver skyline—skyscrapers silhouetted against the frosted foothills.

Movement flickered on the glass. Superimposed over the passing outside world, the distorted reflection of the strange man stared back.

Ashen let out a weak groan. Reflections. Mirrors. She hated them. Almost as much as cowboys and shadows.

Coldness crept over her. She swiveled around to put her back to the bus window, positioning Langhorne's case on her lap before poking the toes of her Converse sneakers into Jacob's thigh. Her friend shot her a disapproving look, but she ignored him to peer over the back of the seat.

The stranger's cratered skin rippled. Underneath his waxy face, his bones rearranged as if his flesh were being stretched over a skull-shaped conveyor belt. A fraction of a second later, his features shifted, and he was normal again.

A deafening throb filled Ashen's ears. She forced herself to turn away. With all of her stupid phobias, she was always prone to getting worked up. Always. At the Home, at school; yet every day, the memory of that night haunted her. The way the shadow thing had toyed with her. Its snapping fangs. Its determination to snuff out her life without a second thought. No matter how hard Ashen tried to cram those thoughts deep down, she couldn't forget. Now, it felt as though she feared everything.

"Jacob?"

"Hmm?" Blissfully unaware, Jacob placed his Walkman on top of her duffel bag. "What's happen'en?"

Her attention lingered on the bag holding her possessions, including her limited collection of paranormal magazines and books, all packed and ready for her new life. Over the years, Jacob and his parents had gone above and beyond—taking her in, feeding her when her mother was at her worst. But what Ashen had just witnessed was on the cusp of crazy. No one would believe her. Most normal folks weren't too keen to side with anything resembling insanity, let alone allow those people to live with them.

"Never mind," she said with a huff. "It's nothing."

Ashen searched for any sign that the bus driver had noticed, but the man remained in an unconcerned, almost trance-like state—his concentration solely on the road in front of him.

Maybe another passenger saw it? With renewed hope, she scanned the rest of the bus. That morning wasn't busy. Two other commuters sat near the middle, but neither looked as though they were headed to an office.

Or a class.

Or any normal job, for that matter.

An elderly woman in a fringed buckskin dress stared through the window at the city. Beautiful beads adorned her chest. Her gray hair, parted down the middle, had been separated into two braids, one of which she twisted between frail fingers.

The other was a young blond man who wore military fatigues of an older style—like something that belonged to a war veteran. Below his rolled-up sleeve, tattoos circled his forearms, the dark ink stark against his fair skin. Ashen squinted at the unclear pattern and the man lifted his head as if he felt her gaze. She blushed. The man smiled.

"Making friends?" Jacob asked. His voice held a slight edge.

"Uh, no." Her face grew hot even though the rest of her was freezing. She indicated to the passengers with her eyes. "Is there some costume party thing today or something?"

"I don't think so," Jacob said. He scowled at the guy in fatigues, then looked to the woman in the leather dress. "Huh. You're right. That's kinda weird."

First, the strange, staring man. Then these people looking like they were stuck in a time warp. All seemed to be visual harbingers of something horrible to come. Ashen was certain of it. She could no longer pretend the signs weren't there. Music continued to play from the headphones, but the thuds of her own heart threatened to drown it out.

"This isn't right," Ashen breathed. "There's a guy behind us—"

"Ah! This is the song!"

"Dammit, Jacob! Listen!" She seized his arm and yanked him closer. "We need to get off this bus. Now."

"What? Why? How're we gonna get home?"

"We'll catch the next one."

She tugged the pull-cord and shoved her friend toward the aisle, all the while keeping a wary eye on the stranger. Jacob frowned at the man, shook his head, and stooped to pick up his Walkman and Ashen's duffel bag as the bus decelerated to pull over at the next stop. The accordion doors opened with a hiss.

"Go, go, go," Ashen urged, pushing her friend ahead.

"Okay, okay! I'm going!"

As they shuffled toward the exit, a booted footstep reverberated in the hollows of the bus. Through the open door, an odd Stetson hat with a large dome appeared, its wide brim low, shading a man whose jaw was patched with neglected stubble. His dark brown duster coat, marred and stained from long use, flowed behind him. Like the rest of the people on the bus that day, his outfit didn't seem to be a costume.

Ashen froze. The air turned to lead. From the headphone speakers, Bon Jovi warbled about being a wanted cowboy. Dead or alive.

"Whoa!" Jacob brimmed with adolescent joy. "Is it me, or

did this guy stroll out of a black-and-white movie?"

Ashen didn't blink. She didn't move. She couldn't. But inside, she seethed. A song about something she couldn't stand was one thing, but this? Mirrors and cowboys might not give Jacob nightmares, but he knew, very well, that they triggered the anxiety that crippled her. She'd spent the past five years paranoid of lurking shadows. Stalking her. Hunting her.

"Oh dang, Ash! Sorry. Forgot." He gave her shoulder a reassuring squeeze. "Do you still want to get off here?"

She shook her head. The cowboy blocked their escape route. There was no way Ashen was getting anywhere near him.

Jacob led her back to their original seat. "He's only a guy in a hat, you know. I'm sure he's harmless."

"Yeah. Harmless."

He laughed. "I get it, Ash. Like, I can't even look at a mirror anymore without getting spooked. But hey, you know, we were only kids. Our imaginations were all in overdrive. Especially on Halloween."

"Sure." Ashen muttered. "Just our imaginations."

"You know, for someone who seems brave, the things that scare you are kinda, well, ordinary. Mirrors. Cowboys. Sad that we can never watch a Western together."

Nerves spent, Ashen could only manage an angry glower.

"I mean," Jacob stammered. "Assuming you ever wanted to hang out. More. Than we do. Now, err, currently."

"Cowboys are lame," Ashen shuddered. "Creepy giant hats freak me out."

In the last seat, the motionless man finally moved. With each step the cowboy took down the aisle, the man responded by grumbling and sinking further and further until only the crown of his head showed over the seat he cowered behind.

A grin flashed through the cowboy's thick mustache. He sat three seats ahead, leaned into the aisle, and ogled the stranger in the final row. The weird man glared back before descending even more.

"Miss." The cowboy tipped his hat to Ashen, then Jacob. "Mister."

The driver maneuvered back into the flow of traffic, and the cowboy winked, faced the front of the bus, and began whistling unfamiliar tunes. Ashen held her breath, willing herself to be calm, her all-in-her imagination mantra looping on repeat in her mind. Meanwhile, Jacob beamed. He pointed at the cowboy and whispered, 'A real John Wayne!' before he went on beaming some more. His delighted expression made him look like a complete doofus.

Behind them, the strange man's dull eyes stayed on the cowboy. Repulsion crossed his features before he slowly turned to Ashen and sneered as he manipulated his bloodless lips to mouth a single, silent word. "Watch."

The man's bones slid beneath his skin again. His eyeballs receded, becoming lifeless, black masses. The bus's overhead lights fluttered off and on, and an inky gloom bled from the man's mouth as if he were gagging on darkness.

Ashen swallowed a rising scream. Maybe she really was losing it.

2

ASHEN: ALONG CAME A SHADOW

Ashen Deming
Born: August 4, 1969
Died: October 31, 1981

October 31, 1981

The afternoon had turned grim. Angry wind howled from the east and slate-gray clouds streaked the edge of the plains, concealing where sky met earth—as if nothing lay beyond and the land dropped off into a doomed, vast void.

Ashen kicked a pebble. It flew down the country road, bouncing until it hit a bump in a tire rut where it changed course, bashed into a tuft of grass, and rolled to a stop.

Even at twelve years old, she could relate to that little rock.

"My parents are driving me to that rich-people neighborhood outside the city again," said the Grim Reaper plodding next to her. He swung his plastic scythe through the air at imagined enemies. "Got full-sized candy bars last year! And only one toothbrush!"

"Yeah, I know, Jacob."

"And since your mom's not taking you trick or treating tonight, we could go together. My parents won't mind."

Ashen kicked another pebble. "Nah, it's okay." She gestured at her school clothes. "No costume, remember?"

"Excuses. You should come."

With a flourish, Jacob took an overly confident slice at the imaginary foe before him. His feet skidded on the sparse gravel. His over-stuffed backpack shifted and he tumbled face-first, hitting the ground with enough impact to pop the bag open, scattering its contents onto the dirt.

"Ow."

Ashen swallowed a giggle. "Are you alright?"

"Yeah," Jacob groaned. He pushed himself up, frowned, and picked up two pieces of his once-whole scythe. "Ah, man!"

She offered her hand. "It's okay. Duct tape fixes everything."

Ashen helped him pick up his homework and class books and notes and drawings and whatever else he had managed to jam into the bag, then slung her own almost empty backpack onto one shoulder and continued home. Jacob followed behind, dusting off his hooded black robe.

"How come you never bring much home?" he asked.

"I get my homework done during lunch. Saves time."

"I know you'll probably say no, but you could always, I dunno, eat instead? With me and our friends?"

The word, "our", didn't ring true. Inside, Ashen frowned. Outside, she smiled.

"Maybe tomorrow."

Jacob gave her a concerned nod and fiddled with his

busted scythe. As reluctant as Ashen acted, she didn't understand why he continued to include her, but she was glad he did. In recent months, she had been escaping to his house so they could play and talk about school. Those few hours were a welcome breather from her normal routine.

She let out a sigh. Deep down, Ashen knew Jacob was her only real friend. Most days she was okay with that. Other days, her chest ached as if something were missing. Of course, her friendship with Jacob helped, but he was one of those wonderful human beings who was always upbeat. Always. After being around him and his constant, unending optimism, she would find herself exhausted to the core, but somehow, her burdens were lighter.

"You know, we could find you a costume, easy," he said. "I have tons of stuff you could borrow."

"Mom is going out. Gotta stay home."

"Maybe you could go to a few neighbors' houses?"

Ashen laughed. "What neighbors?" She scanned the flat landscape of the plains. At the end of the lane, beyond their two houses and the giant cottonwood tree that shaded both of their porches, the roof of the next-closest farmhouse could be seen through what remained of a corn field and a large pumpkin patch.

"No," she said. "No way I'm walking to Old Man Thompson's. He'd probably give me sardines or beans or some other ancient-people thing from his pantry, anyway."

"Prunes!"

"Eww." She scrunched up her face. "What are prunes anyway?"

"Dunno. Shriveled up gross fruit or something. My grandpa loves 'em."

She punted a bigger stone. It missed the wooden post of her mailbox by a few feet. "I'm getting too old for all that kids' stuff, anyway."

"I'm older than you are! By two months!"

"More like a month and three weeks." She stopped at the mouth of the drive leading to her house. "Well, gotta go. Have fun tonight."

Ashen pivoted away and hurried down her short driveway, past the line of trash cans. All the while, she fought back a painful lump in her throat. Of course she wanted to have fun with her friend. She wanted nothing more than to be concerned about her homework and silly school rumors and boys instead of her mother's changing temperament. None of it was right and she knew it, but when was life ever fair?

"Okay," Jacob's sad voice said behind her. "See you, Ash."

Gravel crunched with each of his steps as he trotted next door and up his own drive. When his front door slammed, Ashen paused on her porch and used her sleeve to swipe at her watery eyes. She released a shaky huff, and smoothed her thick, springy curls. No use getting worked up. Jacob was lucky. He got to be a kid and though she was happy for him, she couldn't help being envious at the same time.

Shame swept over her. Hoping that he might have come back outside, she glanced over the fence toward Jacob's house. A bright glare shone from the highest branches of the cottonwood tree that grew between their two yards. As soon as the white light appeared, it faded, vanishing into the drab autumn skies.

Ashen squinted. Maybe it had been a humongous firefly? She'd read about them in a few books, but had never actually seen one. She shook her head, dismissing it. Fireflies were rare in Colorado.

When the light didn't return, she frowned, turned her

key, and went inside.

Even though tornado season had come and gone, the prairie gusts persisted, beating the shutters of the old farmhouse and stealing leaves from the cottonwood tree to fling into the darkness like brittle parchment. The house creaked and groaned as if on the verge of collapse while the shadow skulking in the corner of Ashen's attic bedroom went unnoticed.

Ashen sat cross-legged on her mattress reading *My Side of the Mountain* for the third time. Maybe the fourth time. Either way, she found it far more enjoyable than her current assigned seventh-grade reading. That book was dumb and boring and didn't have a pet falcon in it.

Outside her window, truck brakes squeaked. Her heart raced as she reached for her nightstand lamp. The last time she had been caught reading, her mother had yelled and thrown things, slurring every other word. She had called Ashen a know-it-all just like her father, and when Ashen had talked back, her mother had staggered over and snatched her book away. If Ashen wanted to avoid fishing books out of the trash the next morning, it was best to pretend she was asleep and keep her trap shut.

The glow from the vehicle crept by. Ashen let out a relieved breath, deciding that it must have been Jacob and his parents returning, and went back to reading. A few minutes later, a crackle from the walkie-talkie on her nightstand confirmed her suspicions.

"Ash, you there?"

She ignored the voice and concentrated on the next paragraph.

"We saw your light, Ash."

She rolled her eyes, slipped a bookmark between the pages, and retrieved her walkie-talkie. "Yeah, Jacob. I'm here."

"What're you doing? Over!"

"Reading with Langhorne." Her box turtle lounged beneath a heat lamp in his terrarium by the bed. At the mention of his name, he raised his head, blinked, then scooped up a mouthful of eggshells. With each crunch, the markings above his eyes moved up and down like protruding eyebrows.

"Which book, over?"

"It's about a boy who runs away to live in a hollowed-out tree."

"A tree wouldn't be a very good house. Think of all the bugs that'd crawl in your ears and nose and dig into your brain!" Ashen grimaced as Jacob continued without missing a beat. "Hey, is your mom home yet, over?"

"She's still at the bar."

"Well, my parents wanted to know if you're hungry. Oh! And I scored loads of candy for dessert." An awkward pause preceded a hurried, "Over!"

"I already made myself dinner." Her belly grumbled at the lie. "And you don't have to say 'over' every time we use this thing, you know."

"Sorry, Ash."

The pout in his voice made her soften. "It's okay, Jacob. Can you tell your parents thank you anyway? Please?" She clicked the button again and added, "And maybe we can share some of your candy tomorrow? Over?"

"Yeah, Ash. Sure thing. See you."

She placed the walkie-talkie on her nightstand and pulled the covers around her. Her eyes rested on a framed photograph of her parents taken before her father left. Before her mother could no longer cope. With a heavy sigh, she returned to her book. Her breath hung in the chilled air, and as she turned to the next page, it dissipated into a soft swirl.

A clatter in the yard made her flinch. The faint bark of Old Man Thompson's dog echoed. As everything fell silent again, she stifled a yawn. The long hours of reading had taken their toll. With the heels of her hands she rubbed the sleep from her eyes, blinking hard until her sight readjusted to the dim room.

That was when she saw it. In the darkest recess of the attic, beyond the crude cinder-block shelves filled with books, was a shadow that didn't belong. Hunkered down near her wall mirror, its twisted profile was topped with what appeared to be a wide-brimmed hat.

Ashen didn't own any hats.

Dense air filled her lungs with icy barbs. Her eyes locked onto the shadow as she reached over the edge of the bed until her hand brushed against fake fur. She wrenched up her bunny slipper by one slack ear and, for a moment, hesitated. If the silhouette was a robber, what good was a pink slipper?

She took a breath and chucked the slipper at the shadow. The featureless murk swallowed the pink bunny. When nothing stirred, she fetched her flashlight from her nightstand. As the beam touched the hunched lump, the shadow bled away, fleeing to gray nooks like a swarm of frightened rats, leaving only her backpack and winter coat in a pile on the floor.

"It's just your imagination, Ashen," she whispered over the pounding of her heart. "See? Nothing there. Only a shadow."

She clicked the flashlight off and reached for her book,

but between paragraphs, her eyes wandered to the other side of the room. She squinted. Was the shadow back? Or was her mind playing tricks on her? But when nothing budged, she let herself get caught up in the story, knowing that if she avoided thinking about the dark she'd forget; soon, her mind became lost within the pages.

Until her slipper flew from the attic corner and hit her in the forehead.

Something shuddered within the lingering gloom. The lamps flickered. Frozen, Ashen stared at the shadow rising from its crouch. It lurched toward her. With each step, it grew larger, and its twitches diminished until each movement became more controlled and deliberate. A wispy, sooty aura surrounded an opaque core as fluid as oil and blacker than the darkest night. Beneath its hat, the creature's empty eye cavities narrowed, and it flashed a cruel smile filled with black, spindly teeth.

It wasn't a shadow. It was a monster.

At the halo of light beyond the frame of her bed, it stopped, blocking the path to the rickety attic stairs, trapping Ashen.

Loud static burst from the walkie-talkie. Slapped out of her petrified shock, Ashen dove for it. The monster snarled, and the walkie shattered without anyone touching it. The attic lights blinked out. Claws swiped. They missed her, and the lamps spasmed back on. The creature bellowed and retreated past the boundary, its jaw unhinging to a gaping hole.

Ashen snatched her flashlight. It didn't work. Her clammy hands shook it. Nothing.

Outside the lamp's barricade, the shadow paced like a caged cougar. Subdued light seeped beyond the border, but it didn't illuminate the monster. Instead, the timid rays bent around it, refracting and outlining its furious face as if the thing devoured light itself.

Desperate tears streaked Ashen's cheeks. Frantically, she scanned the room. Steam rose from the bulb of Langhorne's heat lamp, still plugged into an outlet. With every ounce of grit she had, she rolled from her bed and away from the protective circle of light. The creature lunged. She dodged and reached into the terrarium. The hot metal lamp burned her, and she yelped, shaking the sting from her hand while the lamp crashed to the floor, bulb intact.

The sound of metal grinding against metal came from the monster. It was laughing.

A floppy ear peeked from under her bedsheets. Ashen ripped the slipper free and shoved her blistering fingers into it, using it like an oven mitt. She juggled the hot lamp, pointed it, striking the shadow and pushing it into the corner. It let out an unearthly shriek—a tangled blend of screaming horses and deep growls.

"Get back, you—" Her voice broke. "Whatever you are! Get back!"

The lamp's cord dragged behind as she inched toward the attic stairs, pinning the creature with light. She felt around with her bare foot until she found the edge and descended backward, her confidence increasing with every step. Near the base of the stairs, she grinned. The creature hadn't gotten her. She had won.

The cord pulled taut. A distinct pop sounded. The light extinguished and the screeching stopped. As Ashen stared up into the pitch-dark attic, a faint, hummed melody rose from the gloom.

She dropped the useless lamp, catapulted down the last steps, and slammed into the door at the foot of the stairs. The humming swelled. She whipped the door open and launched full tilt down the second-floor hallway. The hall lights failed and the humming intensified, coming closer.

At the stairs leading to the first floor, a sudden dread punched her in the gut.

Langhorne.

She slowed and threw a tentative glance over her shoulder. How could she have forgotten Langhorne? Her turtle, her only other friend besides Jacob, was alone with a beast she'd never seen before. She'd never read about it in any of her books. Not a single one of her teachers, who Ashen already doubted knew as much as they claimed, had ever warned her of the monstrosities that lurked in the night.

The hall lights surrendered. Left in the dark, her eyes darted, searching for any subtle movement. As she reached for the banister, a low, rumbling voice sang into her ear.

"Oh, my Clema, oh my Clema, oh my darlin' Clementine…"

Ashen screamed. The singing persisted. She kicked and punched blindly but not one blow struck the monster. Exhausted, Ashen bent over, panting between sobs. She recognized this song. In fact, she was certain she'd heard it once on a school field trip, but the lyrics weren't quite right.

"Now you are gone…" An invisible hand pushed her.

"And lost forever…" Jab.

"I'm dreadful sorry…" Shove.

Tears flowed down Ashen's cheeks. She crossed her arms in front of her, but the monster kept pushing her, again and again, until her heel teetered on the edge of the top stair.

The singing stopped. With her burned hand, she latched onto the railing, her teeth gritting through the pain. The bunny slipper clung to her, its head drooped as if it accepted Ashen's inevitable doom.

She whimpered, "What are you?"

"A hungry old man," the monster said.

"I don't understand! How come I can't see you now?"

"We are unseen."

Ashen let go of the railing and balled her fists. "What do you want from me?"

Inches from her nose, the creature's face separated from the darkness. "By and by, Clementine. By and by."

With that, the monster gave her a final shove. She fumbled for the handrail. Gravity took control. Her feet went from under her and she tumbled backward. Her shoulder smashed into a step. Pain shot through her neck as she slid to the foot of the stairs.

Crying, she struggled to her hands and knees and crawled. She could make out the frame of the front door through her clouded vision. It was close. She could make it.

A hand crushed her shoulder. Ashen shrieked as fingers bit into her flesh and flipped her onto her back. The creature crouched over her. The brim of its hat brushed her forehead. A deep scar marred the shadow's flesh below one of its eyes. The mark stretched along the monster's serrated cheekbone to its large, bulbous ear rounded like the head of a cauliflower.

The thing's mouth cracked open into a fiendish smile as it pressed its skeletal thumb on her neck, feeling for her pulse. Freezing droplets of water fell from its teeth onto her lips. Its vacant sockets looked into Ashen's eyes as it sang.

"She stubb'd her toe and oh, Kersliver, she fell into the foamy brine."

Heaviness compressed Ashen's chest. A bitter cold pierced her, and she coughed, striving to breathe. Water bubbled from her mouth as she flailed.

She was drowning.

The monster let out a gratified sigh. It tilted its head back, jaw expanding, and inhaled. She fought to keep conscious, but her sight darkened. Her eyes rolled up. Her arms dropped to her sides.

And Ashen died.

A heavy blackness covered her. Jagged stones dug into her back and her eyes fluttered open to a bleak cave. Strands of silver twinkled in the rock walls. Unlit lanterns hung from iron spikes buried in timber support beams, and at the far end, a faint light beckoned. It glimmered with muted colors that coiled around each other in an embrace. Hushed whispers spoke to her, too quiet to discern. But they were delicate. Inviting.

The cave grew dim. Oxygen filled her lungs. A strong scent of alcohol lingered as warmth returned to her.

She opened her eyes. Her mother, a curtain of sheer panic veiling her features, was bent over her, thumping Ashen's chest with her fist. Ashen sputtered, taking in rough, rattled gasps. Her mother got to her unsteady feet. She swayed, leaning against the frame of the open front door, the panic replaced with a drunken daze while a worried Jacob peered in from the porch behind her.

Although the chill in the air had gone, the pain from Ashen's fall and getting pummeled in the chest stayed. Disoriented, she sat up. The vision of the cave was replaced by the farmhouse foyer. There was no trace of the monster.

"Ashen!" Her mother put her hands on her hips. "You tryin' to break your neck? Why're you wet? You trip out of the bathtub? And why's a slipper on your hand?"

Through raspy breaths, Ashen said, "There's a … shadow monster."

"A shadow monster?" her mother asked. She let out a huff that stank of whatever she'd been drinking. "Scarin' yourself on Halloween. We agreed you're supposed to be a grown-up on my nights out, not tryin' to kill yourself playin' around."

Ashen's eyes flicked to Jacob, who looked both uncomfortable and concerned.

"You okay?" he mouthed.

She confirmed with a nod. When she rose to her quivering legs, something moved on the landing above. She sucked in a ragged breath. Almost hidden in the mouth of the unlit hall, the figure of the creature stood, and as she watched, it transformed into a hovering black orb circled by thick, unnatural smoke.

"Mom! Look!"

"Ashen, I—"

"But if you would look!"

"Ashen Deming, enough!" In an instant, her mother's eyes sobered. "You're a big girl now! Stop with the nonsense! I swear, all those books have put crazy ideas in your head and I'm sick of it!"

Tears pricked Ashen's eyes. Her mother wouldn't listen. The only ones who cared about her at all were Jacob and Langhorne.

Her stomach dropped. Langhorne. Her turtle. She had to save her turtle. Overwhelmed by determination, she began to hobble up the stairs.

"Come back here and clean this mess up!"

But Ashen kept going. Each step, she winced, the intense pain in her shoulder recurring at every jostle. Once in the hall, as she threw her slipper down to free her burned hand, she felt a presence next to her. Startled, she pulled away, but Jacob gripped her elbow.

"You should see the doctor."

"I'm fine, Jacob," she said, her tone sharp. "Besides, Mom shouldn't drive. What are you doing here, anyway?"

"I, uh, my walkie-talkie made some weird noises, but it wasn't even on. Then some man started singing, all soft and scratchy. Like it wasn't real. And sorry, Ash, I got scared and called the bar. Told your mom 'cause I thought something was wrong."

"You heard it?" Her question came out more like a demand, and she reminded herself that she shouldn't be cross with him. He was the reason why she was still among the living.

"Heard what?" Fear crept into Jacob's voice. "Ash, you were kidding around with all that monster stuff, right?"

Ashen pointed to the end of the hallway where the orb waited.

For a spell, Jacob stayed silent. Then he whispered, "What is that?"

She didn't answer. The attic door snapped open and the orb flew through, leaving a faint, smoky tail in its wake. The hall lights trembled on.

"Come on," Ashen said.

The two ran down the hall and chased it through the doorway. Jacob shivered beside her as they stumbled upstairs to the dark, frigid attic. Floating in the corner, behind Ashen's bookcases, the black orb waited. Nearby, her mirror shimmered like the light in the cave. Colors flowed into one another, creating iridescent ripples like oil on water.

The orb grazed the mirror, disturbing the colorful patterns, before humming the first notes of its song. At her side, Jacob whimpered, but Ashen felt only rage. Rage that her mother didn't trust her or believe her, rage that her dad would probably never come back, rage that this thing had taunted her in her own bedroom—her own private sanctuary. The one place she felt normal.

Her temper boiled over. She rushed the orb. As the space

between them closed, the shadowy sphere chuckled and flattened itself against the mirror. Gradually, it sank into the reflective surface, but for a brief moment it seemed to labor, as if it were being squeezed through a too-small hole, until it slipped the rest of the way through and disappeared.

The bedside lamp switched on, illuminating Ashen's puzzled face. Her eyelids were irritated and swollen, and a mean-looking bruise had formed on her cheek. She pressed her palms on the cool glass. It was solid. The bright colors had vanished. The monster had gotten away—maybe to come get her some other night.

Her perplexed brows straightened into fierce conviction. She wasn't going to let that happen. Ignoring her throbbing hand, she yanked the mirror from the wall and stomped back to a petrified Jacob. She thrust the mirror at him.

"What do you want me to do with this?" he said, blinking at her as he grappled with the weight. "I don't want it! Didn't you see what happened?"

"Just hold it a second, okay?"

Jacob opened his mouth, seemed to reconsider, and clamped it shut. Limping to the terrarium, Ashen picked up a chilled Langhorne. Grateful he was alive, she stuffed him under her shirt, cradling him close to warm him.

"Okay. Let's go."

Obediently, Jacob trailed behind as he gaped at the mirror. By the time they were back downstairs, they found Ashen's inebriated mother passed out on the living room couch. Since there wasn't any chance of waking her now, Ashen made Jacob wait at the front door while she went from room to room, turning on every light. Satisfied that no murky shadows were hiding in the corners, she hastily threw an afghan over her mother, seized Jacob by the sleeve, and headed outside.

At the trash cans lined up next to the driveway, Ashen grabbed the mirror from Jacob, battling the pain in her shoulder as she hefted the glass above an empty can. She heaved the mirror in, shattering it, and whirled back to the farmhouse. Her nerve began to falter. The sinister house looked as though it would split open, pounce on her, and eat her whole. Trembling, she clenched her fists and started toward the porch.

"You're not actually going back in there, are you?"

Without turning around, she said, "I don't have a choice. There's no way Mom can fight that thing off if it comes back. I can't leave her."

"That thing isn't after her! It's after you!"

Ready to retort, Ashen swiveled to him, but one look at his wide, alarmed eyes made her pause. She pressed her lips together. "Tell you what. If you help me break all the mirrors, I'll sleep over tonight. Deal?"

With a conflicted look, Jacob glanced toward the snoring wafting through the open front door. "Your mom seemed pretty upset."

"She won't remember much by tomorrow." Ashen's own words stung. She forced herself to laugh. "She breaks things a lot. She'll probably think she did it all."

Jacob's smile was as strained as her laugh. "Okay, if you're sure. But we gotta hurry before my parents get worried."

Once every mirror they could find had been destroyed, Ashen followed an insistent Jacob to his house. They mumbled some excuses to his parents, went to his room, and whispered about the monster until the dawn sun rose over the Rocky Mountains. When the grasslands were bathed in golden daylight, Ashen allowed herself to collapse on Jacob's bunk bed and fall asleep.

The entire night, neither child noticed that a different orb, one made of brilliant white, hovered in the branches of the old cottonwood tree.

And it was watching.

3

BEGINNING OF THE END

Dread paralyzed Ashen. The darkness that had been the stranger's eyes spread across the bridge of his nose while the black in his mouth expanded, flowed over his cheek, and took his facial features hostage. As she watched this horror film come to life, she tried to loosen the scream stuck in her gullet, but only labored gasps escaped.

"I reckon that's quite enough, Toad Tibbits. No need to send the girl to a derned sanitarium." The cowboy stood, his once-friendly face tense. Deep lines etched into the man's dusky bronze face betrayed his age, but his eyes were youthful and alive, their luminous yellow-hazel smoldering beneath the Stetson.

Jacob blinked at the exchange as the cowboy sauntered down the aisle past them, stopping a few feet away from the shifting man before putting his hand in his duster coat. "I'd hate to ask more than once."

Fantastic. The psycho cowboy must have a weapon.

Ashen inched lower in her seat, tugging on Jacob's sleeve and dragging him down with her.

"Ya trackin' me?" The pitch of the stranger's low voice mingled with a screechy mechanical hum. As he spoke, beads of sweat glistened along his greasy hairline. "Warders. You'uns know ya messin' where ya ain't belongin'. Ya best leave me ta my prey and mind ta yer own."

"Don't go patronizin' me," the cowboy said. "As soon as I stepped on this here contraption, I knew what you were. Your kind are downright atrocious at concealing yourselves. Y'all have a distinct stink."

The stranger's anger switched to warped amusement. A quiet, deep chuckle trickled through his pale lips.

"Now what's so darned funny?"

The man ignored the cowboy, his laughter growing louder as his open mouth widened. Some of the blackness peeked from the depths of his throat. Jacob flinched. He recoiled from the sight, smashing Ashen hard into the window of the bus.

"Get ofph me, Jacoph!" she said, her face squished against the cold glass.

He muttered an apology and pulled away. While she had been pinned, the cowboy had pulled out the item he'd been hiding away in his coat. As Ashen had guessed—a gun.

Or at least, she thought it was a gun.

Despite Jacob's whispered objections, she wriggled past him and craned her neck around the side of the bench seat. The cowboy's coat blocked most of her view, but she could make out the weapon. It emitted a golden glow that resembled its owner's eyes. Rationally, it shouldn't have been able to fit inside the cowboy's duster. The barrel stretched beyond four feet in length, the width more than triple that of any rifle Ashen had ever seen. As bulky and heavy as the thing appeared, the cowboy handled it with a steady arm as he pointed it at the man's head.

The man the cowboy had called Toad stopped laughing.

"You're really starting to get on my dang nerves," the cowboy said, the crevices in his face deepening. "I suggest you skedaddle at the next stop before you find yourself without the protection of a cold human shell."

Fury exploded from Toad. "We done laid claim ta her!"

"You know fine well you can't lay claim on the living. You best leave her be."

"She's ours!" Toad sneered, his lips pulling away from his yellowed teeth. "Ya and yer Warders got no idea what yer dealing with."

"Is that so? Well, by all means...," with one hand, the cowboy spun the colossal rifle, and the lever-action mechanism cocked with a click, "I reckon you'd best enlighten me."

Toad glared up the barrel. "Thaddeus Glick sends his regards. Ya recall him now, don't ya Macajah?"

The cowboy's eyes narrowed. In one smooth action, he turned the butt of the rifle toward Toad and clubbed him in the jaw. The force snapped Toad's head back. The skin around his bones rippled and a fat shadow wearing a bowler hat separated from the man's body, gnashing its long teeth. Denser than the darkness, the creature dug its claws into its host's flesh and ricocheted back into the body and away from the daylight.

Another cry fixed itself in Ashen's throat. The shadow she had seen as a child hadn't been the only one.

Macajah rested the barrel of the rifle on his shoulder. "Mister Tibbits, as you and I were never formally introduced all those years ago, I reckoned I'd give you what I like to call a deadbeat handshake. Welcome to Denver."

At this, the two costumed passengers rose, each standing to either side of Macajah as if to punctuate the cowboy's statement with their presence.

"Hey!" The bus driver squinted at them through the mirror on the dashboard. "What's goin' on back there?"

As if in response, Toad's cold, corpse-like disguise let out a shriek. Ashen clamped her hands over her ears. Next to her, Jacob shook as the creature's jaw dislocated. Its mouth stretched open like a hinged music box to reveal a monstrous orchestra inside, and the shadow emerged, wincing in the sunlight, laboring to squeeze itself between tongue and skull, grasping at the teeth of the stranger's carcass as if it were pulling itself onto the ledge of a cliff. When it had dislodged itself, it zoomed around the seemingly unconcerned cowboy and his two companions to the front of the bus, leaving an empty body behind.

The driver's eyes widened at the advancing shadow. He yelped and slammed the brakes. The shadow catapulted forward, hurtling into the mirror. Stuck head-first, the creature struggled to squirm its mass through the reflective surface, flopping about until it slithered through and vanished.

The costumed passengers traded brief, surprised looks. Then in quick succession, the old woman seemed to transform into a small orange ball of light. As Ashen sat, slack-jawed at the sight, the blond man smiled at her before he, too, disappeared, but this time into a blue orb, and both pursued the shadow, gliding through the mirror without difficulty.

The bus screeched to a stop. Hands trembling, the driver flipped the hazard lights on, crossed himself, and mumbled about shadows and death and supernatural things taking over the world. He ripped the mirror from its adhesive and scrutinized it, turning it from back to front to back, and crossed himself again.

A rising panic washed over Ashen. She buried her fingers in the seat, trying to comprehend what had happened while the driver stumbled down the steps. Once outside, he collapsed next to a chain-link fence covered with dead vines that bordered one side of the intersection. Beyond lay a jumble of cracked tombstones and monuments. Fairmount Cemetery.

"Was that ... was that what you saw, Ash? As a kid?" Jacob's raspy breaths echoed in her ears.

"You finally believe me, huh?" Ashen rose to quivering legs. "Only took five or so years."

From the floor where he cowered, Jacob grabbed the cuff of her jeans. "Ashen, don't leave!"

"I'm not. I want to see—"

"Don't you care about me at all?"

His words sliced her. Intent on firing back a retort, she spun. Jacob's haggard face met her own. Poor dude looked like a kicked puppy.

Her attempt to keep her tone calm failed. "How could you say something like that?"

"I'm sorry. Please. Don't leave me."

"Jacob, I'm not going anywhere." She helped him to his feet. "Promise. But we're in the middle of the road. We gotta get off this thing. Okay?"

Jacob nodded, but his warm brown eyes glistened with uncertainty.

Nearby, the cowboy examined his glowing gun. He used the front of his coat to wipe it down until he seemed satisfied, then hid it back within the folds of his duster. His amber gaze settled on Ashen. For a minute, they shared an intense stare before the silence was broken by a hoarse whisper.

"Who are you?" Ashen asked.

"Macajah Sloan, though most folks are liable to call me Cage. Are you alright, ma'am?"

Ashen went on as though she hadn't heard him. "Just … stay back. And what was that thing? Is that guy back there dead? And those other people! They just … disappeared! Where are they?"

The cowboy paused as if in thought. When he opened his mouth, instead of an answer, the horn of a semi truck blared. A deafening crash boomed in the cavern of the bus. Its frame buckled from an outside impact, and it tumbled, landing on its side, throwing Ashen. She collided into a bench seat and latched on. The accordion doors peeled back. The windows fractured, exploded, littered the air with tiny daggers. She reached for Jacob. Her fingertips brushed the edge of his sleeve as he slid past her. Her grip slipped on the plastic material of the seat. She fell.

Glass punctured her outstretched palms. She braced herself on the frames between the busted windows and pushed herself to her knees. The ground beneath moved quickly as the bus crumpled, kicking up yellow sparks where metal met asphalt. Frantic, she searched the chaos, fighting to keep herself from slipping between the debris and concrete.

"Jacob!" she screamed. But he and the cowboy were nowhere to be seen.

The bus wrapped around a solid obstacle. It jolted to a stop, jostling Ashen off-balance and into a pile of glass and twisted metal. When she tried to pull herself out, brightness expanded from the wreckage as flames and smoke swelled through the battered metal remains, crawling across the seats and outdated advertisements. The blaze lunged at her and the inside of the bus faded from her vision as everything disintegrated to blackness.

4

INTO THE BELLY OF THE MOUNTAIN

The damp air smelled of dirt. Lying on her back, she opened her eyes to a thick darkness and searched the ground around her. Earth. Slabs of stone. Pieces of rotted wood.

As her eyes adjusted, a distant, dim light revealed a tunnel. Silver veins spiderwebbed through the bedrock, and the walls and ceiling were held up by wooden support beams spaced several feet apart. Each divided section was a perfect replica of the one before, like peering into an infinity mirror; a never-ending passage leading to a faint unknown.

She struggled to her feet and began guiding herself along the rock tunnel, her hands feeling past unlit lanterns hanging from spikes driven into every beam. The far light never brightened, never pierced the dark, no matter how hard she tried to get to it. Hours passed. Her feet ached and her palms were raw from the tunnel walls that clawed at her. She turned away from the light, searching for another exit. Only blackness greeted her.

That was when she heard the whispers. Not coming from the light, but from below. They called to her from under the dirt and stones. They said her name. They told her to give up. To join them. How it wouldn't hurt. She wouldn't have to try anymore. Give up. Just let go.

The voices grew louder. She broke into a run toward the light. Chunks of crumbling timber tripped her and she stumbled, falling face-first. Ahead, rusted cart rails protruded like aged fangs from the gullet of a mine shaft. Voices wafted from the opening, taunting her.

Give up.

Let go.

She crawled to the edge of the hole and stared down into the belly of the mountain. Everything remained still until, gradually, charcoal-gray hues formed into inky black masses. As the shapes climbed the walls of the mine shaft, grinning faces emerged. Hollow eye sockets surrounded by shadowy, tangled flesh peered up, and in unison, the Unseen reached, clamping onto her with their skeletal fingers and dragging her into the pit as she screamed.

Ashen woke in a dimly lit room, clenching a sheet covering her and gasping for breath. The dream had felt real. Her fog-filled head tried to gauge where she was. The smothering scent of bleach and antiseptic mingled with a whiff of vinegar. Muffled voices and hard-soled shoes clipped past, echoing down a hallway outside until they dissipated, drowned out by the squawk of an intercom requesting a nurse in room 215.

The cold of the room bit through the snug sheet wrapped around her. She struggled to free herself enough to sit up.

Fluorescent light trickled through a small, rectangular window set into a door. Wires laced through the safety glass cast a delicate checkered pattern on the tiled floor of a stark hospital room, each vague detail blurry to Ashen's exhausted eyes.

A few stretchers were grouped against the wall. The sparse light illuminated the fabric draped over them like ghosts in the darkness. As Ashen tried to rub the sleep away, she thought back to the wreck before she had lost consciousness. There had been fire. Maybe even an explosion. If any bystanders had been around, the results should have been catastrophic, but each bed stood empty. No sign of the bus driver. No sign of the cowboy, Macajah. And most importantly, no sign of Jacob.

If Jacob wasn't there, where was he? She tore the suffocating sheet loose and threw it to the floor, surprised to find herself fully dressed rather than in a hospital gown. She examined her arms and legs in the weak light. No burns or marks. Not a single scratch.

Pain. She recalled feeling pain. Shards of glass had stabbed her hands when the bus had fallen to its side. Her breath hanging in the chill air, she ran her fingertips over the skin of her palms. Smooth. Unblemished. Gingerly, she touched her face, but no sharp metal pieces had embedded themselves. Nothing felt unusual. No discomfort. No injuries of any kind.

A thought struck her. Had she been there for a few hours? Or days? Had she been here long enough to heal?

The nurses outside grew quiet. Ashen let her arms fall to her sides and they struck the bed with a heavy thump. Puzzled, she felt along the metal frame of a stretcher. Despite herself, she chuckled. Typical. Her lack of social standing couldn't even secure her a real bed.

She rose to unsteady feet and walked to a small sink in the corner of the room. After splashing water onto her face, she filled a paper drinking cup and lifted it to her lips. Her eyes flitted to a small mirror attached to the wall. Instinct kicked in. She dropped the cup and backed away.

On the mirror's surface, a fleeting swirl of dark voids and bright, colorful lights shimmered, embracing her reflection. Tap water dripped down her forehead and across the light freckles speckled on her nose, her face haloed by her rebellious chestnut curls. The accident hadn't touched her face.

Several square cloths had been stacked on a nearby stainless-steel table, so she snagged one, holding it in front of her at arm's length. She tossed the cloth over the mirror, but not before noticing something gleam behind her.

Ashen spun, expecting one of the decaying corpses from her dream. No one was there, but on the far wall of the misty room, silver handles were lined up, each one attached to a miniature door. She made her way toward them and placed a hand on one of the closed doors. It was icy to the touch. A sickening feeling crept over her. Even though her mind screamed at her not to, she grasped one of the latches, taking a deep breath before yanking the door open.

When the vapor cleared within the small refrigerated unit, a long object on a steel tray, concealed by sheer material, became visible. Reluctantly, she lifted the thin sheet, revealing a pair of bare alabaster feet. An official-looking slip of paper encased in clear plastic had been tied around one ankle. On the tag, scrawled details stated that the feet belonged to a Mr. Frank Romero.

She dropped the fabric and retreated, gaping at the cadaver, putting as much space between them as possible. Tripping, she caught herself on the bed she had woken on.

She whirled. Her own lifeless brown eyes stared back at her. A mere shade of who she had been, her body lay, not on a bed or a stretcher as she had thought, but on a gurney. Her nude frame had been mangled by jagged cuts. An intense heat had seared her flesh.

An anguished wail escaped her lips. Her knees buckled. Tears streamed down her cheeks. "I'm asleep. I'm asleep. Wake up, Ashen! Wake up!"

Wisps of smoke coiled around her. Flames flickered, rising around the toes of her sneakers, fluctuating between radiant golds and greens, into cobalt blues and purples before settling into a platinum silver. She staggered back but the sterling blaze followed, smudging the tile floor of the hospital morgue with charred footprints.

"Oh, fantastic," she said between sobs. "I'm in rainbow hell."

A sinking sensation fell like lead in her stomach. An unshakable urge took over. Jacob. She had to find Jacob. She wiped her tears away and jogged to the door, leaving a trail of fire in her wake, but when she reached for the knob her hand passed through it. Dumbfounded, she stopped. When she had been on the gurney, she had felt the starchiness of the sheets against her skin and the coolness in the air. She had touched physical things. She had been able to open the refrigerator.

She tried a second time. Rather than connecting with anything solid, her fingers evaporated into mist, unfocused and wavering, before rebounding into their normal forms. A nervous lump in her throat, she positioned her sneaker in front of the metal door, shut her eyes, took another deep breath, and stepped forward. When her shoe stomped on solid flooring, she opened her eyes to find herself standing halfway in and halfway out of the room. Where her body made contact with the sturdy metal, vaporous particles split into spirals.

She ran the rest of the way into the hospital corridor and turned to read the sign on the door.

Room 303: Body Holding Area.

An invisible force brushed her shoulder. She staggered, searching for the source, but only muffled footsteps walked by. Cautiously, she followed the sounds down the long hallway, looking in each hospital room she passed for any sign of Jacob. Though she could hear pieces of conversations, the hospital seemed abandoned. But as Ashen wandered, glimmering shapes began to materialize. Brilliant whites, darkest blacks, and every hue in between shifted into human forms, glistening like sunlight on water. They bustled from one station to another, gossiping and laughing and breathing.

Jacob faded from her mind and she wept, watching the vivid colors of those who still lived. "Please," she said, attempting to bargain with any hidden force that might be listening. "I need to live. Please, please … let me live."

Something shone at the end of the hallway. At the base of the double doors leading to the parking lot sat Langhorne. Silver light rippled over his shell as he regarded her with mild interest.

"Langhorne?"

When she said his name, the turtle turned and walked through the glass. Not knowing what else to do, Ashen pursued him. As soon as she stepped through the outer doors and into the night, a herd of buffalo stampeded toward her, their fur and horns shimmering with sapphire blues, deep purples, and electric greens. With no time to react, she squatted, covering her head with her arms, and screamed. While the animals ran past, she peeked through the gaps between her fingers, watching as they vanished into the brick wall of the hospital.

Bewildered, she stood and gazed upward. A radiant emission of greens and reds trailed through the night sky. On either side of the street, unfamiliar translucent buildings were layered over the dull architecture Ashen had known all her life, altering the mountain horizon. Although they swirled with the same colors as the buffalo and the people all around her, the extinct structures faded in and out, pulsing between dim and bright.

The intense hues of living, oblivious people walked by a phantom fifties-style hotel and an Old West saloon. On the corner, the image of a house quivered in the gray cityscape. Ashen recalled reading about it years before in a paranormal magazine. An unattended candle had started a fire, burning the home to its foundations and killing the old man asleep inside. Ever since, there had been rumors that the site was haunted.

Ashen meandered among the glowing people, searching the streets for Langhorne. A couple of blocks later, she spotted him near the mouth of an alley, but when she made her way toward him, a white blaze burst in her path, blinding her. She fell to the asphalt as the light's source took shape. A woman, tall and lithe, her skin gleaming like a pale pearl, glided toward her. She had blonde hair, styled into a meticulous updo, her bangs swept to the side with perfect precision. The sleeves of her plain black robe drooped with excess material and swayed to an unheard rhythm.

"Do not be afraid, Ashen Deming," she said, her voice soothing. Inviting.

"How do you know my name?"

"We have been watching you," the woman said, offering her hand. "We have been waiting for you to join us."

Join us.

The dream of the mineshaft came crashing back to Ashen. Contrary to the shadows, this woman appeared to be made of pure light. Other than her black robe, there wasn't anything dark about her, but rather than accepting her hand, Ashen hesitated.

"Trust me," the woman said, her tone soft like silk. "Join us."

"That girl's not to be recruited yet, Miss Callahan," a man drawled.

From the end of the alley, a silhouette wearing a wide-brimmed hat stepped forward, distinct against the changing backdrop of existing and long-departed structures. Remembering the shadows, Ashen ignored the woman's outstretched hand. She got to her feet and withdrew to the sidewalk, weaving between the colorful living souls as despair took hold of her. If the creature from her childhood had come back for her, could this Miss Callahan help her? Could Ashen trust her?

Ashen waited, maintaining her distance on the opposite side of the road. A man sauntered into view wearing some kind of trench coat. A Stetson perched on his head and a thick mustache sat beneath his stately nose. The cowboy from the bus, Macajah. But unlike the living souls around Ashen, this man was solid. A flesh and blood human being.

"You head on back to the station, Constance," he said to the woman. The corner of the man's mouth twitched, but his dense facial hair made it impossible to determine if it was a sneer or a grin.

"Macajah, this girl is freshly deceased," Constance Callahan said. Her soft speech had been replaced by clinical articulation. "The law of the Warders doesn't apply to the jurisdic-"

"Criminy sakes, that's enough bellyaching," he said, reaching into his duster. "You get on back, now. I ain't about to ask you twice."

Scowling, Constance let out a sharp sigh. In an instant, she morphed into a ball of white light and shot down the street. The cowboy kept his eyes locked onto the orb until it became a speck. Once satisfied, he removed his hand from his duster to tip his hat at Ashen as he approached, his coat swishing with his natural swagger. Uncertain as to what to do, she waved weakly in reply. The whole surreal scene looked as though a horse should be tethered to a hitching post in the background.

When the heel of his boot stepped over the yellow line, from around the corner, tires squealed. An engine revved. The front chrome grill of a pickup truck smashed into Macajah, his body exploding into fine vapor. Ashen shrieked as the truck continued down the road, ignorant, leaving behind a golden haze on the night air.

The cowboy, Macajah, was gone.

5

THE DEAD AIN'T SPECIAL

A fine mist still hovered above the pavement as the truck's tail lights slipped around the corner. Ashen staggered into the street. Now that Miss Callahan had left, Ashen's one chance at getting her questions answered had been scattered to the winds. As her panic took root, she heard a husky drawl echo on the wind.

"That's so darned annoying. Ruins the whole of my day."

Tiny spiraling particles embraced one another. The cowboy's form began to emerge, the collected pieces radiating with the same Northern Lights shimmer everything else seemed to be made of. Small flecks were still floating to their proper locations when he cocked his head to the side, one eye locked on her shoes.

"Ma'am, I ain't too sure if you're aware, but your feet appear to be on fire."

She looked down at her Converses. The multicolor flames licked at the rubber soles, curling playfully over her shoelaces.

"Guess you'll be leaving your tracks all over the city," Macajah said, looking on as she inspected each foot. "Reckon we'll have to teach you how to control that."

"Control what, exactly?" she said, her eyes narrowing. "What can you teach me? Do you have a school or a class that teaches you how to be a dead person?"

"That's plain burro milk," Macajah scoffed. As she stared blankly at him, he coughed and raised an eyebrow. "Foolishness."

"No! Waking up in a morgue is 'foolishness'! Running into a man who has some gigantic magic gun is 'burro milk'!"

"Hey, it ain't magic and it ain't a gun. This here is Agnes." He patted his duster where the enormous firearm hid. "My Winchester rifle. The very same that won the West, they say. Well, mostly the same. I opted to stretch the truth some and make my own modifications."

"Fine! Whatever!" Ashen yelled. "I don't care about your stupid gun! I care that I'm on fire! I care that I'm very possibly dead!"

"Ma'am, I suppose I should advise that you're correct. You are, in fact, dead." He focused on Ashen's sneakers, taming his mustache with a weathered hand. "And you're unmistakably on fire."

"But why am I dead? Why am I on fire? What did you do to me, cowboy?"

He raised his hand defensively. "Hold your dang horses a minute. First off, let's get your circumstances square. I didn't do a thing to you. I didn't kill you. Heck, that's just an unfortunate event that occurs on the daily. And you ain't special 'cause you're dead, Little Missy. Everybody dies. You're like all the other bags of bones on this rotating ball of mud."

Macajah tugged down on the brim of his Stetson and continued. "Secondly, I'm none too fond of being referred to as 'cowboy.' It's disrespectful. Tends to vex me something terrible. Granted, when you modern folks lay eyes on me, I reckon that's what you see. But back in my day, most Easterners confused that with being a rustler, which meant a man was a horse thief. As I'm a gentleman and no horse thief, I would be much obliged if you'd call me Cage or Macajah. Or even the formal Mister Sloan."

Ashen scowled. She crossed her arms in dramatic indignation, spun around, and stomped back to the curb. The cowboy followed, punctuating the tongue-lashing he had given her by roughly smoothing imaginary wrinkles from his duster. Ashen's thoughts flitted to her short life. How she'd never go to college, get married, and have children. How she'd never have the chance to become a better mother than her own. How she would never know what it felt like to fall in love.

She hung her head, blinking fast to fight back the tears. In the end, the tears won, spilling out to form fat splatters on the concrete. Macajah looked up from his preening to catch her quickly dab at her eyes. His gaze met hers and the hard edges of his face softened.

"I know this whole affair of dying makes you all-overish and downright afraid," he said. "I can assure you, it'll pass."

The cowboy's words punched her in the gut. Hot tears streamed down her cheeks and she crumpled to her knees in the gutter. A group of the living walked through her as she sobbed. With each passing polychromatic soul, she could see her own body flutter, the tiny fragments of herself folding into uncoordinated loops.

"I can't be dead."

Groaning, Macajah sat on the curb next to her. "I wish that were true, Missy. I really do."

Tendrils of smoke rose from Ashen's smoldering sneakers. A strand of hope laced through her voice. "How is it that I could smell the disinfectant and bleach in the hospital? How could I do that if I'm dead?"

"Well, you still have your senses. You're still a human being. You just don't have a body anymore."

"But I touched things! Objects!"

"There's a reason, but explaining it'll take a spell. For the present, you gotta accept that you're one of the deceased."

At that, she buried her head in her hands. The cowboy nodded along while she blubbered unintelligibly. When her bawling didn't let up, he nudged her. "Little Missy, I gather you're monstrous upset, but I can't understand a dang word you're saying."

She cried all the harder, and Macajah draped his arm around her shoulders and pulled her close, letting her rest her head against him. He let a moment pass before he said, "Truth be told, since my own demise, not a day's gone by where I've not felt that pang of sadness and despair. But, it ain't as bad as it may seem."

"How is this not bad?" she asked, raising her head from his chest.

The corners of Macajah's mustache curled up into a grim smile. "You still exist."

The cowboy let Ashen lean back into him while she regained her composure. When her weeping ceased, he squeezed her arm. "No use wallowing in your own misery, right here in the middle of the street. Come on now. Dust your britches off."

"Where are we going?"

"Got a few folks I'd like to introduce you to," Macajah

said, getting to his feet. "Speaking of which, I reckon I best know what to call you."

"You mean my name? Ashen Deming."

"Ashen, you say? Now, that there is a right proper name for someone on fire."

"Funny."

Macajah offered his hand. "A man's got to try."

Now that she could think with more clarity, Ashen hesitated like she had with Constance. The tawny skin of the man's extended palm was marred with scars and calluses, his fingernails tidy. And even though he was a cowboy, the thing that frightened her the most, she felt safe around him. As though she'd always known him.

She accepted Macajah's hand. After he pulled her up from the gutter, he motioned for her to follow. Without a hint of concern, he strolled down the street, paying no mind to the living people and walking through them as if they were apparitions themselves. Close behind him, Ashen dodged the breathing souls she passed while wiping at her tears with the edge of her sleeve.

"You never said where we're going," Ashen said, avoiding a living man waiting at the bus stop. "Who is it that I'm supposed to meet? Is that Constance lady going to be there?"

"I reckon it's possible," Macajah grunted. "But the Honorable Miss Callahan ain't the one I'm referring to. There's some friends of mine that can help you get accustomed to your new condition."

At the mention of friends, Ashen jogged to catch up. "Wait! Wait! We can't go anywhere yet. I have to find Jacob. Remember? He's the one I was with before the wreck. Oh, and Langhorne!"

"Criminy, who the heck is Langhorne?"

"My turtle," she said, stooping down to scan the area for her pet's familiar shape. "He was here right before Constance showed up. He's gotta be around here somewhere."

"We'll find your reptile," Macajah said as he continued down the street. "And your friend. But not right away."

"But I can't leave!" Ashen said, chasing after him. "I have to know if Jacob's okay."

"There's not a thing you could do about it if he ain't."

She grabbed his arm to stop him. "What are you trying to say?"

"What's done is done, Little Missy." Unease rippled across his features. "Truth is, I'm not altogether certain what happened to that boy, Jacob. However, I give you my word that I'll help you locate him."

"You will? Promise?"

The cowboy nodded but didn't say anything more. Behind him, Ashen tried to keep up, wondering what this was all about. Should she press her luck? Ask any of the thousands of questions stacked up in her brain? She clamped her mouth shut, unwilling to risk chasing him off and not getting any answers. But she did know one thing. Following him around like a lost puppy felt degrading.

As if he could hear her thoughts, he glanced back over his shoulder. The phantom lights of the living and the surrounding architecture mingled in the darkness, highlighting the whiskers on half of his face.

"I assure you—this errand I'm set on is important. My posse has apprehended someone I'm itching to trade words with. Your assistance would be mighty appreciated."

With each footstep, the distance between the morgue and whatever final destination Ashen was being escorted to stretched. They passed industrial buildings and parking lots until the streets gradually evolved into neighborhoods, the rows of identical homes defined against the skyscrapers of downtown.

Layered over existing architecture, the ethereal outlines of buildings that had been demolished long ago wavered with the same purples, reds, and greens that Ashen had witnessed near the hospital. Houses that used to inhabit the city stood proudly once more until their colors dimmed, revealing the dull dwellings beneath. Then, as quickly as they vanished, the vibrant translucent skin reappeared, the visual history altering the cityscape every time she blinked.

The cowboy said few words as they walked side by side. Even though he appeared calm, his hurried steps left Ashen with the distinct impression that he was annoyed—as if she slowed him down—so she quickened her pace to match his stride, ignoring the flaring heat in her calf muscles.

Breaking the silence, Ashen asked, "What's with all the buildings?"

"These here with the colors? They're what I call phantom bricks. An imprint of structures that existed once upon a time."

One of the houses flickered, dissipating into the evening sky, then burst back to its full form. "Umm, are they alive or something?"

Macajah shook his head. "They're connected to a person's emotional currents. If the walls of a place was saturated enough, well, that current remains attached, and that building lingers on long after it's been destroyed. But I reckon they're only an echo. They fade away before coming back again, akin to a memorial."

The flames licking at the cuffs of her jeans glimmered, and in the yards they passed, each tree and blade of grass glowed with the same intense hues as the phantom bricks. But she noticed neither diminished.

"They remind me of the Northern Lights."

The cowboy cracked a smile. "They're awful purdy, ain't they? The Aurora Bor-ree-alis. Signs from God. Some tribes like the Cree call them the 'Dance of the Spirits.' I reckon that moniker's the most accurate."

The stars twinkled over the Rockies as Macajah recounted a story about one of the phantom bricks—a saloon he used to frequent named "The Stray Horse"—and how he'd gotten thrown out after struggling to break up a fight. While he recited his yarn, ranting on about good-for-nothing blowhards that can't insult or throw a punch properly, they reached South Valentia Street, close to where the bus had wrecked. Close to where she had died.

The edge of Fairmount Cemetery came into view. A wisp of light between the headstones—the form of a woman, pale and translucent, wandered, oblivious to them as they approached. The woman opened her mouth in muted wails, her shoulders heaved as she trod in a repetitive pattern. Sorrow washed over Ashen. She didn't notice that she had stopped walking herself until she felt Macajah's duster brush her side.

"Mighty glum, ain't it?"

"I don't understand," Ashen said, watching the woman through a wrought-iron fence. "What's wrong with her?"

"She's a Drifter. Caught up between the spiritual and material. Since they can't rightly control how and when they appear to the living, they're the ones that most often get seen."

"So, she's a ghost?" she asked.

"That's what the living would say, I reckon."

"Why is she like that? Why isn't she like us?"

Macajah leaned against the fence. "You and me, we're aware of who we are and what we are. A Drifter, like that lonesome lady yonder, is different. Some folks can't fathom their death or plain don't want to believe it. So they roam about forever, either where they passed on or where their bones were laid to rest."

"Is that why you said I had to accept it?" she asked, swallowing hard. "Being dead?"

He nodded. "Over time, you could have become like her. An empty husk."

The Drifter circled around to repeat her sequence of motions again, sobbing in the moonlight without a sound escaping her lips. An eerie, silent recording projected on the statues and headstones.

"Could that still happen to me?"

"Little Missy, I don't believe you've got to worry." Macajah tugged on her sleeve to urge her to follow. "You're a mighty strong spirit, but you need to keep it in your noggin that being strong doesn't make you invulnerable. Never forget that even the mightiest souls can crack and break."

"So," she asked, turning her gaze from the Drifter. "What happens to all the bad people?"

The cowboy's eyes darkened and sent a shiver through Ashen. "All folks have a choice to make upon their passing," he said, the foreboding tint of his eye fading. "Most choose to move on. Some stay. Even the evil ones."

Before she could ask what he meant, he started down the road and added, "We've loitered long enough. We best skedaddle."

Ashen had more questions, but attempting to make sense

of everything had made her mind exhausted. The cowboy shoved his hands deep within the folds of his duster, whistling a tune as he walked at a quick clip along South Valentia. When she caught up to him, he threw a sidelong glance at her, golden eyes gleaming, his whiskers sticking straight out from his puckered lips.

Even though the sad woman in the graveyard haunted her, Ashen couldn't help but snicker. His song disturbed, Macajah asked, "Now what, pray tell, is so darned amusing?"

"Oh, it's nothing."

"Well, you got me all interested now, so you best explain."

Shaking her head, she smiled. "Okay, okay. I was thinking that your whistling was … nice. And also that you look kinda like a sea lion."

"I read about those, but I ain't never laid eyes on one," he said. "I ain't the seafaring type. Though I imagine being any kinda lion is good, so I will accept both your comments as well-deserved compliments."

"Seriously, though," Ashen laughed. "I like it. It's reassuring."

"Why thank you kindly, ma'am. Do you have any particular requests?" he asked, then grimaced. "Nothing too modern. I don't much care for some of that highfalutin music they've got now-a-days. It's a grist of commotion to my ears."

"I don't really know many old songs. But don't start singing, 'Clementine.' That song gives me the creeps."

"That there is an old one, true enough. Who taught it to you?"

"When I was a kid," she said, "I saw something that looked like that shadow thing on the bus. It sang to me.

Right before it tried to drown me."

The cowboy's jaw steeled. "It sang 'Clementine' to you?"

"Yeah, but I found out later that it got some of the lyrics wrong." She let out a nervous chuckle. "Like instead of, 'Oh, my darlin,' it sang, 'Oh, my Clema.' Anyway, I've hated that stupid song ever since."

The cowboy's eyes shimmered, but whatever it had been vanished as quickly as it appeared. For the rest of the journey, Macajah didn't whistle.

6

MACAJAH: AGNES

Macajah Sloan
Born: June 22, 1821
Died: August 10, 1879

May 21, 1879

Macajah glowered at his reflection, eyes peering from beneath the wide brim of a Stetson. "I look ridiculous, like I belong in that darned P.T. Barnum's Traveling Menagerie."

Behind him, Abigail appeared, her once ebony ringlets now peppered with a distinguished silver and stacked neatly on the crown of her head. A mischievous grin danced on her lips. "Now, Mr. Sloan, that ain't got a grain of truth to it, and you know it! That color looks mighty fine."

His mustache drooped. "Ridiculous."

"Hush now, Cage. *Eres muy guapo.* And the shopkeep assured me this is what every proper frontiersman is wearing. I even hear it's William Cody's preferred style."

"I don't care a continental about Buffalo Bill, but I reckon he's a derned idjiot if he paid thirty greenbacks for this here hat," Macajah said, jerking the Stetson from his head. "Abbie, why can't we purchase that woolsey yonder and be done with it?"

Abigail looped one lithe arm around his and motioned with the other to the shopkeep. "Because you, my dear husband, old and ornery though you may be, pledged to protect your fellow men for many, many years. And a job well done is deserving of a right decent John B—not some shoddy five-dollar woolsey. Now, we're getting the beaver felt Stetson, and you're not permitted to dispute."

"Mr. Shoenburg, she keeps lamenting that I'm the ornery one," Macajah said to the approaching man, "but I reckon it's the other way around."

The young, round tradesman laughed. "Oh, she only wants the very best for you, Mr. Sloan. And please! Call me Cheap Joe!"

Macajah grimaced. "That don't sound too appealing a title."

"On the contrary!" Joe said, his arms flying up, causing Macajah and Abigail to lean away from the shop counter to avoid being struck by his wild gestures. "You see, after relocating here from back east, I became downright determined to establish the finest shop in Leadville and this desire required a suitable name—one that the good folks would hear and know, right away, that they should choose me to be their favored supplies and goods merchant."

The shopkeep took a deep breath and continued. "However, I concluded rather quicklike that these fellas around here can't recollect much beyond yesterday, thanks to the new saloons being erected at a good clip, so I became determined I needed a moniker that was easy to recall and started referring to myself as Cheap Joe. For remembrance and the like."

"Well, Cheap Joe, you've proven to be a fair and square dealer," Macajah said. "Even though I reckon you're a tad verbose. Suppose I could put a good word out that you treated us right, but we're still green to these parts ourselves."

At this, Joe seized hold of Macajah's free hand and shook it vigorously, forcing Macajah to widen his stance in order to maintain his footing. "Much appreciated, Mr. Sloan! Much appreciated! Having a lawman-"

"Retired lawman."

"My apologies, Mr. Sloan," Joe stammered. "Please excuse my excitement, however, even having a retired lawman endorse my shop is as good as any advert in the city directory!"

"True enough, I reckon."

"Yes! Yes, quite!" Elated, Joe beamed at the couple, his hands fixed on his hips, until he seemed to recall why they were there in the first place. "Oh, my! Let's get back to it, shall we? Have you and Mrs. Sloan settled on a purchase?"

"We'll take this one," Abigail said, attempting to hide her amusement. "Along with that golden-brown hatband there."

"Ah! 'The Boss of the Plains!' Excellent choice!"

A scowl formed on Macajah's brow. "This beaver felt possesses a name?"

Joe nodded eagerly. "Yessir! John B. Stetson's first, and still most popular, design. Protection from the sun, light as a feather, sturdy, impervious to water. Blazes, I even heard tell of men utilizing them as buckets to provide water to their horses!"

"A right fitting ridiculous name for an equally ridiculous item of clothing," Macajah muttered. "Naming your firearm

I fathom, but a dang hat? Outright foolishness."

Abigail smiled and smacked Macajah with the back of her hand. "Cage! You're going to give the poor man fits!"

As Macajah opened his mouth to dispute, the sound of heeled footsteps echoed on the plank sidewalk outside. The bell on the door of the mercantile rang. Joe's eyes flicked past Macajah's shoulder, his ruddy cheeks draining of color, and he lowered his gaze to busy himself with a hatbox for the Stetson. Raising an eyebrow, Macajah looked to the front of the store.

The first man wheezed under the strain of his own weight. After he'd squeezed through the entrance, he shuffled to the side into an empty space, taking his grimy bowler hat off to fan his red, bloated face. A second man, this one wearing a crumpled felt hat, followed. He ducked low to avoid striking his head on the frame of the door. When he stood to his full height, he threw an irritated look at the fat man, stepped to the space opposite him, and crossed his arms in disapproval.

The final man stood in the doorway, silhouetted against the blinding daylight of the bustling streets. His well-tailored, practical clothing gave him a sleek appearance. Head bowed to his chest, he removed his short-crowned topper hat and walked inside, smoothing sparse strands of pure white hair with an aged hand. The remnants of an old scar extended from beneath his eye to his swollen, deformed ear.

The man raised his head as his two hulking companions flanked him. Liver spots dotted the hollows of his temples and dark circles lay beneath his brown eyes. Macajah noticed the gentleman's gaze hover on him and Abigail before shifting to the shopkeep. His slight, frail stature was a deception. Something about the old man reminded Macajah of a giant.

"Mr. Shoenburg." The man flashed a weasel's smile. "I've come for my monthly collection."

"Ah, Mr. Glick, I've not quite procured my required contribution yet, however, business is tremendously improved. I have the utmost confidence that I'll have your funds by week's end."

The higher, yet controlled, pitch of Mr. Glick's voice held a nasal edge. "That weren't our arrangement, Mr. Shoenburg."

"I know, sir. I know. But if you leave me to tend to my current business with these nice folks here, I promise payment to you directly."

"Of course. I ain't about to stand atwixt a businessman and his would-be patrons."

The man showed his toothy grin again, his attention straying from the floundering Joe.

"My word, where are my manners? We ain't been properly introduced yet." He cleared his throat with a phlegm-filled cough and held his hand out to Macajah. "Name's Thaddeus Glick. These two here are my men, Toad and Eli Tibbits."

Macajah assessed the overweight Toad and tall Eli before reluctantly accepting Thaddeus' hand. Though the older man attempted a rigid squeeze, the result was limp and clammy. "Macajah Sloan."

"Sloan? That Irish?" Thaddeus asked with feigned surprise as he regarded Macajah's features and dark beige skin. "Well, I swan! I had presumed ya and yer woman are from other parts? Whereabouts? Southeast somewheres?"

Macajah's expression hardened, his jaw clenched. He felt Abigail's grip on his forearm tighten. "Yep."

"I heard word ya moved out to Solomon Gable's

property, up on the ridge there. That right?"

"Yep."

"My condolences. I was saddened to hear about his sudden demise." Thaddeus' eyes glinted. "Right charitable of him to will that particular plot of land to ya folks. I'd attempted to acquire it from Mr. Gable prior to his passing, but as ya well know, he was a stubborn man. Never budged."

"Yep."

"If'n ya ever have a hankering to sell, I'm certain I can make a grand offer."

"Alright."

Thaddeus pursed his lips and spat out, "Man of little words, ain't ya, Mr. Sloan?"

"Mr. Glick, me and my missus have no intention of selling. We'll be residing on that parcel until we're both no longer for this life."

"I see," Thaddeus smirked. He placed his hat back on his head, adjusting it as he spoke. "Well, my boys and I best be taking our leave. Mr. Shoenburg … I expect yer appearance promptly after Mr. and Mrs. Sloan depart."

"Yessir, Mr. Glick."

Thaddeus gave his hat a tip and exited the store. His two escorts pursued him like detached shadows.

Joe let out a stifled sigh. "I don't much care for that fella."

"Nor do I, Mr. Shoenburg," Abigail said. "His abrupt arrival got my ol' nerves spooked."

"What's your knowledge of the man, Joe?" Macajah asked.

"From what I hear, Mr. Sloan, he journeyed this way from back east years ago. Made a decent living at a trading post somewhere in the plains. Rumor has it he acquired various properties where Denver City stands now by, well, threatening folks to surrender their staked claims."

"Hustler," Macajah growled. "Made a lot of money, I reckon?"

"Yessir. He might as well have located a bonanza."

"Why is he here in Leadville instead of Denver?" Abigail asked. "Particularly a man of his age?"

"I don't believe his age would ever hamper his fondness for riches," Joe explained. "As soon as he caught wind of silver in these parts, he bought up acres of land from the prospectors that founded the town. Us merchants and the like have to go through him for approval, and if an individual doesn't carry the required funding, which is of an inflated amount, well, Mr. Glick presents them with a … generous offer."

"This have to do with the payment he was after?" Macajah asked.

"Yessir. I'm to pay him a set amount, monthly, in lieu of being incapable of paying for the property in total when I first arrived. Most others share in my predicament."

Abigail gave Joe a look filled with concern. "For how long?"

"As long as I dwell here. If I become delinquent, I forfeit my business."

"You won't pay it off in the eventual?"

The shopkeep hung his head. "No ma'am. Regrettably, this is a lifetime debt."

"Heaven's sakes, why would you ever make such an arrangement with that flannel-mouthed tyrant?"

Joe retrieved the Stetson from Abigail and placed it in the hat box. "Young and stupid, ma'am. Didn't have a red cent to my name after the considerable cost of my traveling here, and I was desperate to make something of myself. I sure as heck couldn't turn around and go back."

Looking up at them from his chore, Joe gave a reassuring wink. "Oh, you folks don't need to worry about me. I'll be alright." He placed their parcel on the counter, pausing a moment before adding, "But, please … watch yourselves. For a long while, he's had his eye on that property your old partner left you. I heard tell from a few acquaintances that Mr. Glick has a hunch that earth contains a great deal of silver."

Macajah's eyes narrowed. "How'd this notion of his come about?"

"Unaware, but somewhere he stumbled on the idea. And once he has his sights lit on something he wants, nothing will stop him."

Macajah exchanged a worried glance with his wife. She stood by his side, her head held high and her posture proud, but the fear he saw in her eyes betrayed her. His face burned hot, and he picked up his packaged Stetson, wrapped his arm around his wife's shoulders, and held her close to his chest.

"Much obliged, son. We'll keep an eye out."

August 10, 1879

The stream babbled and sang as it flowed by the cabin. It meandered toward the back of the property, its pace gradually quickening before cascading over a sharp rock ledge and into a freshwater basin filled with cutthroat trout, their green and pink hues speckled here and there within the water's depths.

Nearby, Macajah was putting his shoulder into it, swinging his pickaxe and tearing out chunks of the solid clay ground. He paused to pull a kerchief from his pocket and dabbed at the beads of sweat on his forehead before using his Stetson as a fan.

Through the glare of the kitchen window, he could see Abigail kneading dough for that evening's supper. Her hair had come loose, and she'd flick her head whenever a disheveled curl toppled over and obscured her line of sight. The laugh lines Macajah loved diminished as she concentrated. He couldn't help but notice how serious she looked.

Glancing up, she met his eyes and smiled. She tapped her knuckle on the glass, pointed a dough-covered finger at his pickaxe, pointed back at him, then pointed at the soil he'd been working.

Macajah yelled out, "Alright, alright, ya derned taskmaster! I should've never promised you a vegetable patch—this here is the hardest earth I ever labored over. Gonna take me till next spring to dig one dang ditch!"

He could hear her laughter drift from the cabin's open door and grinned in spite of himself. When he raised the pickaxe for another strike, a distant sound of galloping traveled up the canyon. Four riders appeared from around the bend. Beneath the hooves of their horses, clouds of copper-colored dust billowed, wispy tendrils catching on the mountain breeze.

Macajah didn't recognize three of the men, but he knew the leader. He rested the head of his pickaxe on the ground and leaned on the handle as they approached, shooting a look back toward the house. Abigail stood inside the threshold, rubbing her palms together to roll up extra bits of dough before wiping the excess onto her apron. He motioned for her to go back inside, but she answered with an expression that told him she planned on staying put.

Three men dismounted right outside the cabin. The one

Macajah knew remained in his saddle.

"I wasn't aware Abigail and I were expecting visitors."

"This here is a surprise visit, Mr. Sloan," Thaddeus said.

"I presume a friendly visit?"

"Suppose that all depends. Don't want to jeopardize our blooming friendship."

"That's mighty presumptuous of you. And I ain't your friend."

Thaddeus clicked his tongue in mock disappointment. "Macajah, I could be the best friend ya ever did have." He looked over at Abigail and tipped his hat. "Mrs. Sloan."

The muscles in Macajah's neck tensed. "You leave her be."

"Oh, I wouldn't dream of injuring such a handsome woman. Since it's been a few months since our fated meeting at Cheap Joe's, I merely request that we emend my previous proposals. Even brought up some sample bags for some ore. Saves me and my boys valuable time."

"You and I know that meeting wasn't fate."

Thaddeus smirked. "Well, ain't ya perceptive? Yes, it's true I arranged for our paths to cross to get a measure on ya."

"Well, I've already told you, we ain't in agreement," Macajah said. "It don't matter a lick what you offer or how many times you inquire. We'll not be persuaded."

"You mistake my intent, Mr. Sloan. I ain't here to purchase."

Something in the old man's tone made Macajah more alert, and he tightened his grip on the pickaxe. One of the riders approached Thaddeus and held his hand up to assist the old man with his dismount. Thaddeus took a moment to glare down at the man before he gripped his saddle horn and slid to the ground. He pushed past the rider, swiping his hand away.

"Remind me to find alternate assistance upon returning to town."

Seeing the dejected henchman, Macajah asked, "Where are your other two bruisers, Toad and Eli? Reckon they finally found some sense and located preferable employment?"

A voice from the cabin answered. "We be present, Mister Sloan. We done come by a different route."

Macajah whirled around. Behind Abigail, inside the open door and pressing a glint of steel to her throat, stood Eli. The tall man's large arm was wrapped around her shoulders, and he dipped his head beneath the frame as he maneuvered her outside. Behind him, Toad followed, carrying Macajah's Winchester rifle, Agnes.

Toad inspected the barrel. "This here's a fine gun, Mr. Sloan. Awful fine. Ya don't mind a'tal if'n I hold it a time?" Without waiting for Macajah to respond, Toad raised the Winchester, centered Macajah's skull within the sights of the gun, and winked.

Retrieving his pickaxe, Macajah marched toward Eli and his wife. "You son of a—"

"Now, now, Mr. Sloan," Thaddeus said. "Ya best keep yer distance. Toad here has already drawn a bead on ya. Best if ya remain composed. This'll all be over by and by."

The alarm in Abigail's eyes stopped Macajah in his tracks. "What do you want? For me to accept your offer? Alright. Consider it accepted. But you let my wife go."

"Ya see, that statement leads to the very predicament I desire to discuss. My charitable nature is all wasted away, Macajah. I find ya a disagreeable sort of man." Thaddeus handed some sample bags to two of his other men, his gaze turning to the back end of the property. "Let's take a stroll to that crick yon. Sounds like ya have a lovely waterfall I'd very much like to take a gander at."

His own rifle trained on him, Macajah and Abigail were escorted toward the cliff overlooking the small rapids. All the while, he studied their captors, searching for any weaknesses. Ahead, Eli had seized Abigail by her upper arm. Sunlight flashed off something sticking out of a makeshift sheath attached to the tall man's belt. The bone handle of the knife he'd threatened his wife with.

When they reached the creek, two of the other men moved further upstream along the embankment, kneeling to fill the sample bags with large stones littering the mud. The third one, a youngster no older than twenty, stayed behind. The inexperienced boy wrenched Macajah's arms behind his back and labored to bind the older man's wrists, oblivious to the peculiar way Macajah had positioned himself; knuckles facing each other, fists balled, muscles tense.

"What are you scheming, you rattlesnake?" Macajah muttered to Thaddeus as the boy continued tying and retying unsuccessful knots.

"Ya have a taste for music, Mr. Sloan?" Thaddeus asked. He drew nearer to Macajah, appraising him while he spoke. "I, myself, find music truly remarkable. One song in particular I learnt a long, long time ago at a minstrel show. Awful fond of it. Fastens itself in my head."

"What in the blazes does that have to do with anything?"

Thaddeus smirked. He turned and walked over to where Eli and Abigail waited. Macajah went to repeat his question, but the rope tying him jerked, and the boy led him a few long paces back from the drop. Once there, it didn't take long for the youngster to lose interest in his guard duties. The boy began to pace back and forth, all the while keeping his focus on the Winchester in Toad's grasp, a glimmer of longing in his eyes.

Meanwhile, Macajah's minimal movements went undetected. Jaw clenched, body relaxed, he twisted his wrists, further loosening his restraints, hoping to remain unnoticed.

At the cliff's edge, Thaddeus placed a shriveled hand upon Abigail's cheek. She flinched. A flash of anger rippled across the old man's features and he seized her chin, turning her head to the side to inspect her.

"Fine woman ya got here. Full of spirit, especially one goin' on in years." Abigail tried to pull away, but surprisingly, the old man held firm. "She part injun? Might be why she's so quarrelsome."

"I'm Mexican, you *imbécil*."

"Now, now … that ain't a'tal how a proper lady such as yerself should speak," he said, yanking his hand away. "Even a Mexican one." He wiped his hand with a lace kerchief and looked to Macajah. "I suppose ya married her since she reminded ya of yer own Mexican mama? That about right, Macajah?"

To hide his simmering temper, Macajah kept quiet. When he didn't answer, Thaddeus glowered and beckoned to the two men at the riverbank. "Bring some of them burdened bags over here. I'd like Mrs. Sloan to be my eyes and inspect them, up close, for me."

The men obeyed. Thaddeus opened one of the sample bags. He withdrew a rock. "Now, Mrs. Sloan, does this particular piece of ore appear promising to ya?"

"Don't you dare lay a finger on her!" The rope bit at Macajah wrists, making them bleed, so he worked faster. The more blood, the more likely escape would be.

"Macajah, ya wait yer turn, ya hear? I'm gauging yer woman's smarts." He held the rock a few inches from

Abigail's face. "Well, Mrs. Sloan?"

"I'm no prospector," Abigail said. "I've not the knowledge."

"Well, that there is a shame."

Thaddeus put the rock back in the bag, tying off the top with the crude drawstring stitched into the hem. Holding the bag of ore in one hand, he examined Abigail's apron skirt with the other, trailing his finger under the lip of her apron tie. He gave a tug on the tie, jostling Abigail a bit.

"Now, this is a powerful convenient location to store the stones my boys gathered for me. I'll go ahead and fasten this here bag to ya. Frees ya to look over another sample."

The true horror of Thaddeus' plans hit Macajah. His face burned as he strained against the ropes, all the while staring at the knife in Eli's belt. If he could reach the knife, he thought, he could end this whole ordeal. He could save Abigail.

He pulled with everything he had, his skin raw and torn. Blood trailed down his fingers. Thick drops fell to the parched ground. His right hand slipped out. In one smooth motion, he dropped the rope and barreled toward Eli.

Behind him, he heard the youngster guarding him yelp. The boy's surprise was only temporary, and he sprinted after Macajah. Faster and more agile, the boy jumped on his back, tackling him to the ground inches from Eli's boots. Macajah jammed his elbow back into the boy's nose. The youngster hollered before punching Macajah in the kidneys. Pain flared up through Macajah's back. Winded, he dropped.

Thaddeus shook his head. "You take another step, Mr. Sloan, I'll demand Toad blow yer head clean off."

"No, Cage, *por favor*!" Abigail pleaded, her eyes meeting Thaddeus'. "Please don't hurt him, Mr. Glick. Please."

With a toothy sneer, Thaddeus nodded at Macajah's guard. "Ya there. Gonna manage to hold Mr. Sloan fixed?"

"Yessir. Sorry, sir."

"Good. Now, where were we, Mrs. Sloan?"

The other two henchmen hauled Macajah to his feet. As he struggled, they retied his wrists, as well as his arms, and held him tight to keep him in place. He tried to kick at one of them, but they punched him in the ear until he could no longer stand without aide.

After attaching the first bag of stones, Thaddeus repeated his assault on Abigail, going through each sample his men had collected. He'd taunt her, pulling a lone rock from one of the bags to wave in front of her, then place it back before adding the full ore bag to the rest that circled her waist. The fabric stretched taut with each additional weight, yet Abigail stood, dignified.

Once her apron tie was threatening to tear, Thaddeus stopped. "Now, now," he said, stroking his chin as he assessed his creation. "That there is an attractive belt, Mrs. Sloan, but I believe yer little apron there can't hold much more."

Abigail's eyes were wet as she regarded the old man, but she spoke without fear. "Now that you've had your amusement, Mr. Glick, I am asking you to kindly release me and my husband. We'll depart and you have our word that we'll no longer have any dealings with you."

Thaddeus looked her up and down. The weasel smile crept back, and his voice warbled as he began to sing. "Oh, my Clema … oh, my Clema…"

With his decrepit hand, Thaddeus shoved her in the chest. Abigail staggered back, struggling to maintain her balance as she threw her weight forward. She glanced nervously behind her to the waters churning below.

"Alright, Thaddeus," Macajah yelled, using any strength he had left to fight the men holding him. He fell to his knees. "You made your point clear!"

Thaddeus pushed Abigail again. "Oh my darlin' Clementine…"

"Dang it, Thaddeus!" Macajah begged. "You've won! We grant you the claim. Please, please let Abbie loose!"

Dark eyes met his. "Now yer'ra gone and lost forever. I'm dreadful sorry…"

The old man struck Abigail hard. She took a final step back, the heels of her boots stumbling on the ragged brush clinging to the rock overhang. She screamed and plunged over the edge.

"No! No! Abigail!" Time slowed to a crawl. Macajah felt pure rage pumping through him. "I'm gonna kill you."

"Mr. Sloan, I no longer favor dealing with ya. And a deal such as this is far sweeter when there ain't no funds exchanging hands, don't ya think?"

Thaddeus let out a low whistle and nodded to Toad. The last thing that Macajah saw was Agnes, her hollow barrel smoking.

PART TWO:
ANGER

7

THE WARDERS' CODE

The old woman had been shuffling alongside them ever since Fairmount Cemetery. Although she moved at the same pace as frozen molasses, she'd somehow managed to keep up with Ashen and the cowboy.

The woman had surprised Ashen when she'd first appeared, passing through the closed front door of a single-story home, bewildered, gawking at the painted light dripping from the night sky. Like Ashen's and Macajah's, her form remained unchanged. Solid. Like how regular living people had looked to Ashen back when she was also alive.

They passed another house. A glimmering, colorful silhouette of a living man sat on his front step, a cigarette in his hand. Bats shone as they zipped near the sparse plants and trees in his yard. The man, the bats, even the plants pulsed, the same vivid tones pumping through them in a steady rhythm.

Ashen shook her head as if trying to answer her own confused thoughts. In her new existence, everything was backward. The living looked, well, not alive. And the dead were sometimes fog or mist, like the Drifter in the graveyard, or made of light, like Constance. Or they looked … real.

Ashen's mouth began to shape a question about the woman, but one glance at the cowboy made her snap it shut. A grouchiness cloaked his eyes as he stared straight ahead. She doubted that she would get much of a response. For the last several blocks, anything she'd asked had been acknowledged with a curt reply. Sometimes only a simple grunt.

She peeked back over her shoulder. Since Macajah had not bothered to address the old woman, Ashen assumed she wasn't a threat. Still, she kept a leery eye on her. If that shadow could use a person's body as refuge, like they had on the bus, perhaps the creatures could also hide inside seemingly innocent ghost grannies.

When the residential neighborhoods began to blend with concrete and brick businesses, another man, looking the same as the old woman, exited an apartment building. He ogled one thing after the other, reminding Ashen of how she'd felt when she first left the hospital. The man was fortunate. At least he didn't have a stampede of buffalo charging at him.

"Quackers?"

Ashen whirled to the old woman.

"Quackers?" the woman called again, bending down to peer beneath the low-hanging juniper bushes edging the sidewalk. "Where did you go?"

The cowboy didn't react.

"Should we, you know, help her or something?" Ashen

asked.

"Not a thing we can do."

"But, she's an old lady." A frown touched Ashen's lips. "Isn't helping the right thing to do?"

"There ain't no need to interfere. She'll mosey on fine in the eventual."

Ashen let out a loud huff and marched over to the woman.

"Sakes alive, Little Missy!" Macajah yelled, trailing after her. "It ain't our place!"

She ignored him. "Hello, ma'am?"

The old woman looked up. Her cataracts gleamed. "Oh! Hello, young lady. Have you happened to see Quackers?"

"Who's Quackers?"

"My duck!" The old woman hung her head. "He drowned when I was a little girl. I suppose he wasn't very good at being a duck, but I loved him all the same."

Puzzled, Ashen started to ask about the woman's beloved dead duck when she noticed a thin frost covering the old woman's fingers. Each appendage had turned an odd blue.

"Ma'am?" Ashen grabbed the woman's hands as if her touch alone could warm them. "Are you okay?"

"Oh, my heater's not been working, you see. So I'm always cold. Cold, cold. Even my toes. Cold, cold, cold."

At this, the woman presented her bare feet. They, too, were ice-blue and frozen.

Before Ashen could inquire further, a blinding blue and white glare blasted from the upstairs window of a Victorian house—much more extreme than the variegated tones shrouding everything else. Ashen turned to Macajah.

"Little Missy, you stay put," he said as he drew his Winchester from his duster. He stomped into the yard, rifle ready, and disappeared into the front door.

Left on the sidewalk with the old woman, Ashen stood, mouth open enough to have caught a few evening mosquitoes if she'd still had a physical mouth to catch them with. The old woman looked at her, a sad concern on her face. After a quick shift, something far down the street, something Ashen didn't or couldn't see, drew the woman's attention.

"Quackers!"

With that, the old woman shuffled on, content with following the invisible duck, leaving Ashen alone and staring at the rays of light splintering from the second-story window. There was a crash, then a holler. A thick golden beam shot out from the pane of glass and into the dark Denver cityscape. She bit her bottom lip hard as she debated with herself. What was she thinking? How could she help? She couldn't do anything. Not even touch a doorknob.

With some apprehension, she jogged to the house, thumped up the steps of the porch, and stopped shy of the front door. She paused, willing it to open. Another bang came from upstairs.

"Come on, Ashen!" she muttered. "Pull yourself together!"

She exhaled through gritted teeth, backed up a few strides, and leapt at the door. As she passed through, she felt herself dissipate into floating particles, the motes reattaching to each other on the other side. As her body reformed, a small nearby lamp flickered. The memory of being chased through her childhood home while every light around her died slammed into her mind.

The commotion upstairs continued. Her eyes turned to the ceiling. "In case you haven't noticed Universe, I've had a pretty rough day," she said, a slight groan laced within her plea. "Can you please—with a cherry on top—not let whatever that cowboy is fighting up there be one of those shadow things? That would be great. Thanks."

Ahead, the unsteady lamplight fragmented between wooden railings, casting irregular stripes on a wall covered with family photos. Pushing away her dread, Ashen crept up the carpeted stairs.

Shafts of blue, gold, and white filtered from the gap beneath a closed door in the second-floor hallway. Ashen drew in a deep breath and rushed through, straight into a battlefield. Glowing curved lines and straight beams of light fired back and forth across a bedroom. A ball, blazing white, rebounded off the glass of a framed poster tacked to the wall and flew straight at Ashen's face. She ducked. The light narrowly missed her head.

The cowboy barreled between her and the chaos; his back to her, duster swaying, stance wide. Protective. He held his giant Winchester like a baseball bat, swatting away fragments of light.

"Little Missy, I thought I told you to stay put!" Macajah yelled.

Ashen scowled. So much for being helpful.

"Do we have a visitor?" asked a low voice.

Shielded by Macajah, she craned her neck to peek over his shoulder. On one side of the room was the man who spoke. White light radiated from him in the same way it had from Constance. He wore a fine double-breasted blue suit, his hands up in a brawler's pose. A rugged jawline and sharp gaze, his handsome face was severe, his expression twisted into an ugly sneer.

From the man's clenched fist a white ray shot out toward the opposite side of the room. A barrier of blue light materialized, blocking the beam. Ashen gasped. Behind the barricade was the same tall, blond soldier from the bus. The sleeves of his lightweight green jacket were rolled up to his elbows, exposing the strange markings Ashen had been unable to make out before. Tangles of tattooed barbed wire circled his pale forearms, but instead of being drawn in faded ink, the illuminated illustrations glimmered an electric blue.

"Does it really take three Warders to deal with me?" the well-dressed man asked, bouncing a ball of light in his leather-gloved hand. "That hardly seems fair, wouldn't you agree, gentlemen?"

"We were just happening by, Silas," Macajah drawled. "This ain't no conspiracy."

Silas scoffed. "That's rich, coming from a Warder. Your entire posse is one big intrusion on justice."

"Is that what you call this, Governor Lydford? Justice?" The blond man asked, pointing to the bed behind him. Sprawled out, a young, living soul was fast asleep, oblivious to the ghost war in his bedroom. "He's only a kid! He's not dead!"

Silas Lydford flashed a fake smile. "I've already told you, Max, it was an honest mistake. I had incorrectly assumed he had perished while his parents were away. You've attacked me unprovoked and unwarranted."

The blue luster of Max's tattoos echoed in his eyes. "No, I attacked you because you didn't stop. 'I am here to protect those who cannot protect themselves.'"

"The Warders' code. How quaint."

"All I'm asking is that you back off. Stick to the rules. The dead can't influence the living."

"Perhaps it's time for the Light to break your precious rules," Silas hissed.

"Apparently, the universe says otherwise." The tattoos on Max's arms glowed. The barbed wire pulled away from his skin, becoming tangible, uncoiling into long, vibrant strips. He gripped them like whips, holding lengths of them in each hand. "Because we're the ones with the power."

"Currently," Silas said. He lowered his balled fists to his sides. "Fine. I'll take my leave. But it's amusing how you're always relying on those ridiculous tattoos. Can't manage to fight like a real man, hey, soldier boy?"

Without waiting for a reply, the governor turned from Max. As he approached, Macajah kept both hands on his rifle and moved out of the way. Silas' dark eyes darted to Ashen, who stood dumbfounded in front of the door. The smooth skin between his brows furrowed, and he stopped, scrutinizing the flames licking at her sneakers.

"A newly-dead?"

"Ashen's not yet for recruiting, Silas," Macajah said, ushering Ashen behind him. "Your pal, Constance, already tried."

"Ashen?" His voice held a hint of recognition at the mention of her name. Ashen found herself stepping further away. Silas' eyes squared into a glare. "Double standards. Any newly-dead should be on the table."

"Well, this here newly-dead ain't for debate. Us Warders have business with her."

"Between you and the Unseen, the Light are left with nothing!" Silas spat, his cheeks flushed. "Only scraps! Dregs!"

"Now calm your—"

Before Macajah could finish, Silas struck him with his fist. The cowboy staggered and fell. Silas' fist pulsed, and as he readied his next punch, Ashen rushed forward, wedging herself between the two men.

"Get back!" she yelled. Though her voice quivered, her sterling luster bloomed and a timid, fiery flare sped toward the governor. Silas tried to avoid it, but the flame nicked his chin, leaving behind a tiny singe mark.

"You insolent brat!" he shrieked.

"I'm sorry, I didn't mean to hurt you, I—"

Silas didn't give Ashen a chance to explain. Instead, he launched at her, arms outstretched. Ashen's instincts kicked in. She recoiled, bumping into a small table, scattering a pile of magazines as she fell to the floor. As Silas closed in, she braced herself for impact.

A sudden, loud whinny trilled behind her. Bursting from the wall, a horse sparkling with amber and gold vaulted in front of her, landed in Silas' path, and reared on its hind legs. The governor dodged its front hooves, but when he made another lunge at Ashen, a crack sounded. Electric blue barbed wire wrapped around Silas' face, searing him from chin to nose, the tip of the whip snapping against the perfect skin of his forehead.

The man let out an anguished screech as Max yanked him away from Ashen. The action forced his face to bubble over the wire, rearranging his flesh like oil in too much water. One eye bulged out, his nose flattened and charred, his fragile plasmic features forming into a grotesque abstract painting made real.

"You!" Silas screamed, feeling his face with his hands, his eyes angry. He found the end of the whip and tore it away. The blue wire stuck in spots, ripping up more plasma that created harsh, jagged crevices. "Look what you've done!"

While Macajah rose to his feet, Max said, "I warned you, Silas. You didn't give me much choice."

Teeth bared, the governor growled and transformed into an orb of white light. He hurtled through the shut bedroom door. Macajah and Max chased after him, vanishing into the hallway.

Between quick breaths, Ashen stared at the phantom horse. As she got up, one of the dog-eared magazines she'd knocked from the table caught her eye. Its cover depicted a dark shadow gliding down a staircase while, from the base of the stairs, three witnesses watched on in terror.

She squinted at the title printed in wispy, bold font: "The Truth". Beneath, the subheadline made a chill quiver up her spine: *Detailed Accounts of Dark Forces Persuading Teens to Harm Themselves or Others for the Greater Good.*"

The luminous horse next to her snorted, startling her.

"Hey there you, um, big, big animal," she cooed as she headed for the door, eyes fastened to the large creature. She paused. "Thanks for that, by the way."

The horse nickered and shook its mane.

"Wow," she said, passing through to the hall. "Now I'm talking to ghost ponies."

"That ain't a pony," said Macajah, his head popping out of the opposite wall. "That's Agnes and she's a mare. Now, get your behind in here so I can keep a dang eye on you. Reckon you're liable to cause a heap of trouble if left to your own devices."

After he ducked out of sight, Ashen rolled her eyes. She wasn't the one who had antagonized that guy. She'd only been trying to help. It wasn't her fault Silas held some massive grudge against these "Warders".

She huffed and followed, set on giving the cowboy a piece of her mind. Both Macajah and Max stood in the center of another bedroom while in the corner a full-length mirror shimmered with bright hues. Panicked, Ashen felt herself retreating back to the hallway, but when she noticed neither Max nor Macajah were the least bit disturbed by its presence, she willed herself to a halt.

"Where in tarnation is he?" Macajah asked.

"He must have flown out," Max said. He stuck his head through the outer wall of the house for a few seconds before pulling himself back inside. "Yeah, he scrammed. As long as he doesn't try a stunt like that again, I say we let him go."

"So, does that mean we can leave?" Ashen asked nervously as she gaped at the mirror. "Now?"

"Alright, alright," Macajah said. "Ain't no need to pitch a fit. We'll hightail it directly."

Max gestured at the mirror. "Should we mirror travel?"

The cowboy appraised Ashen's wide, anxious eyes. He shook his head. "Our ornery newly-dead here ain't ready."

As the three tromped down the stairs and back outside, a relieved Ashen asked, "Cage, you said that horse's name was Agnes, right? But isn't Agnes what you called your gun?"

"Yes ma'am. That's also the name of my...," Macajah threw Ashen a disapproving glance, "'Magic rifle' you detest so severely."

"You couldn't come up with something more, I don't know, intimidating?"

"Agnes is a fearsome, frightening name!" Macajah hollered. "That there horse and this here rifle saved you from getting all...," he grimaced, indicating his own face with his hand. "Reshuffled."

The meaning of his words dawned on her. "You mean, if I'd gotten hit by that light, what happened to that governor guy could have happened to me? But we're ghosts, right? Not like it's permanent. Is it?"

"Governor Lydford won't look the same again." Max's face fell. "I was aiming for his arm. Less damage that way. But I missed."

"You did what you had to, son," the cowboy said. He firmly patted Max on the shoulder. "The Light's tactics are getting more aggressive. Ain't your fault Silas is a deranged idjiot."

Max nodded but proceeded to study the cracks in the sidewalk. The neighborhood birds had woken in the lightening gray morning. They chirped, flitting from bare branch to bare branch, an upbeat contrast to the sullen soldier. While the three strolled down the street, Ashen replayed the event with Silas over in her mind. She peeked at Max. Only a few years older than she was, he seemed so sad for someone so young.

"You know, I didn't get to thank you," she said. "For doing what you did."

He raised his gray eyes. Smiling, Ashen added, "And I mean, let's face it, Cage wasn't gonna step in. He's probably too concerned about messing up that massive mustache of his, or thinking about why Agnes is a good name for both a horse and a gun."

As expected, Macajah took the bait. "Little Missy, I have a mind to abandon you right here, right now if you don't acquire some manners."

She raised her eyebrow playfully. "Pretty sensitive for an old, dead cowboy."

"Did you just call me a 'cowboy' after disrespecting my favorite horse?"

A few crickets sounded in the distant duskiness. "No."

"Good," Macajah tugged down on the brim of his Stetson and sauntered ahead of them, grumbling to himself. Ashen held back a snicker. From the corner of her eye, she caught sight of Max, grinning.

8

THE OLD WOMAN AND THE DUCK

The desert sun's weak morning rays filtered through the slits between the skyscrapers, warming sections of pavement in long, golden stripes. In the shade where the heat didn't reach, thick frost clung to the sidewalk. Every time Ashen stepped on it, she expected to hear that familiar, faint crunch underfoot, but instead there was an eerie silence.

Macajah stormed on in the lead, intent on reaching their final destination, while Ashen and Max lagged behind. She frowned in thought. Even though she'd read books and magazines and articles on anything related to the paranormal, she didn't have a single idea as to what lay ahead. Was she supposed to ascend someplace where angels squawked in choirs while playing enormous harps? Maybe reincarnate? Or perhaps she was giving herself too much credit and was destined instead to plummet forever through a dark emptiness.

She'd waited long enough and wanted answers. "Do you

know where we're going?"

"Union Station downtown," Max said.

"The old train depot?"

Max nodded. "I guess you could say it's the Warders' base of operations."

Morning light revealed details on the soldier's military fatigues. The shapeless, combat-practical uniform definitely wasn't modern. Several small canvas bags hung from his heavy-duty tan belt, including a canvas-clad canteen on one hip and a sheathed knife on the other. His trousers billowed over the tops of his mid-calf boots; the drab army-green material clashed with the chestnut-toned leather.

"Are you, um, were you in a war or something?" she asked.

"Yeah, it was something, alright," he said with a laugh. His eyes twinkled, softening the seriousness of his features. He jabbed his finger at a blue diamond patch stitched to the arm of his jacket. On it, the word "Ranger" was embroidered in yellow. "Army. Second Ranger Battalion. A D-Day mission was my last."

"Oh, I'm sorry to hear about—" Ashen raised her eyebrows. "Wait, did you say, D-Day? Like, 'the' D-Day?"

"Was there a different one I don't know about?"

"But," she scanned him head to toe as he grinned back at her. "You're barely older than me!"

He shoved his hands in his pockets and gave Ashen a wink. "We're all the same age here, darlin'. Young and old souls alike. The only timetable we've got is eternity."

An unexpected flush crept across her cheeks. She looked down to avoid any uncomfortable eye contact. Darling? What was with this guy? And the idea of eternity seemed, well, forever. Too massive to wrap her head around. She glowered at her feet, watching the flames lick up her leg with each soundless stomp she took. When she and Max crossed from the sunlit concrete to the shadow of a building, her footsteps remained inaudible, but beneath the soldier's boots, the brittle frost cracked.

Confused, Ashen debated if asking Max about something as silly as sound was worth the risk of turning red again. Once she had formulated her question, she raised her eyes, but a movement beyond the soldier next to her caught her attention.

New, dazed, dead souls strolled alongside them. They seemed like regular people, but there was a hint of how each had perished, just like the blue-fingered old woman pursuing her invisible duck. Although most of these indicators were subtle, others were more obvious: wisps of smoke tangled around a boy's arms and legs, specter water enveloped a lady, seeping growths covered an old man's chest. Visual chronicles of every person's death.

When the old man with the sores let out a phlegmy cough, Ashen winced before glancing at her own silver flames. She guessed getting blown up in a wreck had its advantages. At least her weird ghost power was pretty. It could have been worse. A lot worse.

Behind them, more dead souls followed, congregating on the sidewalks like some odd apparition parade. Their numbers had increased, but something else concerned her. All souls were headed in the same direction. Downtown Denver.

Her sights settled on two teenagers close to her own age. Both meandered along the fringes of the procession. The girl seemed stuck in perpetual shade, as if she repelled daylight, while the other, a boy, seemed to attract it. The two regarded each other for a brief moment, then at the same time, they separated from the group of newly-deads, one heading north and the other south.

New recruits, she assumed, though it seemed peculiar that they had made their minds up so quickly. Ashen could barely manage to keep her mental state in check, let alone figure out what she wanted in her afterlife.

A few blocks later, she and her new companions rounded the corner of 17th and Wynkoop. She stopped in her tracks. The streets were congested with the dead. They streamed in from all directions, each one walking toward a huge phantom brick gate. An arch.

Her mouth dropped open. "That was never here before."

"That there is the old Welcome Arch," Macajah said, making his way through the dead to clear a way to the train station courtyard. "Denver City dismantled it in the 1930s."

Ashen trailed behind Max and the cowboy, weaving between the spirits while she stared at the gate. Situated in front of the courtyard of the old train depot, the once-steel structure glistened like a desert mirage. It was decorated with an intricate metal filigree, and at the crest, old-fashioned light bulbs spelled out the word "MIZPAH". The overall architecture resembled something from Victorian England rather than the West.

"What's 'mizpah' mean?"

"It's a Hebrew word." Macajah said. "A way of sayin' fare thee well."

"So strange," Ashen marveled. "The gate almost looks solid. It's not fading at all."

Macajah only responded with a simple grunt. As they got closer, Ashen could see the inner workings. The arch led to a long, semi-transparent tunnel. Coiled bunches of light and color and voids, wound into tight bundles, stretched through the courtyard and far beyond Union Station. Immediately, she was reminded of her dream of the mine shaft with the unobtainable light at the end. That bizarre dream where she had woken up dead.

At the base, where the colors met the ground and right inside the entrance, feathers fluttered. A duck.

Ashen stood on her tiptoes. She spotted the old lady in the crowd, shuffling with rigid determination. When the woman reached the tunnel's threshold her wrinkled face broke into a broad smile.

"Quackers!"

Without hesitation, she walked through the opening beneath the arch, hunched back stooped low, blue hands outstretched. She scooped up her beloved friend and cradled him close as he quacked happily. The old woman smiled one last time before they both transformed into a faceted gemstone of light. The stone shone with pure brilliance as it split into glassy fireworks that twirled and flew down the tunnel, out of sight.

As soon as the old woman and the duck disappeared, the tunnel expanded, becoming brighter as a steady pulse thrummed through it. When it returned to its original appearance, the next dead soul stepped through the arch, splintering and spiraling along the same path. The tunnel reacted, throbbing with a sentient beat.

"Where did the old lady go?" Ashen asked.

"Moved on to the great unknown," Macajah said, still plowing through the throng.

"Unknown? What do you mean?"

When Macajah didn't answer, Max cleared his throat. "Earthbound spirits, like Cage and myself, don't know what lies beyond. Anyone who travels through the Divide never comes back."

Macajah stopped shy of the arch. "Little Missy, I suspect that there is your missing armored snake."

Fixated on where the tunnel led, Ashen hadn't noticed that a new creature watched from within its depths. At the entrance, behind the shimmering curtain, her turtle waited.

"Langhorne?" A lump formed in Ashen's throat. If it weren't for the silvery luster of his shell, her turtle would look as he always had. Alive.

He blinked back at her.

A pleasant sensation enveloped her brief sorrow. The tunnel pulled her, silently urging her to walk through. Whispering without words that it was the right thing to do. She found herself wondering if her mother was in there. If she was, had she finally overcome her demons? And what if Jacob hadn't survived the crash after all? Was he in the tunnel, too?

She took a step toward the phantom brick arch. The soldier's hand clamped down on her shoulder.

"You might want to go around." Max flashed a friendly smile, but his gray-blue eyes were troubled. As he steered her away from the arch, he added, "Once you cross over, there's no coming back—no second chances to settle unfinished business. But don't worry. Your turtle friend will wait until you're ready."

Ashen's frustration bubbled to the surface. Being dead was bad, getting vague answers to her questions was bad, but somehow, being herded like a wayward child was worse. She gritted her teeth as they passed through one of the arch's side gates. As soon as they were on the other side, she could no longer see the tunnel cutting through the courtyard. Baffled, she twisted away from the soldier's guiding hand to double back, jogging into the waiting crowd. She peered through the arch. The tunnel was still there, but this time, Langhorne wasn't.

"The dead can enter through either side." Max stuffed his

hands into his pockets. "The tunnel goes both ways."

"What do you mean, 'both ways'? And where's Langhorne?"

"He'll be back, Missy," Macajah said, motioning for her to follow. "We're nearly there, so best we get."

Folding her arms, Ashen let out a sharp sigh. She shoved past the two men standing in the side gate and stomped into the courtyard. She swiveled to the arch. That side also led to the tunnel, but this one appeared to extend out into the street where the hordes of dead were gathered. Even the structure of the arch was the same except for one detail. The word "MIZPAH" now read, "WELCOME."

"For some reason, the dead prefer the other side to move on," Max said, coming closer. "But it makes no difference. They just have to pass beneath the arch."

He gave her an uncertain smile, his face clouded with the same sadness as before. She felt her face burn with a combination of regret, anger, and guilt. Ignoring the feeling, she kept her arms crossed and headed toward the Union Station entryway, leaving the two men trailing after her.

"Glad you're here, Cage," Max said behind her. "Before I left for patrol this morning, Fox and John still hadn't gotten anywhere with this guy."

"Ain't surprised. If he's who I suspect, he's always been difficult."

Ashen wanted to ask who they were talking about, but she already knew Macajah wouldn't answer. That seemed to be a new running theme, and although her blood boiled the more she thought about it, she kept quiet as the three walked toward Union Station.

The old train depot initially looked like what she had known in life. But as they approached, the present-day broad arched windows vanished behind a layer of thin film, and the old frontage of square windows quivered into view. A phantom brick clock tower over six stories tall jutted from the middle. A large clockface was attached to each side of the stone structure, the hands pointing to what Ashen assumed was the actual time: a quarter past eleven. In back of the building, spectral trains faded in and out, puffing out multicolored steam as they rumbled by.

Standing outside the front double doors were three figures. The shortest was solid, like Max and Macajah, but the other two had a white ethereal glow. A man's voice rose above the clamor of the ghost train engines.

"Look what he did to me!"

Silas, the governor who had attacked her. The sound of his voice made Ashen stop. Her two companions caught up to her and exchanged a glance before quickening their pace. Ashen willed her legs to move and followed, squinting to see who accompanied the governor.

"Vana, I insist action be taken." The tall woman's soothing tone was familiar. "Can't you see the pain Silas is in?"

The quiet, yet strong voice of an elderly woman spoke. "*Mo'óhtávóéstá'e*, every person sees events differently. I must now speak to Max."

"He overstepped his authority!" Silas yelled.

They were close enough to see Silas' face. The lesion had worsened, as if he had tried to push some of the plasma back in place; the end result looked more like a child had played with too little clay before setting it on fire. Next to him stood Constance, the woman Ashen had run into outside the hospital. The woman who had asked Ashen to join her.

Join us.

"Yes, Silas," the petite elderly woman said, interrupting Ashen's thoughts. The woman wore a fringed buckskin dress, her gray hair parted into two braids—the same woman who had been on the bus the day of the wreck. "You are very particular about your laws. I give my word it will be resolved, but in our way. Not your way."

A muscle in Silas' disfigured jaw flexed. "Fine."

With his final word, he pivoted and marched toward Ashen and the others. Uncertain if he might try and take another lunge at her, she stepped behind Macajah and Max. A few feet away, Silas stopped, glared at each of them with his one good eye, and changed into an orb of white light. The orb hovered for a moment before it shot through the courtyard, past the arch, and darted down Wynkoop.

"Vana, I understand the responsibility the Warders carry." Constance said with a thin smile. Beneath her long black robes, the toe of her sensible shoe tapped. "But you must recognize that Max's actions were extreme."

"Criminy sakes, Constance," Macajah said, taking off his Stetson to smooth his hair. "Max doesn't have to apologize for a dang thing. Silas was interfering with a living being."

Constance's toe ceased. She raised her brow at Max. "Is this true?"

"Yes," Max said. "But you should know the damage I caused wasn't intentional, Miss Callahan. It happened when he attacked Ashen. I had to protect her."

The sting of guilt struck Ashen again. Back at the arch, Max hadn't been trying to control her. He had only been trying to help—to warn her before she made an irreversible decision. Even now, she used him and Macajah as a shield, and she scolded herself for being such a hypocrite. Taking a deep breath, Ashen stepped out from behind the two men.

"It's true. If it hadn't been for Max, I'm really uncertain what your friend, uh, that guy would have done."

"I see. Silas conveniently left that part out." Constance

paused. "Aren't you the girl I met outside the hospital?"

Ashen nodded. The woman's heels clipped toward her without a single hair on her head falling out of place. Something about her makeup and general sense of style seemed stuck more than a decade ago. A white collar peeked from beneath the closure on her robes, starched and void of any frills or embellishments. She tugged at it once before smiling. Her eyes were warm. Ashen smiled back.

"I offer my apologies. Silas' rogue conduct is not representative of the Light," Constance said. "He will keep his distance from now on. I promise."

The woman reached up to fix a few of Ashen's stray curls. The intimate gesture made Ashen flinch. Other than Jacob's poor attempts at flirting, she wasn't used to anyone touching her, and Constance seemed to notice her discomfort. She lowered her hand.

"I'm here at the station frequently," Constance said. She smiled again, her perfect teeth gleaming, before she transformed into a white orb. "If you ever need advice or help, I'll be around." The air around held the echo of her voice as she floated off in the same direction as Silas.

"I reckon the leaders of the Light are announcing their discontent, Vana?" Macajah said, placing his hat back on his head as he watched Constance vanish around the corner.

"Yes." Though the older woman had an unreadable expression, her eyes were merry. "Hello, Hollow Iron. You are late."

"We would have been here sooner," Macajah scowled and nodded his head toward Ashen. "But this one took some convincing."

While Ashen glared at the cowboy, Vana tilted her head. "The young one is the witness?"

"Witness?" Ashen asked. "Witness for what?"

"Tarnation, Missy! You sure do ask a lot of questions!"

"Only because you don't answer them! What does she mean by 'witness'?"

"Reckon if I tell you, it negates the whole purpose of having an unbiased observer," Macajah said as he burst through the double doors into the train station lobby.

Ashen trailed closely behind. "You do see how being vague like this is really, really annoying, right?"

"Quit your derned bellyaching!"

Ashen fumed. "If I'm not here to move on or find Jacob, then why have you brought me here?"

"You're to identify someone. Make certain we've got the right fella."

"Does that mean you had no intention of helping me? You're using me? Then what? Toss me into that arch thing back there and wish me luck?"

Macajah slowed his gait, his booted feet quieting. "No, Little Mis—"

Before he could finish, she turned on her heel and headed back toward the courtyard, pushing past Max and Vana. When she started through the door, Max seized her arm, stopping her.

"Listen, Cage is being a little hard-boiled, is all."

"Don't you get it?" She ripped away from his touch—any good nature she'd had left spent. An intense heat rose from her feet through the muscles of her calves. "He didn't tell me the whole truth. He misled me. Duped me. Tricked me. I could have been out looking for Jacob this entire time!"

As she said the last line something deep within her, like a levee that could no longer hold back a flood, burst. Feelings of annoyance, anger, and sadness blended together. Her tears swelled, teetering on her lower lashes until they grew too heavy and streamed down her cheeks in wet paths. When she had been alive, she'd never wept. But ever since her death, all she'd been successful at was either being completely clueless and useless, or bawling her head off.

A pearly light bloomed around her. Max recoiled. His wide eyes darted down and Ashen followed his gaze. A cry caught in her throat.

The flickering flames around her feet were no longer small. They engulfed her legs and thighs in a sterling brilliance, wrapping their tendrils, pulsing with light and fury, around her knees. Near her waist, the blaze billowed out as if it had been paused mid-explosion.

Fear consumed her battling emotions. "Wh-what's happening?"

"You must calm yourself, young one." The older woman's aged, serene face looked up at Ashen, and as if pacifying a wild horse, she raised her hand—the leather fringe on the hem of her sleeves cascading over either side of her upper arm. "Take deep breaths."

Ashen forced her eyes shut. She focused on her breathing before realizing that she, a dead girl, could no longer breathe and a new panic began to crush her chest. The pressure was so great, she could almost hear her non-existent bones breaking.

"Calm. Breathe. You are safe."

Something in the woman's even tone doused Ashen's fears. The heat in her legs cooled and her breathing returned to a steady, sure tempo. When she opened her eyes, the silver flames had petered out, returning to a tiny flicker dancing on the toes of her Converse sneakers.

"Very good, child."

The older woman was so close that Ashen could make out the craftsmanship of the dress she wore. It was beautiful. Blue and black beads fell across her shoulders in an intricate pattern. Strange ivory pieces, secured to the leather, dangled in a line across the upper portion of her chest.

"Hollow Iron," the older woman said, addressing Macajah. "You will apologize. Now."

"Apologize?" It looked as though another truck had hit Macajah. "Vana, I ain't apologizin'! There's nothin' to apologize for!"

The serenity Ashen had detected on Vana's face had been replaced with a flat seriousness. "And you will agree to assist her in finding her Jacob friend."

"Now listen, I ain't got time for these shenanig—"

"Hollow Iron. You will help this girl."

The cowboy's mouth twisted up beneath his thick mustache. "I likely would have assisted her in kind, anyhow, if she weren't so derned ornery."

"Hey!" Ashen said. "Don't talk about me like I'm not here."

"Oh heck, stop being so disagreeable," Macajah said. "I know you're here. You don't never let me forget." He swept his duster back and planted his fists on his hips before addressing Vana. "Reckon proper introductions are in order. Our witness here is Ashen Deming. Died recently. Smart. Might bit irritating though."

Ashen pressed her lips into a thin line, but before she could scold the cowboy further, the older woman turned to her.

"*Péhévevóonā'o*, Ashen. I am *Vánáhéó'o*."

Blood rushed to Ashen's face. Her anger interrupted and, for the moment, quelled, she asked, "Van-hay-yo? But I thought everyone calls you—"

"Vana. Yes, that is what those who are not Tsitsistas call me." She smiled. *"Vánáhéó'o* means Sage Woman. You may call me Vana. It is okay. It is a difficult name."

"So, are you one of those light people? Like that Constance woman? Or are you a Warder like," Ashen pointed at Macajah, "that jerk?"

"You best hobble your lip," Macajah said.

"That," Max said, maneuvering between the two like an uncomfortable human buffer, "was the Honorable Constance Callahan. She's definitely not one of us."

"You're all Warders?"

"Yes," Vana said. She moved to Ashen's side and wrapped her frail arm around Ashen's waist. "And the Warders need your help."

Ashen stiffened at the contact, but instead of Vana pulling away like Constance had, the older woman held her closer. After an awkward moment, Ashen frowned. "Okay. What do you need from me?"

She allowed Vana to lead her through the Union Station lobby. Though the structure had recently been restored, it didn't reflect any of the renovations. The spacious area was filled with rows of long, high-backed benches with a wide aisle down the center. The benches themselves appeared real, but they occasionally shimmered, betraying their true nature.

The ticket counter and a line of offices were at the back of the room. Each shuttered section had a sign above it. Tickets. Information. Another read Pullman. The one Ashen was being led to, at the end near the rear exit, read, "Telegraph".

Vana stopped outside the entrance to the telegraph room, still holding Ashen. The two men went ahead, walking through the closed door without flinching. Vana squeezed Ashen's elbow before releasing her and motioning to where

Max and Macajah had gone.

"You need my help in there?"

"Yes. It is important, but…"

Ashen had an uneasy feeling. "But what?"

"But you may not like it."

"Great."

Ashen edged toward the door until her nose was within inches of the wooden surface. She held her breath and took a sizable stride. As she filtered through the grainy fibers and thick paint, she peered into a long, narrow room. The furthest recesses were dark, but in the center of the space, overhead, was a boarded-up skylight. Several holes dotted the edge of the wood where slanted rays of sunlight escaped, cutting through the murk to create a circular pattern of beams. Beneath, standing shoulder to shoulder with their backs turned to her, were Macajah and Max.

"No time for games," the cowboy said. "Best you come clean now."

It dawned on Ashen that Macajah wasn't speaking to Max or someone hidden in the far side of the room, but to someone right in front of him. Her view blocked by the cowboy's massive duster, she tiptoed further into the room. Someone—or something—chuckled. She froze.

"Cage," said a low-pitched voice woven with a mechanical hum. "Is that my prey I smell over yon?"

Ashen had heard the voice before. A shiver spread through her. She forced herself between Max and Macajah, breaking through their barricade to rush forward, only to halt after a few steps.

In a chair, surrounded by shafts of light like the bars of a jail cell, sat a shadow figure. His heavy physique spilled out over the arms of the chair and his abdomen rested on his lap, concealing everything but his bulbous knees. Beneath a bowler hat, his bulging face smirked as he glared up at her with his pitch-black eyes.

"No, Toad," Macajah said, placing his hand on Ashen's shoulder. "We've not fetched you prey. We've brought our witness."

9

THE THIRD OFFENSE

Ashen swallowed away a hard lump. "What is that thing?"

"I ain't no thang," the shadow said.

As the monster's features melted and mixed into themselves, revulsion crawled up Ashen's throat. The hard lump returned, and she instinctively shrank away, wedging herself between Macajah and Max.

From the darkest part of the room where the beams of the skylight could not reach, a man spoke. Though the unexpected voice made Ashen flinch, the man sounded nothing like the creature in the chair. He sounded young. Mellow.

"We're growing tired of this, Toad," the man said as he approached, his eyeglasses glinting in the gloom. "This germ is hiding something."

"I know, John," a girl replied. The outline of another, smaller shape emerged next to the man wearing the glasses. Hints of wisdom laced her voice, the mature tone countered by a youthful, innocent quality. "Considering who he's employed by, I expect him to be less than truthful." The girl's ebony eyes flicked up. "Cage? Is this one of the repeat offenders?"

"I reckon, though I've not seen this unfortunate soul in a stretch," Macajah said. "You confirm he's the same from that contraption yesterday?"

"Yeah," answered John. "After he beat feet, Vana and Max apprehended him in the basement of an abandoned house. I have to admit, though, this whole situation seems suspect."

Max turned to a bewildered Ashen. "Do you recognize him?"

Against her better judgment, Ashen moved nearer to the shadow's inky mass. Long, lean fangs curved down past its massive jaws. She shuddered. Though it wasn't the same creature from her bedroom years before, it was remarkably similar.

"I'm pretty certain, yeah. I mean, he sounds the same, but I only caught a glimpse after he, uh, appeared on the bus."

Macajah scratched at the stubble on his cheek. "Before this here fella clawed his way out, he was taking refuge inside a corpse suit. Ain't that about right, Toad?"

Ashen searched the faces around the room, but none revealed any clue to what Macajah's peculiar terminology meant.

"I'm afraid I'm gonna regret asking," she said. "But what, exactly, is a corpse suit?"

The young man named John walked forward and into the light. The spectacles he wore were an older style, the glass set in thick, circular frames of ivory plastic that contrasted with his dark brown skin. He removed them and pulled a handkerchief from the pocket of his plain linen shirt. As he cleaned the lenses, he spoke with a smooth, melodic cadence. "The Unseen, like this man here, have been occupying soulless vessels."

He looked up. As if reading Ashen's confusion, he positioned his glasses on the bridge of his nose and smiled. "Dead folks' bodies. A type of possession, if you will, but the soul has vacated, leaving the body empty."

"They get used like some sort of meat puppet?"

"Precisely."

Ashen turned back toward Toad. "I don't get it. Why take people's dead bodies? Can't these Unseen guys, I dunno, walk around like Warders and be less creepy?"

"Well," John paused. He ran his hand over his tight, curly hair, and when he did, metal tinged against metal. Thick leather cuffs secured with industrial-sized buckles circled each wrist. "The Unseen prefer to hide from the sun and other light while they hunt. They have a natural aversion to it."

The reason for the holes in the skylight became more clear to Ashen. She stretched her arm out into one of the beams that surrounded Toad, watching as the light reflected off her ghost skin. Of course! Light bothered these Unseen, just the same as the creature that had attacked her as a child.

"You may want to keep your distance," John said. "He's not dangerous to us Warders, but he could do some damage to a living person or a newly-dead, like yourself."

Ashen drew her hand away. "Wouldn't this light cage of yours protect me?"

"It's only a security measure," John said. "Assists us in keeping him in check until the sun sets. For now, we'll continue to question him about his new-found abilities, and also why the Unseen have access to so many corpse suits. Seems suspicious."

"Ya best not be falsely accusin', John Porter!" the fat shadow creature bellowed. "I ain't done nothin' wrong! I told ya I ain't touched that feller when he were livin'! Him was dead 'fore I tuck him, ya worthless runaway coon!"

The outburst startled Ashen but before she could back away, the girl who had spoken earlier marched out from the gloom behind John, her eyes brimming with anger. She didn't look to be much older than sixteen. A wide belt was wrapped twice around her slim waist, its purple and white beads woven into intricate geometric patterns. Within the folds of her royal blue frontier-style dress, two wooden hatchet-like handles peeked out, each glowing red. As she reached for them, John placed a gentle hand on her shoulder.

"He's not worth it."

"But, John!"

"Ignorance cannot be reasoned with." John smiled and gave the girl's arm a final squeeze. "You know that, Fox."

Fox pursed her lips and nodded. She pivoted from her initial target, her black, straight hair twirling about her in one motion like a long curtain, and stomped behind John. Letting out a sigh, she began fiddling with something draped below the high collar of her dress. A necklace. Several strands of seed beads, braided together in a chain, supported the weight of a large silver medallion. All the while, the girl glared at the shadow, her eyes emitting a deep crimson. If looks could kill, Ashen was certain that the shadow creature, Toad, would have been dead twice over.

"Like I says," Toad said, grinning at Fox. "I ain't done nothin' wro—"

The echo of Macajah's boots cut him off. "As this here would be your third offense, you best hope you're right." The cowboy entered the cage and bent down, his face mere

103

inches from the inflated Unseen's. "The way I see it, it was you that caused that calamity that led to this young lady's premature demise."

Toad laughed. "Ya Warders, you'uns accusin' and axin' questions, thinkin' ya all mighty powerful."

"And I reckon," Macajah said, "all this bellyaching means you did, in fact, do something nefarious."

"Ya got no proof of nothin', Sloan, and ya knows it."

"So, I suspect you hightailing through that mirror on the bus was nothing?"

The smirk fell from Toad's face. With a blank stare he sat there—a low rumble growing louder from within his girth. As if a switch had been flipped, the creature shot up from his chair and into the air, his bulk shoving Macajah off his feet.

The shadow weaved back and forth to avoid the rays of sunlight confining him. As he darted for the inner wall of the building, Ashen felt Max yank her behind him. The soldier grabbed at each forearm to loosen the barbed wire tattoos, each radiating the same bright blue as when he had fought Silas. Sprawled on the ground, Macajah reached into his duster for his golden Winchester.

The other two Warders' reactions were quicker. The girl with the medallion stood ready, dual-wielding two tomahawks pulsing with a red brilliance. The leather cuffs around John Porter's wrists gleamed. Lime and emerald green twined into lightning that burst from the buckles.

Together, the group struck out at the Unseen, their colorful slashes of light barely missing the ricocheting shadow as they herded him like a runaway bull. When the tip of Max's whip cut the plasma of Toad's cheek, the creature squealed, hesitating long enough for shafts of red and bolts of green to block his escape. He slowed, floating in the middle of his cage, his large frame panting with exertion between his perverse shrieks.

Macajah stood up, clicked his tongue, and pointed the barrel of Agnes at the shadow's head. "Sit. Down. Now."

The shadow whimpered. "I told ya, I ain't done nothin'!"

"The mirror! How'd you use it?" asked Max. "And why were you hunting the living?"

Toad sat in a huff. He lowered his gaze, refusing to keep eye contact with any of the Warders, and rested his arms on his belly.

"This might take a spell," Macajah said, addressing Fox and John. "Go on now. Tend to Miss Deming while we have a little conversation with Toad here."

Fox, still gripping her tomahawks, scowled at Toad as she passed. For a brief moment, her weapons smoldered with intensity as she stowed them on her belt, then she walked through the wall without a word.

The green luster of John's cuffs diminished to a jade haze. He nodded at Ashen and turned the doorknob for her. "After you," he said.

Despite her aggravation at Macajah for assigning her babysitters, she smiled at John, grateful for his attempt at normality. When she stepped through the doorway, Ashen almost bumped into Vana waiting outside. The older woman glanced from Ashen to the Unseen. There was a trace of recognition as the door to the telegraph room shut, but her look vanished when Fox, wearing a serious expression, placed a hand on Vana's shoulder.

"He's one of them, isn't he?" Fox asked.

"Yes," Vana said.

"Who is that guy?" Ashen asked.

Vana frowned but didn't say anything more. She squeezed Fox's hand before retiring into the main room of the train station alone.

Once Vana was out of earshot, Fox said, "A bad man."

Ashen shuffled from foot to foot. She felt out of place. Overwhelmed. Her eyes fell on the pendant hanging from its beaded chain around Fox's neck. It was expertly crafted. Inlaid with purple and white shells, the silver had been shaped into the likeness of an animal. A fox.

Ashen struggled to think of something to say. "Yeah, that Toad guy seems pretty ... not so great." She paused, then finished with, "Umm, your necklace is cool."

Fox regarded her. "Thank you."

The three stood in awkward silence. John cleared his throat. "I suppose we should formally introduce ourselves. I'm John Porter, and this is Katie Matheson."

"Katie? I thought her name was Fox?"

"Angry Fox is my tribal name."

"Oh. Well, that's a...," Ashen searched for words again, "... nice name. Should I call you Katie or Angry Fox?"

"I no longer have a preference," Angry Fox said as she headed toward Vana on the other side of the room.

Ashen's eyes followed the girl. "Did I say something to offend her?"

"Nah," John said. "She's a softy. Takes time to get to know her." When unclear fragments of Angry Fox and Vana's quiet conversation floated across the lobby, he adjusted his glasses and turned to Ashen. "I deduce you're not accustomed to being supervised by strangers?"

"Not really." The heat in her feet intensified as she gestured at the flickering interior of Union Station. The lobby had grown more populated with living souls as lunchtime approached, and the people rushed about, oblivious to the ghosts and the afterlife all around them. "I mean, I get that I'm young and naive and all, but I can take of myself, even in this new reality."

"Being dead is a lot for anyone to deal with," John said. "You'll catch on."

"When?"

"Eventually?"

Ashen sighed. "Wonderful."

He laughed. "I certainly didn't intend to rattle your cage, Miss ... Ashley, was it?"

"Ashen. Ashen Deming. Nice to meet you."

"Likewise." John said. He pointed his thumb at the closed door of the telegraph room. "I suppose we have a while to wait. Care to accompany me on my duties, Miss Deming?"

She shrugged and, not knowing what else to do, followed him, dodging what living souls she encountered. Nearby, the two Warder women, heads lowered, sat together on a phantom bench, their hushed tones drowned out by the sound of John's footsteps echoing against the white marble walls of the lobby. Angry Fox's concerned gaze flicked to John and Ashen as they passed. John nodded once and disappeared through the front doors of Union Station.

Before going outside, Ashen hesitated and peered back over her shoulder. Vana's aged face was contorted with grief. There were no tears, but her utter despair was coupled with something not unlike rage. Whatever wound that creature, Toad, had inflicted was fresh.

Even though Angry Fox's hands were clasped over the older woman's, the younger girl's focus hadn't strayed from Ashen. When their eyes met, Ashen held up her hand and gave her an uncertain wave. The medallion shimmered around Angry Fox's neck as she nodded back.

The early afternoon sun blazed down into the courtyard. Ashen winced in the brightness. At the front, the glimmering Welcome Gate stood out against the neutral canvas of washed-out pavement and concrete like a half-finished painting. While the newly-dead flocked to the opposite side, waiting for their turn to move on, multicolored forms of the living hurried from one light rail platform to the next.

"Is that older lady okay?" Ashen asked.

"Vana? Yeah, she'll be alright. We'll help her out with her usual responsibilities for today." John paused. "In normal circumstances, I'd be out patrolling or following leads on offenders."

"So, Warders are cops?"

"I guess so, yes. We police the departed." John raised his eyes to the Welcome Arch. "We also protect the Divide's entrance."

"Why? Seems pretty fine on its own."

"The arch itself can't be harmed, but there are some souls that need protection from it."

Ashen leaned against the door. "This is all way too confusing. Aren't all the dead supposed to go through there?"

"Not earthbounds. Once we decide to stay, we remain on this plane."

"So why'd you stay?"

When John spoke, his voice was husky. "Have you ever heard of Langston Hughes?"

Ashen shook her head.

"He was a poet. A man I admire greatly. After I died, I started the long trek from Limon to Denver—pursuing that weird attraction I guess we all feel upon death." He removed his glasses and used his shirt to buff the lenses. "Not long after I began my journey, a poem by Langston Hughes kept replaying in my brain—about how Justice is a blind goddess. And something in me snapped. I became furious … and I turned around."

John got quiet as he polished his glasses. The very air around the two ghosts felt electric. Tense. Ashen didn't dare speak.

"You see, I was falsely accused of a crime I did not commit, but I knew who was responsible. So I went back, and for the next fifteen years, I haunted that man. I made my own justice." John put his glasses on. "Every earthbound has their reasons for staying."

Before John could elaborate, there was a loud crack of thunder. Dark clouds, full of doom and displeasure, had formed over the Rockies. "That's unfortunate," he added, frowning. "The sunshine was promising. Hope Cage and Max get somewhere with a few less hours of daylight."

The day wore on. Living people sprinted to catch the next bus or light rail before the inevitable downpour. From the front steps of Union Station, while she kept a wary eye on the impending storm, Ashen watched the colorful forms scurry through the courtyard. Her mind wandered to Jacob. She hoped more than anything that he was one of those living lights.

When the clear patches of sky turned the color of faded candlelight, Angry Fox walked through the front wall of Union Station. Her face was sullen; so serious for one so young.

"How is Vana?" asked John.

The young girl began to fiddle with her medallion, flipping it from back to front to back again. "She's as well as can be expected. As well as any of us when faced with our pasts." She cleared her throat. "She told me Silas was here."

John's expression now mirrored Angry Fox's. "Glad I

missed him."

"She also said he attacked the newly-dead," Fox said, gesturing toward Ashen. "Max intervened. Apparently required some force."

"How much force?"

A mischievous smirk pulled at the corners of Angry Fox's lips. It was as close to a smile as Ashen had seen. "From what I gather, he'll not be victorious in … what are those absurd charades called? Beauty pageants?"

A full grin crept to John's face. "Fox, that's vicious."

"He deserves it, wouldn't you say?"

"Wow. Do any of you not have any crazy baggage with some other dead person?" Ashen asked. She stood and crossed her arms. "Also, please stop referring to me as newly-dead. That's just—"

"Disrespectful?" John finished. As Ashen blinked in surprise, he smiled. "It appears Macajah has already made an impression on you."

As Ashen sulked, a wall of black clouds rolled overhead, blotting out what daylight remained. Long shadows layered on top of each other as the darkening sky shifted and churned into swirls of golden-green and charcoal-gray. Lightning flashed. Thunder rumbled. It began to rain.

"A tornado?" Ashen asked, her eyes wide. "Kinda early in the season, isn't it?" A funnel hitting downtown Denver was unheard-of. If it was big enough and managed to touch down, there might be a lot more newly-deads like herself lining up at the Welcome Arch.

Neither Angry Fox nor John answered. Instead, they each took up a fighting stance; Fox gripped a glowing tomahawk in each hand while close by, both of John's cuffs gleamed. A heavy curtain of mist formed to the north. A whistle, distant at first, howled longer and louder as it approached. The low repetitious beat of a lumbering steam engine rumbled. Brakes shrieked.

From within the fog emerged the largest locomotive Ashen had ever seen. A matte jet black, it floated off the ground, its massive smokestack billowing out inky phantom smoke, its cowcatcher attached to the front cutting through the haze like a mouthful of sharp teeth. Above, rivets circled the edge of a round, thick piece of forged metal faced with a brass plate—the number 191 stamped in the center. Rather than illuminating the path ahead, its single square headlamp devoured light, not unlike the twenty black orbs flying alongside the wheels of the train.

"No. It's not a tornado," Angry Fox finally said. "Tornadoes are less aggravating."

10

ENGINE 191

The train slowed. Although she tried, Ashen couldn't rip her eyes away from the black orbs. Memories piled on top of one another, every detail from the night she drowned in her farmhouse foyer crushing and smothering the next with its weight. There was no mistake. The monster that had attacked her had changed into an orb exactly like these. She wondered if the Unseen creature from her childhood was among them.

Her fear grew, her focus cutting from one orb to the next, scrutinizing each as they flew in an erratic procession; the small and fast zipped around and through the phantom locomotive while those that were bigger flanked either side, drifting along at differing speeds. There seemed to be no method to their movements. No organization. Only random disarray.

The largest of the group sat on top of the headlamp. Different from the others, a deep purple shimmer, nearly undetectable, rippled across its surface as it teetered on the apex. When the train shuddered to a halt, it transformed until the crouched form of a shadow creature, an Unseen, materialized. From beneath its rumpled hat, it peered down at Ashen and the Warders, its sunken eyes ingesting light like the headlamp it was perched on.

The rest of the Unseen orbs altered into dark silhouettes of men and women. All wore hats from different time periods. A lady's frontier bonnet, a simple baseball cap, a glamorous topper made of velvet with a collection of ostrich plumes jutting from the side. One of the creatures adjusted what looked to be a Civil War cap, but since everything was cloaked in black, Ashen couldn't tell if it was for the Union or the Confederate Army.

Although relieved none wore the same wide-brimmed squat style of the monster she'd witnessed as a child, a new, cold terror took over. Five years ago, it had only been one creature. Now, Ashen was confronted with twenty, maybe more. Who was to say these weren't a threat? She glanced at John and Angry Fox. At least this time she wasn't alone.

The Unseen on the headlamp stood to its full height. Every part of its tall, lanky frame looked sharp. Severe. It bent down, its pointed knees low, and launched itself into the air, landing with little effort a few feet in front of them. Ashen flinched, but the two Warders next to her didn't budge.

The creature regarded them. "Where's my kin?"

"Your brother's fine, Eli. Cage and Max are doing their due diligence," John said, stepping forward. "Strange. It's not like the Unseen to be out before sunset."

"Light don't agree with us, but it ain't botherin' us no more, neither. Not like it used to. Mister Glick's been workin' us fierce with recruitin'."

"Recruiting?" Ashen asked. She had a sinking feeling. After her encounter as a child, she'd pored over books and articles, all mentioning creatures like these Unseen, like the Drifters, like the Warders, like the Light. It had all been so close to reality, yet still so far away. And the magazine declaring, "The Truth"—the one she'd seen in the boy's room where she'd first met Silas—kept leaping into Ashen's mind. Dark forces were at play, but which of these groups were the ones preaching the greater good while bullying the living? All of them? None of them?

"The more souls the Unseen or the Light recruit," John answered. "The more powerful they become."

"What about you guys?"

"The Warders' power comes from the Divide."

"Warder!" Eli interrupted. "I ain't here ta be teachin' lessons. I'm here ta fetch my kin."

Angry Fox moved next to John. "Eli, you're well aware of the punishment if he did interfere with the living."

"He ain't done what ya says he done. Even if'n he did, ya let Mister Lydford git. You'uns ain't got no right ta be holdin' him fer the same."

"That was Silas' first offense," Angry Fox said, the tomahawks in her grasp glimmering. Red light accented the white of her knuckles. "This is your brother's third."

"Ya can't let her do that ta him!" Desperation twisted the Unseen's voice. Ashen's two companions glanced at each other. Their expressions reflected steel, but underneath, there was an inevitable dread. Whatever punishment lay ahead for Toad, the Warders took no pleasure in it.

John spoke softly. "You know our rules, Eli. Our laws. You need to prepare yourself for the probability of his exile."

"A fate worse 'un this, ya mean," Eli said, scowling as he gestured at the world around them. "I'm present fer Mister

Glick, true enough. But I'm here fer me, too. I'm askin' you'uns ta reconsider."

"You weren't concerned about others when you were a living man," Angry Fox said. "And neither was your brother."

At this, Eli's face altered to a mask of misery. He lowered his head to stare at the ground. "I ain't askin' fer forgiveness. Just fer a clean slate, fer Toad's sake."

The click of heels sounded on the sidewalk behind them. "There are no clean slates for the dead."

Ashen and the Warders whirled. At once, Constance Callahan materialized, her brilliant white light washing out the black of her judicial robes as they billowed around her slim frame.

"Hello, Katie," Constance said to Angry Fox before her gaze flicked to John, then Ashen. "Ashen—I advise you stay clear of that man, John Porter. He's a dangerous killer. Why the Warders allowed him in their ranks, I'll never understand."

When she spoke, John turned back to Eli. A ripple of stoic indifference crossed his features. "As I've stated before, Miss Callahan—I'm innocent."

"The Honorable, if you please."

He cleared his throat but didn't correct himself. With a thin smile, Constance said, "Of course. I shouldn't expect such niceties from a Warder, especially one such as yourself." Without waiting for a reaction, she switched her attention to Ashen and her forced smile became a genuine beam. "I've come to speak to Ashen privately. Is this acceptable?"

While Angry Fox stood by, frowning, John sucked in a breath. He nodded. "Fox and I will check on the status of Eli's brother."

The whole time he spoke, Constance never looked in his direction. It was obvious she wasn't waiting for his approval. Jaw set, John lifted his eyes to Ashen and gave her a sad yet reassuring smile.

"We'll be back in a few minutes," he said to her.

Eli looked up. "Many thanks ta ya."

"We'll discuss his fate with the others," Angry Fox said, stowing her weapons in her skirt. "But your gratitude at this time may be premature."

As she and John headed toward the Union Station entrance, Constance draped her arm around Ashen's shoulders and began to guide her away from the Unseen's phantom locomotive and toward the Divide.

"Have they been treating you well?" the woman asked when they were out of earshot.

"Uh, yes?" Ashen looked back at Eli. Surrounded by his mob, the Unseen stood as if he were a statue, his empty sockets fixed upon the backs of John and Angry Fox as they disappeared through the double doors.

Being brought closer to the Divide made Ashen's stomach lurch. The yearning she had felt when she'd first arrived grew stronger, and she found herself searching for Langhorne as they neared, hoping he was there to greet her. She frowned. Her turtle wasn't beneath the arch or waiting at the feet of the throngs of dead.

Constance stopped. "Have you considered the Light's offer? To join us?"

Join us.

Snapped from her daze, Ashen blinked at her. "Not really. Sorry, I mean, the only thing I've been thinking of is finding Jacob."

"That's your friend, isn't it? The one from your accident?" Constance asked. She smiled. "Perhaps he's more than a friend?"

"Oh, no! Eww. No, nothing like that. He's like … my brother."

"Perhaps he has moved on." The woman indicated the Welcome Arch. "Without you."

Ashen winced. The idea that Jacob had abandoned her hurt. "He wouldn't do that," she said, but her own words didn't sound convincing. "I'm sure he's alive. Somewhere."

"Well, you should start in the last place you saw him." Constance fixed another of Ashen's curls. "Follow the breadcrumbs from there."

Constance let her finger trail down Ashen's cheek. The invasive move left Ashen conflicted. For years, she had craved the same caring affection from her own mother—affection that this stranger managed to give with little effort.

"Once you find him," Constance said. "Do you know what you will decide?"

"Move on, I guess," Ashen said. "I mean, I appreciate your offer and all, but I don't think I'm really cut out for this."

"Losing an asset such as yourself would be a pity."

"You've gotta be joking. Ever since I died, I've been a disaster, not an asset."

"Oh, Ashen! A lovely, learned girl such as yourself could never be a disaster." Constance said. "I understand this place isn't for everyone, but I do hope you take as much time as you need. One shouldn't rush into such big decisions."

The judge's smile melted, her attention drawn to Union Station. John and Angry Fox were making their way down the front steps toward them, and as they did, Constance let out a strained sigh. She pulled Ashen into a sudden embrace. It was a kind gesture, and Ashen knew it, but she couldn't prevent her body tensing. In return, she gingerly patted Constance three times on the back.

"I wish you luck," the judge said in her ear. "But before I leave, I will give you one final piece of advice." She released Ashen to hold her at arm's length. Her features had darkened to a serious sternness. "Do not trust anyone. Not Macajah. Not any of the Warders. Especially," she said, glaring at John, "not him."

Alarmed, Ashen narrowed her eyes at John. "What? Why?"

But instead of answering, the judge transformed into a hovering white orb. Constance's voice chimed from within.

"Remember what I said. Don't trust anyone."

After she spoke, the judge's orb darted down 17th Street. Left alone, Ashen stood in the courtyard with her mouth open, staring after her.

"Is she still attempting to recruit you?" John asked as he approached. Angry Fox peered from behind him.

"Yeah," Ashen said. She looked to each of them. They seemed trustworthy enough, but other than Jacob, she had never been a great judge of character. With Constance's warning ringing in her ears, she couldn't help but wonder if her intuition was as bad in death as it had been in life.

"Have you accepted?" asked Angry Fox.

"Oh. Uh, no. I've got other priorities right now."

"Your friend," John said. "Which reminds me, Cage said he'll assist you with your search, as promised, after he releases Toad."

"He's been making empty promises for a while." Salt sprinkled Ashen's tone. "And Cage isn't actually thinking of letting that guy go, is he?"

"This is Toad Tibbits' third strike, and considering his awaiting punishment would be irreversible, Cage offered him a trade. Tibbits delivered." John removed his glasses and rubbed his eyes with the back of his hand. "I'll go give the good news to Eli before we head inside."

As John walked off toward the Unseen, Ashen felt herself shaking. Was the cowboy out of his mind? How did he expect Ashen to move on through the Divide with the threat of that fat shadow breathing down her neck? Maybe she'd get lucky, find Jacob alive and well, and get out of there before anything bad had a chance to happen.

It was as if Angry Fox could read her thoughts. "Believe it or not, we Warders are not imbeciles."

"Wait, I never said—"

"What I mean is we are confident that Toad is the one who assaulted you, but please understand that the information he provided Macajah is valuable. It may help us to better protect the vulnerable."

"Ugh, I get it," Ashen said with a huff. "I mean, I don't really like it, but I get it. Anyway, that slimeball Toad is nothing compared to the first Unseen guy that attacked me."

"Macajah mentioned that. Was he the one who sang, 'Down by the River Liv'd a Maiden' to you?"

"Well, he sang 'Clementine,' but good to know the old cowboy butthead bothers to listen sometimes."

A smirk curled at the corner of Angry Fox's mouth. "It's essentially the same song. 'Clementine' is a parody—a more modern version of 'Maiden.'"

"It's like a hundred years old, isn't it?"

"To me, that is relatively modern," Angry Fox said, her smile broadening.

The steam whistle blared. As the rumble of the locomotive grew, the black shadows of the Unseen changed back into their orbs. The last to join them was Eli. He faced John, gave him a single, deep nod, turned toward Angry Fox, and did the same. He transformed, floating up to balance on the headlight as the locomotive trundled through the courtyard where it vanished into the advancing dusk.

John headed toward Union Station. As the two girls followed, Ashen asked, "I won't have to get close to the Unseen guy again, right?"

"No need to fret," Angry Fox said. "We won't allow him near you."

"Good to know. I just keep thinking of the whole, 'lost and gone forever' bit of that song he sang."

"Gone and lost forever."

"Same difference. Still freaks me out. That part is pretty fitting right now."

"Do you know 'Amazing Grace'?" Angry Fox asked, slowing down.

"The song? Yeah, of course."

"It had importance to my people. They were quite fond of it, so whenever I feel melancholy, I recite, 'I once was lost, but now am found.' I find it calms me."

"I gotta admit, you seem like a lot of things, but sad isn't one of them."

"Darkness is a part of everyone. I conceal mine well, but the sorrow remains," Angry Fox said. Her eyelids fluttered for a moment before she lifted her head high and picked up her pace. "At any rate, if you agree to keep my secret, newly-dead, I'll be certain to conveniently forget that you referred to Macajah as a cowboy. Agreed?"

Ashen smiled. "Agreed."

11

MONSTERS

The rest of the posse's chatter ceased when Macajah and Max exited the small room with their prisoner. The shadow creature marched ahead, his wrists loosely bound, wincing whenever the lit barbed wire touched him.

"Quit your squirmin', Tibbits," Macajah drawled. "Unless you're determined to cause yourself permanent damage."

"This here thang's on too tight," Toad said.

"No, it ain't. You best keep your trap shut before I gift you another deadbeat handshake."

Toad huffed, his black eyes roaming the open lobby. Next to the main double doors, waiting with the rest, stood Vana. When the Unseen's sights settled on her, terror transformed his face and in a panic, he backed up, seeming to forget about the wire singeing the plasma near his hands.

"Ya keep that thar heathen away!"

His massive bulk collided into Macajah and Max. The two Warders responded, each moving to either side to grab one of his round arms and drag him toward Union Station's entrance. All the while, Vana's gaze never faltered.

"No!" Toad yelled. "Ya injun here ain't makin' me no Drifter!"

Cold penetrated Ashen's core as she thought back to the ghost in the cemetery, alone and weeping in the night. She flicked her eyes to Vana. A throbbing orange light bloomed around the older woman, but her expression was serene. Regal. Downright graceful. Even though she didn't show any sign of malice, Ashen found herself reeling back. Something about Vana reminded her of a bomb on the verge of detonation.

"Vana's not making you a Drifter, you derned idjiot," the cowboy said. He shoved Toad toward Max and tipped the brim of his Stetson. Max nodded before ushering the Unseen out into the darkened courtyard.

Macajah sauntered over. "Pay him no mind, Vana."

"Yes, Hollow Iron. He is a little man."

"Did he provide anything more on how he was able to use mirrors?" John asked.

The cowboy let out a rough grunt. "P'shaw. Seems as though our Unseen friends have stumbled on more souls for power. Toad vows it's due to increased recruiting, but I suspect there's more to his tale. Newly-deads movin' on through the Divide have dwindled, true enough, but that don't explain why the Unseen have had a surge."

"And we're still releasing him?"

"Not much choice. I made a bargain and I intend to keep my word. I reckon if we're gonna enforce our laws, we best abide by the same rules."

Max's head popped through the doors of the station. "Cage? Some Unseen are here."

"Thaddeus with them?"

"Unconfirmed. There's two of them, though. One's Eli."

The thick stubble on Macajah's cheek twitched. "Suppose we ought to get this over with."

Ashen followed the posse out to the courtyard. In the twilight, the glow from Max's blue barbed wire emphasized the outlines of the soldier and the Unseen as they led the way toward the Divide.

Quickening her pace, Ashen caught up to Macajah. "What did you mean about Vana making Toad a Drifter?"

"Never you mind, Little Missy."

"But isn't a Drifter like that lady we saw—"

"I said never you mind."

The cowboy's curt dismissal made Ashen seethe. More secrets? More lies? For what purpose? Her blood boiled, its angry rhythm pulsing through her as she thought about Constance's warning. How could she trust any of the Warders when they continued to keep her in the dark?

The heat within her grew. Silver flames burst from her forearm as she reached out, grabbed hold of the cowboy's sleeve, and jerked him to a halt. A burning handprint branded the leather of his duster, but Macajah didn't flinch.

"Oh, no you don't, you stupid cowboy! You're gonna give me some answers!"

The man whirled, his golden eyes beneath the Stetson lit. "I ain't playin' games, Miss Deming! You don't gotta be stuck here with the rest of us earthbounds. You're free to head yonder to that there arch," he said, pointing at the Divide with his bronze finger. "Pass on through, unscathed, and get all the answers a soul could ever want. You've no idea what a grand gift you possess!"

"If you're so bitter about being here, move on! Change it!"

"I wish I could," Macajah said. His brow creased and his stern tone softened. "But that ain't possible now."

He lowered his head. Though the brim of his hat hid most of his face, the lights of the city danced across his mustache and quivering bottom lip. When he next spoke, his voice was thick.

"I apologize."

"Keep your apologies." She tried to force confidence into her trembling words, but witnessing the cowboy's vulnerability was like watching an unbreakable fortress crumble before her eyes. "It's probably better if I find Jacob on my own."

Without a plan in mind, she stomped off, unaware of where she was headed. All she knew was that she wanted—needed—to get away from the Divide, away from the Warders and the Unseen shadows and every other perplexing detail of her newly-dead life. After a few strides, she felt the cowboy's hand clasp on her shoulder where her spectral blaze hadn't spread.

"I am sorry, Little Missy," he said. He let his arm fall to his side. "I reckon I let my worries get the best of me. Once this exchange with the Unseen is over, if you'll have me, I would be mighty appreciative if you allowed me to fulfill my promise. Assist you in locating your friend. On my honor, I'll do what I'm able to assure you don't get stranded here like the rest of us."

With that, he pivoted and trudged off toward the arch, past Max, who looked baffled, and Toad, who had a giddy smirk plastered on his bloated face. Ashen's temper reduced to a simmer as she stared after him.

"Hollow Iron is a difficult man," Vana said. Her hand, small and delicate, patted the back of Ashen's arm and lingered there. "But he is a good man."

"Why does he have to be such a pain?"

"He misses those he loves. We all do."

The simple statement sank its teeth into Ashen. Her gaze flicked to Max before she turned to Vana. Behind the older woman stood John and Angry Fox. Within each Warder's expression, torment and sadness dwelled like a private, unspeakable story that they couldn't bear to share. An unadulterated truth.

"Can someone here please be straight with me?" Ashen said, the fire in her arm subsiding. "What did Toad mean about being made into a Drifter?"

Vana linked her petite arm around Ashen's and guided her toward the arch and Macajah. The rest of the posse walked alongside them. "When I was alive, I was a sage. A wise woman of my people." While the woman spoke, Ashen's emotional knots released, her anxiety lessening. "When I died, something remained."

John leaned toward her. "For Warders to maintain the balance between the factions—the Unseen and the Light— we needed a form of punishment in the event someone broke the rules."

"The three strike thing?"

"Precisely. Vana has the unique ability to make spirits forget who they are—to turn them into Drifters—and that constant threat scares the hell out of most ghosts."

The woman in the cemetery had appeared as though she were in agony. It was a sight Ashen hoped she'd never have to see again. She thought back to what Macajah had said. How over time, if Ashen didn't accept her fate, she would become like that lady. A husk.

"Isn't that cruel?" she asked.

John shook his head. The luminous blue from Max's barbed wire reflected off his lenses. "There are worse things that can happen to an earthbound spirit. Over the years, Vana has enforced that punishment in only a few extreme cases. What she does is relatively humane."

"I guess I don't get it. Like, did a bearded dude in the sky give her this ultimate authority or something?"

"Like most things here, no one knows." John smiled, but it seemed strained. "There are theories, of course, on how this is all supposed to work. Deities. God. The universe. When we die we all know, deep down, we're supposed to pass beneath that arch and move on, but when we choose not to, we're left to our own devices."

"You mean we're on our own?"

He gave Ashen a shrug. "In the end, I surmise it doesn't really matter. We've found a new purpose. Protect those who cannot protect themselves."

With every step closer to the Divide Ashen took, the stronger her urge to cross over into the wild light became. That pull, that feeling of the tunnel being her destiny, was as strong as it had been when she'd first seen it. It felt like eons, not mere hours, since then.

Ahead, Macajah waited at the threshold. As Ashen trailed behind with the rest of the posse, she avoided thinking about or looking at the spectral tunnel, instead focusing her attention on the two figures near the cowboy. Right away, she could tell one was Eli, the tall Unseen from the train. He hovered over a much smaller, hunched shape. When the posse reached the creatures, the light from Max's barbed wire revealed something Ashen hadn't expected. She stopped in her tracks.

An ancient man peered back at her. At first glance, Ashen might have assumed he was one of the many random living souls who dashed here and there throughout the courtyard, but the man's hollow eyes, waxy skin, and lack of vibrant spirit colors gave away his disguise. He emitted darkness.

"My, my ... how ya've grown, Clementine."

Clementine. Gone and lost forever. A flood of memories. Before she could warn Macajah and the rest, the old man shuddered. His skin deflated and draped from his bones. A shadow hand stretched out from the mouth of the corpse suit, yanking itself up, exposing the flat crown and wide brim of a hat. The creature grew, expanding as it slithered from the gap, standing to its full height and dwarfing the tall Unseen next to it. All around them, the screams of living souls spread as the old man's empty body collapsed into a heap on the sidewalk like discarded rags.

Angry Fox muttered under her breath with ferocious intensity. She withdrew her tomahawks, each burning with a vivid red. John's cuffs gleamed green, but he kept them lowered.

"Thaddeus Glick." Macajah said the name as if it left a bitter taste in his mouth. "Always a pleasure."

"Here to fetch my man. Ya tell yer injun gal to cease her … barbaric tendencies."

Sighing, Macajah waved Angry Fox back, locking eyes with her. Fox glared, giving a terse nod to the cowboy, but didn't stash her weapons.

"I reckon you can lay claim on him," Macajah said. "Though I'm none too convinced you'll be wanting him returned."

The expression the massive shadow wore was emotionless. "What do ya mean, Mr. Sloan?"

"Toad let slip you Unseen kind are using our mirrors on the regular."

"He did, did he?"

Raising his hands defensively, Toad blubbered, "I ain't done nothin', boss, I swears! Them Warders was torturin' me!"

"If your idea of torture is getting asked questions before

being let free, you're one yellow-bellied coward," Macajah snapped.

"I ain't afeared of ya, Cage!" Toad yelled, his voice laced with unease.

"It's fine, Toad. Just fine," Thaddeus said in hushed tones. "Now, ya come on over here with me and ya brother."

The heavy Unseen looked relieved as Max freed him from his restraints. Wincing, Toad rubbed where the barbed wire had been and shuffled over to where Thaddeus and Eli waited in front of the Welcome Arch.

The tall shadow scolded Toad. "I oughta whack ya solid."

"Apologies, Eli. Mister Glick," the fat man muttered, hanging his head to stare at the ground.

Thaddeus' spindly fangs broke into a wide grin. "That's alright, my boy. Quite."

He wrapped his colossal arm around Toad's shoulders and pulled him close. They glided, side by side, toward the Divide's entrance. All the while, Thaddeus whispered in a rhythmic cadence, assuring Toad he had nothing to be concerned about, but as they drew nearer, Toad became more rigid, his vacant sockets narrowed with uncertainty.

In a rapid movement, Thaddeus seized the back of Toad's skull and shoved him forward. The fat shadow could only yelp as he flailed toward the Divide. Eli hollered, reached for his brother, but it was too late. Toad fell inside, the edges of his shadowy form singeing; layers of himself peeled off like charred strips of paper. He looked back through the arch at Eli, his face crumbling to ash.

While pieces of Toad flaked away and vanished in a swirl of colorful energy, the hollows of the tunnel reacted as it had when the old woman and her duck had entered. But instead of an immediate return to its original state, it grew broader, more powerful; its pulse beating like the swing of a relentless pendulum that showed no sign of stopping. Its flowing colors became so bright that Ashen threw her hand up to shield her eyes, and when she thought the Divide might detonate, its energy fizzled, dying down to its previous appearance.

Eli lashed out and struck Thaddeus square in the chest. "Why?"

"I ain't got the patience to deal with squealers."

"He were my blood!"

"Ya best quieten down, Eli, less ya desire the same."

The blackened features of Eli shifted. Purple shimmered below the surface. He crossed his arms and turned from Thaddeus and the posse, retreating to the fringes of the courtyard where he discreetly swiped at his eyes with the back of his hand.

Sirens echoed in the distance. Thaddeus grinned. "These livin' beings certainly get worked up by a little ol' abandoned corpse. Reckon we best light out." He eyed the puddle of old man flesh on the ground. "Shame. Unassuming feller like him was mighty helpful. Too bad he's rotted and too far gone now. Could have used him to acquire other ... volunteers."

"Volunteers?" Ashen repeated before she could stop herself. She winced. She could feel Macajah's steely, disapproving scowl.

The Unseen didn't clarify or seem to notice. He took a few paces toward Eli, paused, cocked his head, and regarded Ashen. "Clementine. I remember ya were such a lonely girl. Unfortunate ya didn't turn dark. My first failure." He tsked. "Oh, I recall Toad saying something about a feller with ya on that metal rig?"

Her heart sped up. "Jacob? Is he okay?"

"I'm doubtful he fared too well. Ya best see for yerself."

"Wait! What does that mean?" Ashen pleaded, feeling Vana's grip on her tighten. She wrenched her arm away and jogged cautiously after him. "Where's Jacob?"

Ignoring Ashen, Thaddeus glanced over his shoulder at Angry Fox. With one of his long, bony fingers, he felt along his cheek and the ugly scar that extended to his deformed ear. "Oh, and Katie. I was always fond of that medallion of yourn. See ya around … by and by."

Angry Fox growled. Thaddeus grinned and slapped Eli hard on the back, and the two transformed into black orbs, the smaller one tinged violet. An aura of smoke twirled around them as they hovered a moment, then darted down the street, vaporous tails trailing behind them like comets in the night.

12

ANGRY FOX: THE TRAIL WHERE THEY CRIED

Angry Fox
Born: March 18, 1823
Died: June 1, 1839

May 25, 1838

Katie Matheson walked in the stifling Georgia heat. It felt as though she had been walking for months, but it had only been a few days. She tugged at the high, ruffled collar of her calico dress, wishing she had worn something lighter the day the militiamen came.

Her hand carefully patted over the corkscrew curls framing her face. At least, they used to be curls. They now hung in limp sections. She imagined she looked like a tattered drapery. Or maybe a drenched mule. Since she no longer had her looking glass to check, she supposed it didn't matter. Katie sighed.

"It will be okay," her grandfather said.

"They forced us to leave. Where are they taking us?"

"To the lands the prophets foresaw."

Katie ground her teeth to stop herself from saying anything more. After the initial terror of armed men entering their home had passed, all she felt was anger. Even though she wasn't allowed time to gather her belongings, she did manage to grab her leather satchel as she and her grandfather were forced out by a few bayonet-wielding volunteers. Those same men dawdled, rummaging through drawers and cupboards and pocketing whatever they desired for themselves while Katie watched and waited to be escorted away.

Still, there was a grain of hope. Perhaps she would see some of the cities and towns she'd read of and fantasized about in the books by the Europeans. Those fantastic stone structures from her father's homeland that stretched into the sky and blotted out the sun. Exotic places where everyone had blue eyes and yellow or orange hair. Sometimes green eyes. She'd never seen anyone with green eyes and wondered if the color was actually as vibrant as fresh grass.

She pulled her practice embroidery from her sleeve, dabbing the piece of linen along the nape of her neck to catch a trickle of sweat that had crawled along her scalp. The cloth was already dingy, the precise silk stitching dull against the yellowing fabric, and she frowned as she folded it to protect the work as much as possible.

"That there's purty."

Katie spun to a young man. A Georgia militiaman. He was small and slight like she was. She guessed he was European, maybe the same kind of people as her father. Even though his skin was fair, this boy was darker eyed, his hair curly and wild. His gaze had an edge, but when he smiled, his features softened.

"Thank you," she said coldly, turning her back to him.

"That yern work?"

"Pardon?"

"Did ya stitch it?"

She tried to hide her aggravation. "Do you find it impossible to believe a savage such as myself could create it?"

"Ya ain't lookin' like no savage I ever seen. Don't sound like none, neither. Look right and proper."

A smile played at the corners of her mouth and she peered back at the boy. "Thank you."

"Welcome." He returned her smile before adding, "Name's Teddy."

"I'm Katie Matheson."

Confusion crossed Teddy's face as his eyes flicked to Katie's grandfather. "Yer pa thar don't look like no Matheson."

"This is my grandfather. My father is a Scotsman. A trader."

"I am called Black Fox," her grandfather interjected.

"What's yer white man name?"

The old man stopped. The traditional turban he wore only added to his height and, although aged, he towered over the boy. As he regarded Teddy, he let his hand wander to the top of his hunting shirt where, beneath, Katie knew his silver fox pendant was concealed. After a moment, he replied with a voice that sounded strained, yet proud.

"I am only called Black Fox."

The old man put his arm around Katie. As they continued on the trail, she glanced back. The boy, Teddy, stood at the side of the trail, a single hand resting on his hip, staring after her.

August 11, 1838

"You must eat," Katie said in English.

The failing firelight emphasized the wrinkles of her grandfather's face. He no longer looked like the same man. Every aged valley and hollow had deepened and grown darker with each passing day.

Black Fox picked up the bowl of government rations from the dirt. When he handed it to her, his hands had a tremor.

"You eat it. I cannot."

He spoke in Cherokee as he had done since their arrival. Even though the guards in the military stockade were getting increasingly impatient with Black Fox, he refused to use their words.

"At least take the medicine," she urged back in their native tongue.

"If the white men let us forage, we could make better."

"Grandfather, it took a great deal for Teddy to acquire this."

The old man grimaced. "You should not trust that boy."

"He's not like the others. In any manner, being his friend might help us survive."

The embers from the small fire were reflected in the luster of her grandfather's eyes. He studied her for a few moments and when he next spoke, his voice sounded thick and ragged.

"You are too much like your grandfather."

"Willful, you mean?"

He gave her a sad smile. "A warrior."

He removed the silver medallion from around his neck with his trembling hands. The weight of it dangled in the dimness; the wampum fox eyes glistened against the black of night.

"This belongs to you now," he said.

"Grandfather, I can't-"

"It is yours."

With reluctance, she leaned forward as he draped the necklace around her neck. The medallion lay on her chest with the heaviness of the world. When he pulled his hands away, his fingers, cold as ice, brushed her cheek.

"Tie that securely to you," he said. "Hide it so the white men do not see it. It is valuable."

Katie did as instructed. Once she covered the medallion with her high collar, she reached into her satchel, withdrew a small vial, and tried to hand it to him.

"No, young one. Give it to the red dress woman. She is more ill than I."

Worried tears stung her eyes as the old man lay back to rest against the small pile of their belongings. She swallowed, nodded, and crawled to the opening of their blanket tent. Ducking beneath the overhanging edge, she turned to glance back at him.

"Grandfather, what is the woman called again?" she asked, but only Black Fox's shallow, rattling breaths answered. Lips pursed into a thin line, she exited the tent and quickened her pace toward the woman's small shelter, nestled next to the tall, timber wall that imprisoned her people.

The glow from the dying fire cast grotesque shadows. Other people stirred beneath their makeshift dwellings, all in varying degrees of wakefulness, but aside from the occasional cough from one of the many sick, the camp was silent. Even the wildlife in the nearby trees didn't dare speak.

As she approached the front gate of the stockades, the evening air grew more tainted, stinking with rot and disease intensified by the hot temperature. A horrid stench Katie couldn't escape. It made her think she'd never smell anything other than death for the rest of her life.

Even though her embroidery was now nothing more than a grimy rag, she tugged it from her sleeve and covered her nose. Close to where a few guards were posted, a line of bodies waited to be buried at dawn. Though she averted her gaze, she noted there were at least six; more today than there had been in a week. Perhaps longer. She hoped she wouldn't recognize any of them and moved to hurry past, but out of the corner of her eye, she caught sight of a familiar red fabric.

Startled, she almost dropped her embroidery. It was same pattern as the kind woman's handcrafted dress. For months, the vibrant red had been a beacon to Katie. Something bright in the monotone gray of the camp. Now, the woman who wore it, the one who had helped her and her grandfather find the lengths of material that now protected them from the scorch of the sun, lay in the midst of the dead, her forehead still slick with sweat. She had perished like so many before her: the gentle man who had shared what clothing he possessed with the children of the camp; the little boy with the large, brown eyes rimmed in feathery lashes; the newborn who had only lived a few days.

Their names. Why couldn't she remember their names?

The tears began to well. Katie swallowed them away and squeezed her eyes shut, trying to make her hands cease their quaking. She pivoted from the bodies, keeping her eyes closed, refusing to open them again until she had walked a few slow, careful steps.

Then, she ran.

November 17, 1838

The frozen ground bit through the dirty rags wrapped around Katie's feet. The torn scraps of fabric did nothing to stave off the cold. Every part of her had become numb, but within her deadened senses was a tinge of dull pain. A reminder that she was still alive.

Beyond the wagon in front of her, as far as she could see, were a few hundred of her people. She glanced back whenever there was a random cry or cough and met the eyes of several hundred more. Next to her, a toddler sobbed. Puffs of frosted air trailed from his open mouth. His older sister cradled the boy's thin frame as she stared into the distance. Although the girl was younger than Katie, she looked like an ancient sage; an old soul crammed into an adolescent body.

Katie's gaze rested on the wagon ahead. In the back, a few heaps were covered in blankets. The previous evening, while she and her people attempted to sleep, the first snowstorm of winter had struck. Fierce, freezing winds riddled with sleet tore at their shelters and through their inadequate clothing. When dawn broke, Katie had checked on her grandfather. He did not move. He did not breathe. So the soldiers had collected him and put him in the back of the wagon. They told her there wasn't enough time to bury him in the icy, hard earth and that she would have to wait. So she walked, step after endless step, clenching her fists and stumbling through the mud and snow while her grandfather's fox medallion thumped against her chest.

Some soldiers rode past and barked out commands. When the procession of her people slowed, a handful of soldiers dismounted, approached the stopped wagon, and unloaded her grandfather's body—along with the rest of the dead—and lay them, side by side on a mound near the trail.

"I'm awful sorry, Katie."

Her eyes flitted from the bundled bodies to Teddy's face. It had been two weeks since the wood timbers of their prison camp had been set ablaze by the military in a feeble attempt to avoid the spread of disease, but despite the rough conditions they had endured after leaving the burning corpse of the stockades behind, the dark blue coat of Teddy's new American Army uniform was immaculate. Every night, by the light of the fire, Katie watched as he diligently cleaned away whatever had soiled the wool during their travels.

Katie lowered her head. "You tried to help us. Thank you."

"If'n you'll let me, I'd like ta help ya bury him proper."

"Yes. I'd appreciate that."

Teddy motioned to another soldier and together, the two men carried Black Fox up a short incline and placed him on the snow beneath a beech tree. Katie followed, dropped to her knees, and attempted to dig with her hands. The ground was solid, so she gave the frosted crust a half-hearted whack to break through to the muck below. Nothing budged. She tried again with a little more force. Nothing. Tears began to prick her eyes, but she bit them back. In a burst of frustration, she balled her fists and punched, cracking the ice into shards that left tiny cuts across her knuckles. She ignored the wounds, hitting over and over again, each strike harder and faster than the one before until only a white powder smeared with pink blood remained.

She was interrupted by Teddy's hand gripping her shoulder. "We got us a shovel. Ya go on now and say yer farewells."

Mechanically, Katie rose, walked over to her grandfather's body, and uncovered his gaunt face. When she saw the pallid tone of his skin, a guttural moan escaped her lips. She crumpled to the snow and caressed his cheek as she cried, letting the icy tears stream down her cheeks. A year prior, Katie's father had gone west to trade, leaving her in Black Fox's care. Now, she had to say goodbye to the only family she had left.

Everything now felt like a waking dream. Unusual details jumped out at her, like how blinding the snow was, how the gnarled beech trees swayed, how peaceful the woods were. Her reddened eyes roamed. At the base of the nearby tree grew a large rose bush. Coated in frost, it had tangled itself around the trunk, its evergreen leaves glistening from what sunlight filtered through the gray canopy above. A few long, wild vines had dropped and stretched across the snow, and sprinkled among its thorns were bright crimson colored rose hips. A rare, autumn bloom of white flowers with golden centers created a halo around the old man, embracing him.

Taking care not to trample the flowers, Katie removed the blankets from her grandfather's body, undid his wampum belt, and tied it around her own waist before attaching his tomahawks to the suede loops. As she hid the handles of the weapons as well as she could within the folds of her skirt, the wails from the toddler she had been walking next to sounded from the trail.

"Wish that child would hush," Teddy said behind her.

Katie turned to him. "He's very ill."

"Reckon so, but his cryin' cain't do nothin' but invite more heartache." The young man's eyes reflected surprise. "Ya wearin' yer grandad's belt?"

"Yes. I want to keep it."

"Fair enough. Welp, we dug as deep as we could. Ground's mighty hard."

She withdrew her embroidery from her sleeve, wiped at her face, and nodded. The men heaved Black Fox into the shallow grave. A painful sting of loss returned along with Katie's tears. She let them flow unhampered while the other soldier shoveled. When her grandfather was buried, Teddy removed his military-issued hat and walked over to her, but before he could speak additional words of comfort, something caught his attention. His eyes narrowed.

"What's that?" he asked, pointing at Katie's neck. Without thinking, she clutched at her collar and her fingers felt the fox's polished wampum eyes peeking out at Teddy from between a couple of loose buttons.

"My gran- grandfather's," she stammered, shoving the medallion out of sight, her gaze darting to the other soldier by the tree trunk. He remained preoccupied as he knocked mud off the shovel. She hoped he hadn't noticed their exchange. "He gave it to me a while ago."

"He did?" Teddy said. Frowning, he cocked his head and gave a terse nod at the handles of the tomahawks. "Ain't never seen them before, neither. Ya have them this whole time, too?"

"No, I took them from Grandfather just now." She lowered her voice. "Please … don't say anything. Please. They're heirlooms and all that I have."

"Why ya ain't never say nothin' about that thar silver? Ya hidin' it from me?" His tone held an accusatory edge, but there was something more. He sounded hurt.

"I, no, I didn't," she whispered, perplexed at his reaction. "I simply didn't think to mention it."

"Thought we was friends."

"Of course we are! I didn't mean—"

The other soldier walked back toward the trail and they paused to study him as he passed. Once he had moved further away, Katie sighed.

"I'm sorry I kept it from you, Teddy. Truly. I didn't mean to upset you."

Teddy's hard, dark eyes looked at her and after a short moment, he flashed her a strained smile. Katie shivered. There was a chilliness to his grin, something colder than the weather, that hadn't been there before.

"It's alright, Katie," he said. "Ain't no harm. But ya best be cautious and keep them things outta sight. Ya don't know who ya can trust."

December 4, 1838

Reverend Daniel's song, as breathy as an exhausted sigh, drifted through the camp. It was too quiet at first—lost among the wails from Will Uke, the little boy from the trail whose illness had worsened during the last few weeks. As the reverend's words became clearer, Arly, the boy's sister, rocked her tiny brother in her arms like a newborn as she hummed along.

Amazing Grace, how sweet the sound,
That saved a wretch, like me.

The tune echoed against the wall and ceiling of their latest shelter, Mantle Rock; a vast sandstone arch carpeted with frosted moss. While a handful of soldiers kept watch for runaways, Katie and some of her people, wrapped in their government-issued blankets, huddled together around the sparse campfires. There hadn't been enough room for everyone under the stone bridge outcropping, so the rest of her tribe camped in the snow and formed an endless line of families all along the road they'd walked in on.

In an attempt to warm her nose and keep the heavy smoke at bay, Katie used what remained of her embroidery to cover her lower face. On the other side of the campfire sat Teddy. The young man's eyes were shadowed by his hat, his mouth turned down into a frown, his right leg nervous, bouncing up and down in a rhythmic twitch with each shrill cry from the small boy.

I once was lost, but now am found,
Was blind, but now I see.

Little Will shrieked louder. Teddy slapped his palms hard against his knees and bolted to his feet.

"I cain't listen to this no more!"

"'Any longer'—not 'no more,'" Katie corrected, her voice muffled by her embroidery.

A brief, black cloud touched Teddy's expression before his frown broke into a smile. "Thanks to ya, Miss Katie. If I'm to be a right proper merchant to *Californios,* I reckon I best learn to talk, err, speak like a gentleman." He paused. Mouth closed, he ran his tongue along the front of his teeth in thought. "I'm gonna take the boy and his sister down the road a spell. One of the other fellers said there was a doctor not far off. Maybe they can quit his bawlin'."

"How long will you be? What if the ferry comes for us?"

Teddy laughed. "Berry's Ferry ain't-" He broke off and sighed. "Isn't. It isn't gonna be unstuck any time soon. That thar river's surface is froze near solid. We're stuck here a stretch."

He tipped his hat to her, buried his hands in his coat

pockets, and walked over to where Arly and Will sat at the far side of the camp. Katie couldn't quite hear what was said, but she could see fear and concern reflected on Arly's face. When Teddy reached out for her hand, the girl's initial instinct was to envelop her brother in a protective embrace and recoil.

It was Teddy's reaction that surprised Katie. A gloom darkened his eyes, and in a split second, he snatched Arly's wrist and hoisted her and the boy up as if they weighed nothing. Once Arly was standing, cradling Will close, Teddy flashed his chilly smile, pressed his hand against her upper back, and guided her into the mouth of the woods and toward the road.

"We'll be returnin' directly," he called over his shoulder. They trudged through deep snow between tree trunks and dead foliage, shrinking to moving specks in the wilderness until they gradually disappeared. As Will's cries diminished, Reverend Daniel started another verse of the song. The rest of Katie's people under Mantle Rock joined in, but their words were not English, like the reverend's. This time, they were in their own language.

U dv ne u ne tsv,
(He said when He spoke,)
E lo ni gv ni li s qua di.
(All the world will end.)

Katie stared into the fire, watching its flames lick at the sodden wood, and tried to push Will's screams from her mind. The boy had been keeping her awake most nights. On those rare occasions when she managed sleep, her own fantasies of her father finding her and rescuing her from the horrors of the trail woke her anyway.

She wondered how much longer they would have to wait for the ferry. With the harsh winter came harsh weather. Two miles away weaved a mighty river, but it may as well have been an unscalable barricade. For the past few weeks, the ice had prevented most of her tribe from traveling to the opposite shore. Teddy was right. There would be no more crossing until it thawed, and even then, Katie wasn't certain how many of her people would proceed. Many of the elders refused to go near the waters, believing them to be a gateway leading to a land where spirits dwelled. To proceed west was to walk into death itself.

A sound came from the woods. It was Teddy, his blue uniform trousers soaked from the knees down—the front of his coat sullied with muddy leaves and snow. His face had turned a pale gray, but his hands were bright red and chapped, as if someone had squeezed the blood from his veins and forced it all to settle into his fingers.

"That didn't take very long. Where are Arly and Will?"

"They, uh," his eyes briefly locked with hers before he sat and began rubbing his hands together above the fire. A few fresh scrapes were highlighted in its light. "The doc said the boy needed to stay so he could give him regular medicine and all."

Katie got up and placed Teddy's battered hands in hers, dabbing at the cuts with her embroidery. "Are you okay? What happened?"

The darkness in the young man's eyes fell. He squeezed her hand, holding it for a moment before pulling away.

"Took a tumble in the snow is all. Everything's fine, Katie. Just fine."

She sat next to him and turned her old embroidery over, examining it, running her fingertips over the design she had spent hours stitching. It was almost destroyed, soiled with dirt, sweat, and Teddy's crimson bloodstains that now mingled with the faded brown ones of her and her people, each serving as a reminder of yet another lost.

Death may lay west, she thought, but her people weren't immune to dying where they were, either. The Europeans were forcing them to stay in the severe conditions for as long as possible—as if they wanted them to perish. There had been one night, as they waited for Berry's Ferry to break free, when twenty-two had died from exposure:

Darcus Downing
Kell
Rising Faun
Aggie Silk
Feather-in-the-Water
Stomp About
Sein McCoy
Nacy Hicks
Eliza Heldebrand
Luther Moore
Path Killer
David Israel
Leaf
Up-the-Branch
Gammon Prichett
Susannah Foster
Sharlot Vickory
Laughing Girl
George Bear Meat
Sally Mayfield
Archilla
Proud Man

Twenty-two. And this time, Katie remembered all of their names.

"Teddy," she said, crumpling the linen into a ball.

"Yeah?"

"Please don't call me Katie anymore."

He looked at her, puzzled, but said nothing as she threw her embroidery into the fire.

"My name is Angry Fox."

April 27, 1839

From her location at the top of the bluff, the earth was like bare flesh. Gone were the serene mountains and dense forests. Instead, Angry Fox gazed upon a flat, unfamiliar land bathed in sunlight; the greenery of her Georgia home had been replaced with burned ochre and parched golds. Recently built cabins and homesteads were sprinkled here and there, but they looked unnatural, as if her people were intruders who didn't belong.

"Everything changed in eight-hundred miles," she muttered.

Her horse answered with a shuffle. "Woah, boy." Angry Fox leaned forward in her saddle to give him a firm pat on his withers. "No need to be anxious. We're leaving soon."

"Ya set on a name for that thar colt?"

Teddy stood at the base of the stunted ridge. He squinted up at her, the reins of his mare in one hand, his eyes shaded with the other.

His deceptively childlike voice caused Angry Fox to sit bolt upright. "No, not yet," she said, finding her grip tightening on her saddle horn. She relaxed her hold. "I was thinking Echota."

"After the town ya come from? Purty name," he said, nodding. "Welp, come on. Got everything we need."

She forced herself to smile, trying to reason through her doubts as Echota carried her down the short bluff. It was times like these where Teddy seemed so harmless. Even kind. But she couldn't ignore how her people had been avoiding him. She couldn't forget the fear etched into their expressions whenever he was present. While some of the soldiers had been sympathetic, Teddy could be a little volatile. Impulsive. Her people's reactions were instinctual and understandable. But they didn't see how he'd treated her since they had arrived at Fort Gibson; those moments when he allowed his soft nature, his vulnerability, to show. Her people didn't know him like she knew him.

As Echota's hooves kicked up dust, Black Fox's words echoed in Angry Fox's mind.

You should not trust that boy.

By the time she and her horse had reached Teddy, he had settled in his saddle, brushing smudges of dust from his new clothes.

"Thank you again for helping me, Teddy. It means the world to me."

The young man grinned and Angry Fox's worries dissipated. It was the same warm smile she remembered from the day they had met, eleven months before.

"Passin' west through injun country, meetin' yer Pa so I can learn my trade." He lowered his head and added, "Glad ya bein' my companion and all. Don't forget—yer helpin' me, too."

Guilt tugged at her. She flicked her eyes from him to the skirt of her dark blue dress. "You know, you didn't have to purchase the horse as well as my travel clothes."

"I couldn't allow ya to wear them rags no more."

"'Those rags any more.'"

Teddy winked. "That's what I said."

"You're a headstrong man." She sighed. "Regardless, I'm no damsel in distress. I would have found a way."

"Not a doubt ya would've, but ya know fine well the government paid me handsomely for my services. Might as well use it."

He clicked his tongue, dug his heels into the mare's sides, and steered his horse westward.

Angry Fox squeezed Echota gently with her legs until the horse broke into a trot. When they caught up to Teddy and his mare, she asked, "What did you decide to name your horse?"

"I've always been fond of the name Clementine. Like the way it sounds on the tongue."

After a few paces, she took a final glance over her shoulder. By the time her tribe had arrived at Fort Gibson, their losses were great. Too many old had perished and too many young had joined them. Now, they had new land, but though they were a people with a vast past, they had no future.

Angry Fox was determined to change that. With every stride Echota took further from her tribe, she felt she was being ripped apart; she didn't want to leave, but she couldn't stay without finding her own past. Without finding her father.

June 1, 1839

Teeth gritted, Angry Fox dropped her leather satchel to the floor. She scanned the dim room. The surface of the writing desk was bare. Furs and blankets, folded in a neat pile, were stacked on top of the rope mattress. In the corner, on the mantle of an adobe fireplace, sat a lonesome brass candlestick, its flame lit and flickering from the steady breeze blowing through the open door. All of her possessions had been packed and readied that morning.

Everything except her tomahawks.

Her frustration bubbled as she pawed back through the blankets, shaking each before tossing it to the side. They had to be there. How could she have misplaced them?

A bang sounded outside. Heart racing, Angry Fox hurried to the doorway. Across the fort's courtyard, near the upper level billiard room, two fur trappers were buckled over at the waist, laughing. One swayed back and forth, gripping the stock of a smoking rifle while the other, more stable man struggled to help keep his friend upright. As they escorted each other down the stairs and toward their quarters, Angry Fox retreated back into the gloom and out of sight.

She sighed, relieved, and returned to her search, but a growing, frantic feeling began to take root. If those men were already so influenced by whatever rotten whiskey they were serving at the billiard room's saloon, she had to hurry. It meant there wasn't much time.

"Lookin' fer somethin'?"

Startled, she whirled, shoving the blankets behind her, and immediately winced at her own lack of subtlety. The petite frame of Teddy stood in the doorway, his overgrown curly locks rippling in the prairie night air, his eyes glinting beneath his wide-brimmed hat, the one that he'd won from a poker game. His newest trophy.

Angry Fox hated it.

"Ya got somethin' thar?" He took a step into the room.

"No, no," she said, forcing a smile. "You surprised me while I was tidying up, is all."

His gaze shifted from her to the empty writing desk to the discarded blankets, before traveling to her satchel, its contents spilling out onto the wooden floor planks. Angry Fox followed his stare. A lump rose in her throat, and as she knelt to sweep the items back into the bag, she attempted to swallow it away.

"Ya always collect the total of yer effects when yer cleanin'?"

"Oh, you know how fond I am of efficiency." Her voice cracked a little. She cleared her throat, but kept her focus lowered. "Did you do well?"

"Lost some. Won most. Got ya a fare-thee-well gift."

Before Angry Fox could process Teddy's words, something soft landed on the floor in front of her. She reached out, and her trembling, timid hand felt the silky pelt of a black fox. She peered up at him and hoped her features feigned ignorance rather than worry.

"What do you mean, fare-thee-well?"

"I ain't lackin' brains. I figured a while back ya were itchin' to run off." He paused, his delicate hands making a dramatic flourish in the air before pointing toward the eastern grasslands. "Abscond."

A dense quiet cloaked the room. After a few moments, Teddy crouched in front of her and regarded her with an emotionless glare. Without intending to, Angry Fox leaned away from him, chancing an anxious glance at the wide-open door behind him, and when her eyes met and locked with his, his lips cracked open, revealing a huge grin.

"No needin' to be afeared of me."

"What? I'm not-"

"I understand." The grin lingered while he stood. He offered his hand. She studied it, forehead creased, and when she didn't budge, he let out a huff. "Come on, now. I ain't mad at ya. When yer Pa weren't ... wasn't here when we arrived, I reckoned ya didn't have much mind to be stayin'."

Frowning, she slipped her hand into his and rose to her feet. "But I thought you might-"

Another rifle blasted. Alarmed, she jumped. Faint howls of laughter pealed from outside the fort's walls.

"Are ya set on tonight?" Teddy asked as the commotion died. When Angry Fox nodded, he sighed. "Fair enough, but them fellers out there've consumed a great deal of coffin varnish. If yer gonna flee in the dark of night, at least allow me to escort ya beyond the reach of their firearms." He studied her slight frame and added, "As well as their carnal appetites."

She hugged the fox pelt close. Women were a rarity at Bent's Fort. Ever since Angry Fox's arrival, she had garnered a great deal of male attention, none of which she welcomed. Her rejections only succeeded in making her a target for the worst of them. There had been a few evenings where she had stayed awake till dawn. Filled with fear, she would listen while an inebriated soldier or trapper or explorer tried to force his way into her quarters, keeping her tomahawks at the ready in case the knotted lock she'd fashioned on the door didn't hold.

It was only a matter of time until something horrible happened. Angry Fox knew it.

"Ya go on now and finish up," Teddy said, heading toward the door. "I'll fetch Echota."

"No, I can't possibly accept."

"Ya won't be survivin' long in the hot sun without a horse. That trek will take near a month on foot, and ya know it."

"He's not mine to keep. I'll be fine."

"Nonsense. Ya keep the horse."

He smiled and Angry Fox's distrust began to melt. When she had discovered her father had left Bent's Fort months ago, she'd felt lost. Alone. Meanwhile, Teddy fell into the frontier life with ease, finding ways to manipulate the susceptible in order to fund his desire for fortune, growing more cold and distant each day. Witnessing this shadowy side dominate him—a shrewd, cagey side prone to cruel outbursts—only made her feel more out of place. All she wanted now was to be with her people.

"You have been very kind, Teddy. Thank you."

"Obliged," he said as he started outside.

"Oh, Teddy—I seem to have misplaced my tomahawks. Have you seen them?"

The man stopped. "I've not, but the entrance here to yer quarters was unshut earlier. Perhaps one of them travelers wandered in for a souvenir from a genuine half-breed." He rubbed at his own neck. "At least ya have the good sense to always wear that silver piece. Safer."

A flash of emotion darted across the man's face, something Angry Fox couldn't quite gauge. A strange shiver crawled up the nape of her neck, making her thankful Teddy was insistent that she take Echota. Though he was a skilled rider, she was better and could outride him if he became more threatening than those men's firearms.

"Meet ya in the corral," he said, smiling, and Angry Fox managed a nervous nod in return.

As soon as he disappeared into the dusky night, she rushed to finish packing, giving the area another thorough search. Teddy had to be right; some disreputable frontiersman must have robbed her. She slammed her satchel on the bed, planted her hands on her hips and muttered curses to herself, annoyed that she could have been so careless. Without her tomahawks, she felt vulnerable. She didn't like that feeling.

A swift gust blew into the room. Light danced on the

mantel, casting barbaric shadows on the walls and into the corners. The ornate holder the candle perched upon glimmered with a muted golden gleam. It looked out of place in its rustic surroundings. Angry Fox picked it up, feeling the weight of it as the flame ebbed, wavering with each movement she made. It was heavy. Solid.

She removed the stick at its base. The hot wax dripped down over her fingers as she used her other hand to chuck the metal candlestick holder into her satchel. With one quick breath, she blew the candle out.

Other than the occasional firearm blast disrupting the prairie blackness with a rapid orange flash, the fort appeared welcoming. A sliver of moonlight illuminated the grassland as the two traveled further from the hoots and hollers of the drunken men. All the while Angry Fox stayed alert, watching for any sudden changes in the man riding alongside her, but he remained quiet on his mare and rarely spoke.

They weren't far from the fort when Echota let out series of aggravated snorts. Angry Fox gave him a reassuring pat on his withers, but by the time they were approaching a safe distance, his snorts had turned forceful as he thrashed his head, his mane creating wispy shimmers in the night.

"Easy, easy," she said. Her fingertips traced along the edge of the leather fender beneath her leg, down to the stirrup, and over to the cinch that secured the saddle. The strap was slack. She tightened it. As soon as she did, Echota let out a shrill squeal. He reared up on his hind legs, and Angry Fox threw her weight forward and held tight to the saddle horn.

"Colt thar gettin' spooked?" Teddy asked.

"Woah, boy!"

With one hand, she relaxed the cinch. Echota's withers shivered, nostrils flared as he blew out panicked puffs of air, but once the strap drooped away from his underbelly, he calmed.

"Lucky he didn't throw ya."

Angry Fox stroked Echota's neck, her worried thoughts crowding out all others. "That's so unlike him."

"He's still green. Likely I tacked him up poorly. Apologies."

"I doubt it's that. Regardless, he's settled now. I'll ride on. I'll be able to see better at dawn."

"Ya know fine well a loose saddle's dangerous, particularly in the dark. Best stop to correct it." His mare, Clementine, began to rake the earth with her hoof, so he gave a firm, severe tug to the reins. The unnecessary force made her head whip back. "I can help ya if'n ya need."

"I'll be fine," she said, the dim light hiding the scowl on her face. "You go on—return to the fort."

"Yer an independent woman, but I wouldn't be a proper gentlemen if I abandoned ya 'fore I knew yer safe."

Angry Fox nodded, but the nagging, aching warning flared throughout her. Before she slipped to the ground, she unbuckled her satchel attached to the side of the saddle and pulled it open. A hint of the candlestick gleamed in the pale moonlight.

Past Echota's hindquarter, she could see the shadowy figure of Teddy sitting on his mare. She tried to keep him in her line of sight while she hunted blindly, feeling along her horse's shoulder and down to his belly, and when she stopped where the cinch had been, Echota snorted and stomped his front hooves.

She frowned. There was something wet on Echota's coat. After pulling her hand away, she put her palm up to her nose. The faint scent of metal lingered.

Puzzled, Angry Fox seized the cinch swaying beneath her horse, but as soon as she clamped her fingers around the worn hide strap, she felt a stabbing pain. She jerked back, shaking her hand to get the sting out, sucking air between her teeth. The pain subsided, and she unfastened the cinch with a quick tug and held it up. What little light existed glinted off the exposed, squarish heads of horseshoe nails. On the opposite side, the nail tips poked through the leather, their ends clipped short, sharpened, and moist with her horse's blood.

Dropping the sabotaged cinch, she shot a look beyond Echota's frame. Clementine's outline could still be seen, but Teddy was gone. Eyes wide, Angry Fox took a few, slow steps closer to her open satchel. When her hand clutched the column of the candlestick, a familiar voice whispered right next to her.

"By and by."

Angry Fox wrenched the candlestick free. She swung. The ornate brass connected. Teddy staggered on unsteady legs, his own ear clasped, and screamed. It was a shrill, enraged scream, one that sent Angry Fox reeling as she stared in horror.

"Ya no-good squaw!" he screeched. He tore his wide-brimmed hat off and threw it down, revealing a thick, ugly gash trailing from ear to cheek, stopping beneath his eye. Locks of his curly hair stuck to the swelling remnants of his ear. He regained his footing and blinked his glassy eyes hard, squinting to focus on the candlestick caked with blood in Angry Fox's grip.

He lunged, knocking her to the ground before she could

react. Teddy's hands wrapped around her neck. He was strong, far stronger than he appeared, and in a matter of seconds, she was struggling to breathe. Buzzing static filled her mind. She clubbed his shoulder, then his injured ear with the candlestick but he didn't flinch, his wild eyes, barely discernible in the dark, brimming with white-hot fury.

He snarled, teeth glowing. "Ungrateful! I give ya all, but it's not good enough for ya!" He punctuated this by bashing her head into the ground.

Blood dripped from his wounds onto her skin. Her vision slipped into a fog. She tried to speak but she couldn't make a sound. He slammed her once more against the dirt and rocks beneath, got up, and snatched her medallion, yanking on the beaded chain until the silver clasp broke.

"We'll consider this payment," he said. From a suede pouch tied at his waist, he pulled out a kerchief, stuffed the medallion into the pouch, and tied it shut.

"Teddy," she managed, her voice hoarse and raw.

"Ya nothin' but a deceiver. A deserter." He walked to his horse, using the kerchief to dab at his face before ripping something from his bag. "That's unacceptable," he said. As he returned, she could see he held her tomahawks, one in each hand.

"Teddy," she croaked. "Don't."

"Ain't nobody callin' me Teddy now." He readied the tomahawks to strike. "My name's Thaddeus."

PART THREE:
BARGAINING

13

INTO THE LOOKING GLASS

Brass letters spelling out the word 'Baggage' were attached to the thick, white molding above the entrance to Union Station's luggage claim. Ashen paced back and forth at the threshold, the flames on her sneakers more energetic and licking higher, leaving silvery rainbow footprints burning on the grimy tile.

She stopped, crossed her arms, and spun to Max and Macajah. "I'm not going down there."

"Tarnation, Missy!" The cowboy sounded irritated. "It's a looking glass, not some … tall-tale monstrosity! We need to use the darned thing to help us find your friend."

From the lobby behind Max and Macajah, Angry Fox muttered, "If Thaddeus left anyone to find."

Ashen scowled at the girl, fighting a lump in her throat that she couldn't swallow away. Thaddeus. She felt in her gut that he knew something. He had dangled Jacob's welfare just outside her reach, toying with her like a predator with his victim.

"Hobble it, Fox!" Macajah said. "Truth is we don't rightly know what that scoundrel cooked up."

A fleeting moment of sympathy washed over Angry Fox's expression before her face turned hard and proud. She glanced at Ashen, then at John and Vana, who eyed her with a look Ashen recognized. It was the same as the one her mother used whenever Ashen had disappointed her.

"I'm ... sorry," Fox said. "I've known the man for a very long time. He lacks even a single thread of decency."

Ashen tried to shut the Unseen creature's words from her mind, but Angry Fox's remark generated imagined scenarios. Thaddeus had had no qualms trying to murder Ashen when she had been a helpless child. He also didn't hesitate when forcing his own kind into an abyss of the unknown. There were no lines he thought twice about crossing.

Was he torturing Jacob?

Was Jacob even alive?

Tears threatened to spill out. Ashen blinked them away and said, "It's okay, Fox. No problem."

Angry Fox nodded. It was a slight gesture, but Ashen found it as reassuring as an unspoken apology.

Max stepped in front of her and blocked her view of the mirror. His fair, angelic features made her forget her phobia, if only for a moment, and her breath caught as he bent down until his concerned eyes lined up with hers.

"Ash, Cage and I would like to go with you. Assuming you'll let us."

Macajah chimed in. "I did promise to help you, Little Missy. I'm a man of my word."

"What about them?" she asked, her gaze shifting past Max's shoulder to the three standing in the lobby.

"The rest of the posse will stay here," Max said. "They need to take care of a few things."

Her hands began to shake. She rubbed them together to make them stop. "Can't we, you know, fly off like the Unseen? Poof into a ball of light or whatever?"

"Heck, if you wanna squander half the day getting there," the cowboy said. "For long distance travels, this way's more efficient. Just as purty, too."

She let out a heavy sigh. "Figured."

Max smiled. She noticed that whenever he smiled, his eyes smiled, too. He cleared his throat. "So, you ready?"

"No, but I'm going anyway."

He grinned. "That's my girl."

Ashen's body froze. Her cheeks burned. My girl? If Jacob had called her that, she would have smacked him and been annoyed for weeks. But hearing Max say them sent a weird sensation fluttering where her stomach used to be.

She hurried to change the subject. "Umm, what do I do again?"

"You have to think of where you want to go," Max said. "Windsor Lake."

"But a lake's not a mirror."

"True, but it's reflective, so it works the same."

"If I have to do this, can't we portal someplace closer to where the bus wrecked?" she said, crossing her arms in an attempt to comfort herself. "A mirror in a nearby house or something?"

The soldier shook his head. "Hopefully, we'll find your friend without any issues. But chances are, we'll need to track him down by questioning any living people around. For that, Cage and I need to be materialized." Ashen threw him a perplexed look and he laughed, adding, "We'll look solid. Same as we did on the bus the day you died."

"Little Missy, quit your delaying," Macajah said. "It'll be less suspicious if we meander from the lake. It's quiet there in the mornings. Less witnesses to notice us, and it'll likely confound any other folks who may be watching."

Watching? Before Ashen could ask for clarification, Max placed his hand on the small of her back and guided her into the corridor. A sizable floor-to-ceiling mirror, framed in ornate gold, stood at the end of the hall. Multicolored curls quivered across the surface, but neither her image nor the images of her companions were captured in it. Instead, only the busy train station showed. A constant stream of breathing souls streaked from one side of the building to the other, each living person unaware that a group of ghosts waited in the corridor, the newest and youngest of the bunch scared beyond anything of a simple mirror.

After a moment, Ashen gritted her teeth and marched forward with quick strides. Her eyes followed the colorful ripples that bounced from edge to edge, distorting the reflection of Union Station. As she drew closer, she caught glimpses of something beyond the shimmers. Stars, galaxies, planets.

Dread crept up on Ashen. A few inches away from the glass, she stopped. "I'm not gonna get lost in there, am I? These are like portals, right?"

"I ain't too absolute on what a portal is, but you're not gonna absquatulate, if that's the meaning you intended."

The dread Ashen felt sunk its claws into her. "Absquatulate? That sounds ... really, really not good. Like, the polar opposite of good."

"Hold your horses, Missy. Means you're not gonna disappear. You mosey on through and see for yourself."

She threw a worried look at the cowboy. He tamed his mustache with one hand, his Stetson casting shadows on his face, making it unreadable. Next to him stood Max, his grin wide and warm. Her anxiety melted away, replaced instead with confusion, then embarrassment. She pivoted back to the mirror to hide her warming cheeks.

"You can do this."

The mirror and her fears had distracted Ashen so thoroughly that she hadn't noticed Angry Fox move next to her. Her blush reignited.

"No, I can't."

"You're no damsel, Miss Deming." A rare smile played on Angry Fox's lips. "You're a capable, independent woman. You can do this."

The girl's maternal approach coupled with her youthful look mystified Ashen. When she had first arrived at the station, Max had mentioned how, upon death, they were all the same age, but whenever Angry Fox spoke it became clear that she had been a spirit for a long, long while. Perhaps longer than Macajah or any of the rest.

Ashen managed a quick nod, trying to crowd out her doubts by concentrating on Angry Fox's little pep talk.

"Yeah," she said. "Definitely not a damsel."

Ashen pressed her palm against the glass. The colors of the mirror reacted, rebounding at a touch she couldn't feel, and the surface trembled with colorful waves as her fingertips grazed the surface. She leaned forward. The waves sloshed over her hand, up her forearm to her elbow. She pressed on, took a deep breath, and thought of Windsor Lake as she plunged into darkness.

Pressure in her mind blossomed to an inaudible boom. Afraid her skull would fall off or explode, she clasped at her temples. Her weightless body twisted, rotating through an undefined void, the thoughts in her head wandering through a maze of pain. Was she floating in outer space? Or maybe she had accepted her dead fate and this was what dying felt like.

A lifetime seemed to pass until the pressure abruptly dispersed and she broke through the other side. She floated up and out of Windsor Lake. The sun peeked over the Rockies, bathing everything in a golden pink light. Green and purple pulsed at a regular rhythm through tree limbs, and when the occasional spring leaf settled on the glassy water, the resulting delicate ripples warped the mirrored serenity.

The calm lake stirred. Macajah's Stetson appeared first as he rose next to Ashen, his form repelling the water struggling to cling to him. Other than the liquid dripping from an invisible field around him, he looked as he always had: dry and dusty, like he had returned from a lengthy journey through the drought-afflicted plains. Once out of the lake, he smoothed his duster, descending until his boots rested on the water's surface, and then strolled with a nonchalant gait to the shore.

Still hovering, Ashen watched as Max came through, the water interacting with him in the same manner. He drifted for a moment before his chestnut leather boots landed on the lake as if it were made of solid rock. He glanced up at her and winked.

She could feel herself blushing again. The blushing thing was getting irritating.

"Come on down from there, Missy," Macajah hollered from the beach.

"Uh..." She examined her blazing sneakers dangling above the lake. "How, exactly?"

"It's basically the same as going through the mirror," Max said. "Mind over matter. Think of walking on the lake. Then, you walk on the lake. Like this." He demonstrated, the resulting ripples disturbing the water as he stomped beneath her.

"Oh. Sure. Fine. Do that. Makes sense."

She bit the inside of her lip, focused, and willed her feet to move. Nothing happened. Both Max and Macajah shouted out tips and ideas to her, but none worked. She stayed where she hung, pinned in midair, feeling silly and helpless. After a while, she kicked her legs at random, moving her arms in odd midair dog-paddling motions until she combined the two in frustration.

"What the heck do you think you're doing?" Macajah bellowed, holding his sides. "You ain't no dang border collie!"

"Ignore him." The corners of Max's mouth turned up as he attempted to stave off the laughter. He offered her his hand, but she swatted him away.

"I hate you both," she said bitterly.

Letting out a deep sigh, Max tugged on the cuff of her jeans. Her glare never ceased the whole time she dropped to the lake's surface.

"You're overthinking it." He turned to head to the shore.

She followed him, pouting. "So what if I am?"

"Little Missy," Macajah said from the bank, his thumbs hitched in his duster's pockets and a big grin plastered on his face. "You ever contemplate the act of breathing when you were a living being?"

"Only when I had the hiccups."

"But in your day-to-day, breathing is a natural thing. Don't require a lick of brain power, does it?"

"Guess not."

"Let this come naturally," Max said. "It's like a muscle that needs training. Eventually, you won't have to think about it any more."

The soldier wrapped his arm around her shoulders and guided her toward the trail. Still cross, she shrugged away, but Max pulled her closer to whisper in her ear.

"I have faith in you."

14

WINDSOR LAKE

As the three ghosts walked along the lakeside trail, birds swooped between trees and lake grass, streaking the sky with vivid color. Tiny insects flitted from plant to plant like dancing miniature candles. Even the smallest microorganisms had their own living glow, making the water sparkle.

A loon wailed. Max's tattoos flared electric blue and Macajah reached into his duster, allowing a sliver of Agnes to show between the folds. The rifle's gleam mimicked the cowboy's brilliant amber irises. After no danger presented itself, both men appeared satisfied.

"You guys are a bit jumpy, aren't you?" Ashen said with a smirk.

"Can never be too cautious." Max surveyed the surrounding area. "Knowing the Unseen are up to something worries me."

"I'm in agreement," Macajah grumbled. "Thaddeus and

myself have a history, so to speak. And this whole dang affair doesn't set right."

The cowboy frowned and squatted at the edge of the lake. Ashen peered over his shoulder. Fish were gathered, huddled in the shallows, burrowed beneath the silt to stave off the crisp, early spring air. But the mirrored surface had caught an image she had not expected.

The muted features of Macajah stared back.

Ashen shoved the cowboy to the side, almost knocking him off-balance as she crowded next to him. She searched for her own likeness, but only Macajah's lopsided grin greeted her.

"Your reflection," she said. "You're materialized? How?"

Macajah grunted and swiped at the tranquil waters. Fish scattered, the resulting turbulence distorting his image. Cupping his hand, he captured some of the liquid before letting it dribble through his fingers.

"Hey! How'd you touch water?" she demanded, unable to hide her accusatory tone, trying to figure out the trick as Max came up behind her, his reflection clear in the morning light. She looked back at him. "I can't see myself. Why don't I show up like you guys?"

Max opened his mouth to answer, but Macajah stood, shaking off droplets before wiping his hand across his chest, leaving a damp print on the worn leather of his duster. "We see ourselves because we believe—we know—we exist. That's your first lesson. Believe."

"Obviously, I exist." She targeted Macajah's massive mustache in the water and slapped at it. Her attempt failed. "I mean, I'm here, aren't I?"

"If you truly believed, you'd see yourself in this here lake, or succeed in touching it. As you're not achieving either, my horse sense tells me you've not quite accepted it yet."

"What's there to accept? I mean, this whole explanation is weird. The Divide, mind over matter, you guys, the Unseen." Ashen took another half-hearted swat at the water. "Like, what if I'm dreaming it all?"

"You best start believing." A grimness crossed Macajah's face. "Remember what I told you back when we saw that poor woman back in the cemetery?"

"I could become lost." The thought of the silent, wailing spirit circling her own grave made Ashen shudder. "That I might become a Drifter, like her."

He nodded. "And if that happens, you won't remember who you are. Becoming a Drifter is the afterlife's version of insanity, and like I said, everyone who dies has a choice, even if they may not be of sound mind to do so."

"But if Vana can make people into Drifters, does that mean she can also bring them back? I mean, it's reversible, right?"

"To her credit, she's tried many a time," Macajah said. "But a lost soul's condition is most likely permanent." Before he continued, he glanced at Max. "That said, I am aware of one that returned from that fate."

The soldier eyed the cowboy and shook his head in a curt no. Macajah nodded in return, his lips pursed to a flat crease.

Max cleared his throat. "I'm going ahead. Scout the location. Make certain we're not walking into some sort of trap." As soon as he finished speaking, he diminished into a bright blue orb and shot off over the lake toward South Valentia Street.

Ashen sprinted a few paces after him. "Wait!" she yelled, but Max's orb had already made its way through the sagebrush that grew along the opposite edge. When his blue light winked out of sight, she stopped, turned to Macajah, and threw her hands in the air.

"What was that all about?"

"Smart fella. Thinks ahead. A soldier through and through."

"Come on, Cage. I'm not stupid. I saw your secret exchange." She let her arms drop to her sides. "Why'd he go off by himself? I mean, I don't like heights much, but why don't we turn into one of those floating balls and, you know, glide or float or teleport after him?"

Macajah's face scrunched up. "Reckon I don't know what a teleport is, but it sounds a might bit disturbing."

"Teleportation! Ugh, never mind. I keep forgetting you're from, like, Old West times. Probably don't know anything about pseudo-science stuff."

"I ain't no idjiot, Missy! Fact is, I'm mighty fond of the subject of science. Even rustle up a publication from time to time, and I'll have you know I'm a sizable admirer of Nikola Tesla. Used to haunt him at his experimental station down in Colorado Springs." Macajah's grumpy disposition melted. He hung his head. "I suspect there's a ... possibility ... I may be the reason why the poor fella took to conversing with pigeons."

"Sorry. I figured science wouldn't interest you."

"Best you not assume a thing." The cowboy gave her a dismissive wave. Morning rays from the sun made Macajah's flesh blush with life. Ashen gazed at the backs of her own hands, but the same light that kissed the cowboy's skin filtered through her bones, thrusting her into a perpetual fog.

"You ready to skedaddle? Or are you gonna glower there, all judgmental-like?"

"What?" she asked, her eyebrows drawn together. His focus stayed on her feet. She looked down. Fine, silvery fire flickered over the toes of her sneakers, but a different movement shimmered beneath. A bright, colorful fish swam below the gentle ripples of the lake.

Ashen shrieked and sprinted toward Macajah. Once on the solid shore, she panted and said, "I thought I was on the ground!"

"You're bein' ornery and not listenin'. Since you believed you were on sturdy earth, your non-body followed suit."

"Believe?" She rolled her eyes. "Ooh! Maybe if I clap my hands enough, I'll resurrect myself!"

Under the brim of the Stetson, Macajah's features clouded. "I ain't never heard tale of that ever working, but if it'll get you out of your fix, I reckon it's worth a try."

"Why do I end up with a mentor who only reads science books?" Ashen muttered.

They strolled the embankment together without speaking. In the lake, fish were becoming more active, livening in the warmer daylight. Next to the trail, several militant multicolored ants carried bits of leaves and grass, all marching in a straight line. Even the dead old cowboy looked like he still breathed. Everything around her lived.

Everything except her.

As if he could read her thoughts, Macajah broke the lakeside silence. "Becomin' accustomed to death differs from fella to fella, or young lady such as yourself. Best to start at the beginning, Little Missy. What's your first recollection after your demise?"

"I saw a freakin' dead guy."

"Now, now. None of that hasty balderdash. Think back to when you first came to. Before you saw anything using your spirit eyes."

"I woke up on a gurney."

"On it? So, you were touching it?"

She glared at Macajah. "Yes, I was lying on it, which

171

generally requires one to be physically touching it."

"You keep on being a smart alec," he said, his eyes narrowing to slits, "and I'll abandon you right here."

"Sorry."

"Now, did you touch anything else?"

"The latch on the ... dead person freezer. I opened it and saw a guy's feet."

"And then?"

She concentrated on the glassy surface of the lake. "I guess I was in shock. I could only stare at his feet and that tag around his ankle and I backed away, fast, until I ran into the gurney I woke up on. And then I turned around and saw myself."

"Your dead self?"

She nodded, kicking a flaming sneaker at a fish exploring the shoreline, but her foot passed through without disturbing the water. "Yeah, I mean, it was me ... my body and all, but it didn't look like me. Didn't look real. Like a Halloween decoration. A bad replica or, like, a mannequin."

Macajah studied her as she toed at the lake. "And after that?"

"Couldn't touch anything. Couldn't open the door to get out. Nothing."

"Except the floor?"

She turned to the cowboy, confused. "What?"

"The floor, Missy. I reckon since we met, we shambled over ten miles together. Not a once did you sink on through the concrete and wind up in the Orient."

Panic swelled in Ashen's chest. She had never questioned her ability to walk, or to stand, and the longer she considered this, the shorter and quicker each breath became until, slowly, she began to submerge into the beach.

Macajah grabbed hold of her arm, stabilizing her, but her

legs and feet felt as though they dangled in nothingness.

"Don't go contemplatin' that notion too long," the cowboy said. "You gotta believe, to know without a shade of doubt, that you can do whatever you dream up."

She closed her eyes, swallowed hard, and tried to hold back her fear; to think of anything but falling through the world. But no matter how hard she tried, her mind kept reverting back, imagining herself tumbling through layers of sediment and molten rock, from one continent to the next for eternity.

Scared and trembling, her eyelids flew open to Macajah, still holding her afloat.

"I can't think of anything else, Cage!"

"You gotta!" He hefted her higher until she could see the concern, burden, seriousness, all wrapped up in his blazing scowl. "Little Missy, you hold out a fool's hope that you'll become tangible again. That's a dangerous desire. In the eventual, the realization needs to strike that you'll never again be a living being. If you don't, you risk being caught in an eternal torment you can't escape. Lost. It's a mighty fine balance, as fine as a frog's hair, to know that you're dead, accept it, and still believe that you exist."

The memory of the hospital mirror, her reflection clear and real in the wavering glass, engulfed her. She had assumed, believed, that she was alive. That she lived and breathed as she had before. It was only after she had seen her body...

"Now repeat after me." Macajah pointed at his own glimmering face in the water. "'I, Ashen Deming, am dead, and I still exist.'"

"This is stupid."

"Criminy sakes! Say it anyway before I have a mind to let you plummet to the moon!"

She sighed. "I, Ashen Deming, am dead. I still exist."

"Good. Now repeat that and ruminate on making yourself appear. Believe what you're saying."

She looked where she assumed her eyes would be and whispered, "I, Ashen Deming, am dead. And I still exist."

Macajah released her arm. She hovered a moment before sinking into the sand.

"Cage! Don't let go!"

"Ashen Deming!" The cowboy whipped his Stetson off and threw it to the ground. He bent down within inches of her face, his glowing eyes wild. "You will not become a Drifter on my watch, ya hear? You repeat those dang words and mean them!"

"I still exist!"

Her descent halted. She kept chanting the lines like an incantation until she rose up and out of the ground. Within the reflection on the ankle-deep lake water, a commotion of churning particles clutched at each other as they formed her deep brown eyes. Gradually, the freckles on her nose appeared, spreading across her cheeks, up her temples, and into her raised eyebrows.

The cowboy's chest puffed up. "Reckoned you had it in you, Missy. Your first materialization."

Ashen turned her disembodied head, examining her profile, noting that most of her scalp and neck hadn't appeared while Macajah brushed the dust from his Stetson and placed it back on his head.

"Well, the back of your noggin's missing, as is your carcass, but the rest of you should show in due time. With some practice, you'll control it—off and on—at will."

"My first materialization?" Ashen repeated, her stuck mind catching up. "Do you mean someone could see me right now?"

Macajah smiled. "If'n by someone you mean the living, then yes, although you'd give them some mighty powerful night terrors on account of you looking like a partial floating skull. Fortunately, no living folks come round these parts this time of the year."

She nodded in response. Out of the corner of her eye, she registered movement. Her hair had emerged — chestnut curls reacting to the soft breeze. She took a few steps out onto the lake, sinking slightly before the soles of her sneakers rose to the top, and knelt down. A little more of her face and head peered back. It felt like years since she'd last seen herself and now that she could, she felt indifferent, as though observing a complete stranger.

A frown touched her lips. The same action echoed in the water. She smiled, and like an old friend, her reflection smiled in return. With an invisible hand, she reached into the lake. A cold sensation coiled up her wrist, and when she pulled her hand back, small dewdrops of liquid clung to her, rolling to her fingertips until they dripped off, returning to the lake in fluid halos.

"A dang good start, Missy!" Macajah clasped his rugged hand on her shoulder. "Mighty proud."

"I think I may finally be getting over my mirror phobia," she said, standing. "Well, assuming some Unseen guy doesn't pop out at me."

"For Thaddeus and his gang, traveling by mirror is a recent development. I reckon you're safe enough."

Ashen laughed. "I guess when you've been around for a hundred years, five years is considered recent."

The cowboy's expression turned puzzled. "Five years? What in tarnation are you yammerin' abou —"

Macajah's head snapped up. From the far side of the lake, the fringe sagebrush rustled and Max's blue orb appeared.

His movements were slow, almost sluggish, weaving back and forth as he hovered.

"Max?" Ashen jogged forward a little. "Oh no, Cage. Is he hurt or something?"

Macajah didn't answer. He withdrew Agnes, aiming a shot beyond Max toward any pursuing threat. The blue orb approached, settling at their feet before the sullen soldier materialized. He glanced at Ashen with an expression that she couldn't quite put her finger on.

"What's wrong?" she asked. "Is it Thaddeus and the Unseen?"

"The Unseen aren't there," Max said, refusing to look her in the eye. "We should probably head back to the station."

"But what about Jacob?"

Upon hearing Jacob's name, Max paused and focused on the ground. After a stretched moment, his pale eyes, full of pity and sadness, flicked to her. "It's probably best if we go back."

"No," Ashen said, tears brimming. "Show me. Show me what you found."

The muscles of his neck flexed. He nodded, turned, and walked toward the cluster of naked trees and brush that bordered a dried-out canal. Ashen and Macajah followed. As they crossed over to a paved path, she wiped at her cheeks, muffling her sniffles with the back of her sleeve. When they were about to reach South Valentia Street where the bus had crashed, Ashen hoped she had misread Max. That he had seen something—a bad sign or clue—but nothing definite. That maybe Jacob was okay.

The street, at first, appeared as it always had. The empty path and road ahead were bathed in high desert sunshine. Nearby, Fairmount Cemetery leered from behind a fence, the chain link suffocated by twiggy vines covered with tiny green shoots; new life growing from last year's remains. Any signs of the wreck had already been cleared away.

A roadside tree cast its gnarled shadow upon the asphalt. In its darkened confines, a thick mist carpeted the street. It hugged the ground, hanging in the parched air like an out-of-place oceanside fog. Ashen ignored her two companions and walked timidly across the road until she stood over the hazy swirls. Within, a form began to take shape.

A sob caught in her throat. On his side lay Jacob, wispy and translucent, hugging his knees to his chest. His image emerged, writhing, screaming in soundless agony, and Ashen dropped to her knees—her mind extinguished to darkness.

15

Max: Operation Neptune

Max Churchill
Born: April 9, 1924
Died: June 6, 1944

June 6, 1944

The dawn was covered in a filthy gray. Max bailed out encroaching sea water with his helmet, his grip tight to keep his hands from shaking. With every helmetful he tossed overboard, the choppy sea reciprocated tenfold; its smothering waves reached up and over the wall of the British Navy's LCA, tumbling the boat like a toy in a bathtub.

The wind shifted. Artillery smoke mingled with vomit. Max's stomach lurched. Earlier that morning, while he had struggled to swallow an apple and a chocolate bar, the rest of the US Army Rangers had stuffed themselves on the feast provided by the HMS *Amsterdam*. Crammed into tiny landing crafts, those same, well-fed soldiers now swayed with each six-foot swell, retching every few minutes to add to the putrid stew of sick and water that sloshed against their Corcoran jump boots.

A hollow boom from a battleship sounded behind them. More followed, and huge shells cut through the sky like brass eagles, the air around them distorting, pushing down on the men in the boat. A soldier named Benjamin Henry stared fearfully at the projectiles. A recent Ranger recruit, he had joined them in England, claiming he had volunteered on his eighteenth birthday, but Max guessed he was a few years shy of that. Either way, he was like the younger brother Max never had. He couldn't help but admire the kid. Private Henry embodied innocence and optimism and everything the war wasn't.

Max stopped bailing to give Henry a firm pat on the arm. "They won't hit us, Private."

"I know, sir. Just didn't think they'd be so close."

"Be glad they're covering us for the assault, Henry. Scaling Pointe du Hoc and disarming those guns will be tough enough. We can use all the help we can get."

"Yes, Corporal."

The rising sun filtered through the gloom and revealed the impending shoreline. Their destination was three miles away, obscured by a wall of thick, white haze. In the lead, surveying the line of cliffs ahead, the stately silhouette of their commanding officer, Lieutenant Colonel Rudder, stood on the raised platform edge of LCA 888 as if he were Washington crossing the Delaware.

The rough water of the Channel had already taken its toll. Max squinted at the handful of landing craft and DUKW amphibious trucks that remained of their flotilla. Right after launch, Captain Slater's LCA had been swamped and the men aboard pulled to safety. A DUKW carrying the ladders had sunk, then one of the supply crafts. Some of the British coxswains that piloted the LCAs had tried to get to the soldiers in time, but they had only managed to save one.

Max's face steeled. If the sea itself killed them so easily, what chance would they have when they reached the shore?

He noticed Henry's eyebrows knitting up. The boy's eyes glazed over, a small moan escaping his lips, and he quickly looked down.

"Something on your mind, Private?"

Henry sniffed but didn't look up. "Yes, sir ... well, how's it you're so calm? I mean, you gotta be scared, right?"

"Sure, we all are. But I've got an advantage."

The private raised his head, his misty eyes wide at the possibility of a more seasoned soldier's secret. "What advantage, sir?"

"Don't let on to the Army, but I can't see a lick. No real detail at a distance. Suppose close combat suits me best. Not a lot to fear when you can't see them shooting at you."

Henry seemed confused. "Can't see them, sir?"

"Nah. Eyesight is lousy. Eyeglasses don't help, so I run like crazy, straight at them, until I can give them a knuckle sandwich."

A few of the enlisted men chuckled as Henry exclaimed, "The guys are right, sir! You're completely nuts!"

Max laughed. "The Germans don't expect it, that's for sure."

Low-flying engines rumbled overhead. Dark shadows of Flying Fortresses and Liberators soared in formation through dense clouds. The forty planes flew so close to each other that Max figured any of the aircrew would be able to step outside and walk from one outstretched wing to the next.

A man named Clemmons took off his helmet before gazing upward. An orange diamond with a numerical two inside had been painted on the back of the outer shell. The number of their battalion. "Quite a sight, ain't it, Corporal?"

Max tried to focus his poor eyesight on the target as the planes dropped their bombs. The enemy's beach defenses lit up. Belated audible blasts trailed out to the sea. Smoke billowed, the glow of fire refracted into orange and red streaks, and although the shore blazed, the mass of the damage trailed inland, away from the beach.

"Damn," Clemmons said. "Hope to hell they took some of 'em Krauts out."

The planes had waited too long. Max pursed his lips and set back to bailing. "Put your helmet back on, Clemmons. Almost in range."

When the battleships had ceased firing, someone tapped him on his shoulder. It was Private Edlin, a massive, broad man. "Something's funny, Corporal," he said, pointing a sausage-like finger at the cliffs. "That don't look like our objective."

As soon as Edlin spoke, the form of Lieutenant Colonel Rudder in the lead landing craft motioned wildly at his navigating coxswain.

"Oh, no." Max thrust his map into Edlin's hands. "Check the shape."

"We're about," the big man paused, grunting once before indicating an area along the coast, "here."

"Pointe de la Percée. Wrong point." Max scrunched his eyes at the A-11 watch on his wrist. "Supposed to land in a few minutes. We're not even close."

The lead LCA 888 made an abrupt right turn. The rest followed suit and Max hunkered down, smacking each of the enlisted soldier's helmets, forcing them to sit on the wooden benches.

"We're officially in the Germans' range, gentlemen! Keep your heads covered! Don't be an easy target!"

Maneuvering through the men, Max huddled at the bow between the coxswain's and bowman's armored shelters and looked over the bow ramp. They were moving parallel to the shore, less than three hundred yards away. The enemy was perched at the top of the cliffs. An occasional sharp whizz of artillery fire sounded over the LCA. Max held his breath. He hoped that the bulk of the German forces were occupied elsewhere. A minute passed before commotion echoed from above. A louder, more distinct ping hit the metal plate of the boat. They'd been noticed.

"Stay down!"

The cloth-ripping sound of a German MG 42 came from the cliffs. The GIs had nicknamed the machine gun Hitler's Zipper, and its constant, distinct whir caused Max's blood to freeze. A spray of bullets skewered the water and peppered the side of the craft. Dread grew in the pit of his stomach.

One private rose from the bench, preparing to return fire. His helmet peeked over the wide edge of the LCA.

"Private!"

Max's heart raced. He reached to yank the man down, but too late. A bullet pierced the private's ear and through his skull. His body crumpled to the bottom of the boat.

After he'd checked for a pulse, Max pushed the man's corpse to the side, as far out of the way as possible. He loosened the dead man's helmet and used it to cover his dull eyes. He heard Private Henry next to him gulp down a panicked gasp.

"Shallow breaths, Henry! This is why we stay covered!"

Machine gun and rifle fire pummeled the armor-clad vessel for three miles, then the Germans lobbed mortars, their explosive shells hitting the craft with concussive blows. A high pitch reverberated from a solid hit. Max clamped his hands over his ears and peered through the crack between the ramp and hull as a mortar bomb hit a DUKW ahead of them. In a futile attempt to avoid enemy fire, the men threw themselves overboard, but either the jarring shock or the weight of their gear caused them to remain limp in the water. Max closed his eyes, listening for any sign of life amid the chaos, but the wreckage of the DUKW stayed silent.

Seventy yards from the beach, the belly of the LCA scraped against sand and shingle.

"We're supposed to head west!" he shouted.

"Lieutenant Colonel Rudder's order!" the British coxswain yelled over the noise of the blasts. Inside the armored LCA shelter, the Royal Navy soldier revved the engine. When the boat didn't move further, the man shook his head and waved Max off. "Can't get any closer, chum! Stuck on a crater!"

Max glanced at the blurry, distant cliffs. Their location was too far away—and when he picked up the saturated grappling rope, its additional weight confirmed it would never reach the top of the precipice. He let the rope fall to the floor. Perhaps the others nearest to the point had managed to keep theirs dry.

"Okay, D Company! This is it! As soon as that ramp opens, hustle!"

A few men nodded. Some crossed themselves, whispering prayers. Others, their stance rigid, embraced their plastic-encased guns. They had nothing else to hold on to.

The bowman lowered the ramp. Time slowed to a stop, yet everything quickened.

Deafening thuds of Max's own pumping blood hushed the battle. Each man was shoved forward by the rest, some tripping over the dead body of the private. They jumped off the ramp and into the water, their bobbing heads fighting the current, feet struggling to reach the bottom.

Large obstacles called hedgehogs stuck up from the sands. The six-foot-tall steel rails resembled neglected crosses that had been tumbled over by a gust of wind. Positioned near one was the hazy frame of the lead LCA. Its rocket-propelled ropes fired toward the Germans' position. The LCA's ramp fell open. A shot discharged. From the top of the cliff, a dark smudge plummeted, silhouetted against the tawny clay.

Bullets pelted the marbled froth of the waves. Tubular fountains shot high into the air. Max pushed more men forward, urging them to take cover, but two men paused at the threshold as the projectiles drew near.

Max shouted a warning, his voice muffled; foreign. With each impact, the men's bodies spasmed and twitched until they collapsed at the bottom of the ramp, one on top of the other. The waves pulled and released their lifeless limbs in a morbid waltz.

He heard a cry. Behind him, Henry stared on, mouth turned down in horror. Lead battered metal. On instinct, Max grabbed Henry and another soldier's arm and threw himself over the ledge of the landing craft, splashing into the sea with the two men in tow.

Churned gravel muddied the water. Arms and legs flailed, grappling heavy gear. Shots shattered the surface. Each bullet arched, slowed by the sea, and halted after a few feet. Henry wrestled with his life jacket, his mouth wide, yelling, choking on salt water. The other private surfaced as another volley of bullets hit, but they were too close this time. The surrounding area turned pink.

Henry began to lose consciousness. Max yanked at the

knife in his belt and cut through the leather strap binding Henry to his life jacket. He caught him by the collar, forcing his head up, and shook the boy.

"Keep just above the waves, Private! Use the water as protection!"

Henry coughed and nodded, his eyes filled with tears. Max took hold of the boy's arm, jerked him to his feet, and kept low as he dragged Henry through the rising tide toward the nearest Hedgehog. They huddled behind the steel in the waist-deep surf, the air thick with the stench of iron and rubber and fuel and smoke. Floating corpses littered the Channel. Max avoided the GIs' faces.

On the beach ahead, Rangers carrying portable rocket launchers and rope ladders raced toward the cliffs while grenades hailed down. The boy next to him trembled, flinching at every explosion. Every shot.

Max seized the chin strap of Henry's helmet and locked eyes with the soldier. "Can't stay here, Private! The only ones staying on this beach are the dead or those who are gonna die! Now, move!"

An expression of nervous determination replaced the fear. The boy nodded again, and the two readied themselves. They rushed forward, wading through the murky shallows, and broke into a waterlogged run once their feet touched shingle. More Rangers from other landing craft ran alongside them. Some men were struck by grenades or artillery, but the rest kept moving, sprinting past the screams and cries for medics and mothers.

The earlier bombing from the battleships had toppled the face of the cliff. The men who had arrived first were using the mound to take cover as they set up portable rocket launchers. Max and the rest ran up the mud pile. As the Rangers pressed themselves against the clay wall, heads peeked down at them, throwing grenades and shooting at those who gathered beneath.

A German soldier aimed his rifle.

"Push in!" Max yelled, his voice cracking—anxious. He hoped that the German was a bad shot.

A large boom blared from the English Channel. Pieces of rock and earth rained on them, showering the Rangers' helmets as British and American artillery pounded the top of the crag. The Germans yelled and the dark shapes above retreated out of sight.

Edlin and a few other solid brutes began to scale the wall, stabbing their knives into the clay, using the exposed hilts to climb as they reached from one hold to the next. There was a blast behind Max. A rocket-propelled grapnel soared overhead, its hooks catching on the military debris that lined the ledge, leaving a rope, heavy with water, dangling from the cliff's apex.

While more grapnels flew toward the cliff, Max grabbed the slippery rope in front of him. A few rope ladders lay unused on the sand. He pointed at them.

"Why aren't we using these?"

"Not long enough, Corporal!"

Max growled and dug the toes of his boots into the wet clay. Some of the Germans had made their way back to the cliff's edge as he ascended, but the constant shelling from the battleships, along with some Rangers providing cover fire beneath, kept many back.

A German cut through one of the ropes. The men that hung from it screamed for help, hunting in vain to gain purchase before they plunged to the beach below. Above and to the right, Max could see Henry moving up the steep muck.

"Faster, Henry!"

The light frame of the private responded, his nimble legs clambering up behind Edlin, who still climbed without the aid of a rope. Reaching the top first, Edlin pulled himself over. His burly arm reached down for Henry, lifting him without effort, and the two men scrambled over the ledge.

Artillery thundered. Soldiers yelled in both German and English before an explosion. Soot and dust floated overhead, billowing around Max, then silence.

Max hauled himself over the rim, searching for any sign of his men. Edlin lay wounded in a crater readying his weapon, his frantic eyes darting to the Germans holed up in their bunkers. Nearby, Henry knelt, a German's Luger pistol pointed at his head.

In an instant, Max got to his feet and ran full tilt toward the German. The man gaped, his expression shocked. A shot rang. Raising the Luger, the German pointed it, but Max tackled the man full-force and threw him to the ground. The two wrestled, rolling into razor sharp coils of barbed wire and metal remains along the edge of the cliff. The wire sliced at them as Max bashed the German's hand into the ground until his grip loosened, and Max tore the Luger from his grasp, flung it to the beach below, and elbowed the man hard beneath his chin.

There was a loud crack. The German's head snapped back, and a searing, tingling heat throbbed in Max's thigh. Dizzy, he punched at the German's throat. He missed. The German overpowered him and flipped Max onto his back, tangling them both in more wire, and began to strangle Max. Everything turned gray.

Another shot. The German fell, dead, on top of him. Strength spent, Max struggled to push the full weight of the man off. Barbed wire bit into his flesh. He looked to the burning pain. The hilt of a Hitler Youth dagger protruded from his thigh. At some point during the fight, it had dislodged. His fatigues were soaked with his own blood.

The femoral artery. A death sentence. He wanted to go home. What would his mother think?

He sat up.

The guns they were meant to destroy pointed from concrete bunkers.

From the bomb crater, Edlin's rifle smoked.

On the ground before him lay a dead boy named Private Benjamin Henry.

Max lay back on his barbed wire mattress. It had been a pointless objective. An illusion. The guns weren't real. Sticking out from the bunkers at the tops of the cliffs were telegraph poles, not gun barrels.

So many had died for guns that didn't exist.

October 18, 1948

Cobalt-blue clouds abandoned by the setting sun loomed overhead. A boy held fast to his little sister's hand as he led her along a muddy trail marred by tire tracks and booted feet.

Her whining protests echoed in the approaching dusk. "Why must we go this way, Philippe?"

"Because, *ma petite soeur*, this way's faster."

"But I don't like it. It's scary."

Philippe rolled his eyes. "Nothing to be scared of."

"But all the soldiers! And Papa says we shouldn't go this way!"

"They're only graves. Graves can't hurt you. And you know we're late. Papa's gonna be furious."

She whimpered. He felt her resist as the military cemetery

came into view. The American and German sides had been divided by clumps of gnarled, warped trees—each crouched and ready to pounce on their prey of wooden crosses in perfect lines. Row after row of graves stretched and disappeared into a border of dark shrubs.

Philippe forced a smile at his sister. "Not far to go now. Almost there."

He squeezed her hand. She managed to smile back, but her eyes were swimming with concern. The failing light now cloaked the trail with shadow and he quickened his pace, ignoring the white crosses as he concentrated on avoiding puddles and navigating from one dry patch to the next.

Philippe didn't like the graveyard, either. As they passed, he glanced at a section where shovels were sticking up from piled earth. His father had told him that since the war was over, the American soldiers were either going to be relocated to the bigger cemetery in Colleville-sur-Mer or sent back to their families. When Philippe asked if the Germans were also being sent home, his father only shook his head sadly.

The hard soles of his sister's boots scraped on bits of rock as she darted forward. She closed the short distance between her and her brother in an instant, colliding into Philippe's backside and burying her face into his hip while she wailed.

"Hey, quit messing about!"

"A soldier! It's a soldier!" she sobbed, giving his belt a series of panicked tugs.

"What? There've hardly been any soldiers here for years, you know that."

She stopped, raised her tiny hand, and pointed toward the edge of the cemetery nearest to the trail.

"A soldier," she said again. The concern she'd shown before had hardened to a frightened seriousness. She stood, shaking, staring at her brother, refusing to look in the direction she pointed.

He let out a heavy sigh and gazed off into the growing night. "*Ma petite*, there isn't anyth-"

His words caught in his throat. He took a few steps back and rubbed his tired eyes.

A mist circled one of the crosses. The vapor became more opaque and shifted into the shape of a man wearing Army fatigues. Barbed wire bound his arms and torso. His expression was one of anguish. Through parted lips, he yelled silently, and his image shimmered as he rounded the cross again and again, repeating each action as he had before.

Although Philippe's feet wouldn't move, he wanted to run. A moment passed before he realized his sister was yanking on his arm, urging him to leave, but his eyes stayed locked on the soldier. Other wispy figures began to appear, filling the graveyard with hundreds of the repetitive dead. A German soldier with half of his helmet missing. An American holding his own insides. Another man, unrecognizable, engulfed in spectral flames.

With his sister's hand in his own, Philippe remembered how to run.

PART FOUR:
DEPRESSION

16

FINDING JACOB

Time smothered everything in fog as fringes of the day fell away. In the west, fingers of night clawed from behind Pikes Peak, tearing out chunks of cobalt-blue sky to reveal its star-spotted innards.

Full days had passed since she had found Jacob. Tiny shards of glass were all that remained of the bus crash, and in their reflections, Ashen had lost track of how many times the sun had risen and set. She resented their presence. They littered the asphalt, strewn upon the road like unwanted garbage. Those shattered pieces of her and Jacob's deaths were reminders that their lives had meant nothing. They had been erased.

She sat on the curb and cradled her folded knees. Tears streamed down her face and an intense, searing throb surged through her as she stared at the faded image of Jacob, crumpled on the ground, screaming in silence. He wavered in and out of focus, more defined in the evening, but muting to a dull glow at first light. As punishment, she forced herself to watch. Watch as her friend replayed his actions over and over like a busted videocassette stuck on repeat.

She thought of how she had treated him. How she had never said anything kind, or told him how much she appreciated him. Jacob had always been there for her. Always. And now, even though she could see him right in front of her, he was gone. She might never get the chance to make things right.

Macajah had left at some point. She wasn't sure when, but she became vaguely aware whenever he returned. Every time, he never said a word—he'd only sit next to her. After a moment, he'd drape his arm around her shoulder, hug her to him, and then he'd disappear again.

Max, however ... Max stayed. Always on the periphery, he waited; keeping his distance, giving her space, but never leaving.

About a week went by before Macajah spoke. One late afternoon, he arrived after a long absence and settled himself on the curb. The cowboy scanned her feet, then her legs and arms while rubbing his jaw, his bristles softly scraping across his palm.

"How're you holding up, Little Missy?"

Ashen didn't reply. She didn't know what to say. Everything seemed pointless.

In an attempt to avoid him, she turned her head away. Hanging on the edge of her vision, a silver glimmer caught her attention, startling her. The small flames that once curled around her shoes had swelled larger than they had at Union Station, engulfing her entire body in a pearl-gray light. The phantom fire twirled around her hands, dissolved to a weak flicker, then rebounded to its original brilliance.

"What's happening?" she whispered.

"You're gainin' strength," Macajah said. "I reckon the process hastened on account of you being grieved."

"Is that a bad thing?" The memory of Toad disintegrating in the Divide entered her mind. She slowed her breathing like Vana had taught her. "I'm ... I'm not gonna burn away or anything, right?"

"You'll be staying in a single piece," the cowboy said. He stretched his legs and thumped the heels of his boots in the street. "So to speak, I suppose. But those flames gaining power means you're running out of time to move on."

"What do you mean?"

"You recall that attraction you experienced back when you saw the Divide and your armored snake friend?"

Ashen nodded. Her impulse to follow Langhorne had been a difficult thing to ignore.

"Well, when us specters first expire, we all feel that almighty yearning to enter that arch. We know somewhere deep, deep down, that's where we're destined to be."

"What happens to the people that go?"

"Ain't certain. A great many souls pass through unharmed, some having longer to decide than others. Everyone's different, but there's a finite amount of time to determine if you want to stay, or go, all peaceful-like."

Her eyes, wet and raw, rested on Jacob. "And if I stay?"

"If you don't move on, you become an earthbound spirit like the rest of us. Those energies of yours will get mighty potent, not unlike what you're starting to possess. But there's a catch."

"What?"

"Those who decide to stay can never enter the Divide," he

said, his drawl huskier. Darker. "If we do, we suffer a ghost's death."

"What we saw happen to Toad—that would happen to you? Or me, if I ever changed my mind?"

"Yes, Missy. We cease to exist."

They sat quietly as Ashen considered this. Jacob ... the Drifter. She couldn't leave him now, even with the looming threat of being stuck here forever. Assuming there was anything at the end of the Divide, she'd always know that she'd abandoned him and that he remained behind, in pain.

"Cage?" she asked. Her voice quivered as she fought the stinging tears that blurred her vision. "Why did you stay?"

"I reckon I could recite our code to you. Say it's my duty to protect those living souls who can't protect themselves, but that ain't entirely accurate." Macajah paused as if to search for words. "My wife, Abigail, wasn't there when I'd located the Divide. So I waited. Couldn't stomach traveling to the unknown alone and leaving her behind. Eventually, I figured bein' a retired lawman and all, I'd do more good staying put."

"Oh."

"Carried a fool's hope we'd find each other again, but what's done is done," Macajah said. "For the present, know that Max and me, well, we're mindful of how miserable this whole affair is. The prospect of you losing yourself pains us."

Her lip trembled. "You mean if I become a Drifter."

"Little Missy, that there would be an awful tragedy."

Tears came easily now. "It doesn't matter if I do. There's no one left to remember me."

"It dang well matters! It matters to us! Particularly to a certain protective young fella who's taken to becoming your personal guardian angel." He bent his head to the side, indicating Max a few yards away. The soldier fiddled with his fighting knife, flipping it by the blade and catching it again, a haunted concern within his gray eyes. "If you ask me, of all the ghosts you may meet, he's the one that can give you a fragment of hope."

"Hope? How is any of what's happened hopeful?"

"That's the funny thing about hope," he said. "You never know what dark place it'll shine from."

After his cryptic response, Macajah rose, tipped his hat, and sauntered off, his leather duster swaying in his wake. When he passed Max, he raised an eyebrow that vanished beneath the Stetson's brim. The soldier waited, watching as the cowboy formed into a golden orb, floated off toward Windsor Lake, and winked out of sight.

A stern seriousness was reflected in Max's features as he approached Ashen, but even when he sat next to her, she continued her self-punishment, unable to tear her eyes off Jacob writhing at her feet. Max, as far as she could tell, did the same. The sun dipped behind the Rockies and the street lights blinked on, washing out the road with a circle of bleached pale yellow.

After a quiet while, she glanced at Max, finding that he wasn't looking at Jacob as she had assumed. Instead, he focused on something beyond, past the chain-link fence surrounding the dusky grounds of Fairmount Cemetery to the Drifters wandering inside. The lost ghosts were more visible in the gathering dark. For the first time, Ashen noticed how many there were. Their numbers were in the hundreds.

"Are you okay?" he asked, his gaze following a Drifter aimlessly circling a headstone.

"Yeah," she said without looking in his direction.

"I'm sorry. About your friend."

"It's not your fault."

"I'm worried. About you."

She tried to smile. "I know."

"I...," he paused like he was trying to find the right thing to say. "I don't want the same thing that happened to me to happen to you."

She looked at him, confused. "What do you mean?"

"Back at the lake, do you remember how Cage told you he knew about a Drifter that came back?"

"Oh! I'm so stupid!" Ashen blurted. If a Drifter had managed to come back, then that meant..., "I completely forgot! Who is he? Where can we find him? Or her? Is it a her?"

"Uh, well," he flashed a grim grin. "You won't have to look far."

"Wait," she said, her eyes widening. "It was you? You used to be a Drifter?"

"That's why I'm concerned. It's a slippery slope once you start—"

"Why didn't you say something earlier!" Anger dominated her sorrow. "Jacob's been here in agony and you've been ... been sitting there, playing with your stupid knife!"

He raised his hands in defense. "It's not like that at all, I swear! I just can't remember how I snapped out of it."

"Oh, of course." She toed a pebble with her blazing silver Converse. "A possible solution presents itself and not one of you knows a thing about it."

"That's not fair, Ash. It's not like I can compare notes with other ex-Drifters. If that were possible, I would have done that ages ago."

A slew of emotions bubbled up in Ashen. Embarrassment. Frustration. Regret. It wasn't Max's fault. It wasn't his responsibility. Yet, here he was, protecting her as she mourned. Supporting her even as she lashed out at him. Why did he have to be so easy to like?

"I'm sorry, Max. For losing my temper." Ashen kicked the pebble out into the road. At the sight of the bouncing stone, she felt a sliver of satisfaction. "I know you're trying to help."

"I get it. It's okay," he said, rubbing the back of his neck. "Trust me, I feel pretty useless. I mean, I can remember the day that I died. Clearly. I remember D-Day and getting to the top of the cliff. I remember the guys in my battalion. I remember getting stabbed. After that, things get a bit murky."

"Something must have happened. You managed to break the spell or whatever, which means there must be something we can do for Jacob. Right?"

He hesitated. The furrow between his eyebrows deepened. "I recall utter hopelessness. Emptiness. But, there's not much else until I 'woke' here in Colorado. Took a while before I eventually put two and two together. Found out I'd been in Normandy for over four years. One of those temporary soldier cemeteries. I guess after the war ended, my body got sent home to be buried on the family plot."

"Okay, well, what's the first thing you remember? When you woke up?"

"My mother's voice," he said, a reminiscent smile on his face. "She kept saying how she was proud of me. How she was glad I was finally home."

Max's smile dissolved. He turned and peered into Ashen's eyes. She shivered.

"I hope you don't think I intentionally kept this from you," he said. "I would have said something sooner, but I didn't want to give you false hope. I don't understand why it happened in the first place."

"It's okay. It's, ugh, I want to help him. I want to make up for being…"

Unable to finish her sentence, she broke eye contact and began to rise from the curb. Max hurried to stand before her, offering his hand to help. She accepted this time, slipping her hand into his, feeling the warmth and the rougher texture and the lines of his palm—and beneath, a throbbing pulse. He seemed so real—aware and cognizant—yet here he stood, an ex-Drifter.

Her eyes flicked to Jacob. Somehow, she had to fix this.

Ashen took a few shaking steps forward and got down on her knees as if she were coaxing an injured animal. In front of her, curled up in the middle of the street, was her friend, his mouth wide open in torment.

"Jacob? Jacob, can you hear me?"

She reached out for him, but her hand passed through his spirit, colliding with the asphalt below.

"I can't even touch him."

"He doesn't know you're here," Max said.

She shook her head, blinking rapidly to slow the tears. "But I can touch you. You feel real."

Max knelt next to her. "Both have to be aware of the other's existence in order to connect. The more you're certain that someone, or something, is there, the more real it becomes."

"You're home, Jacob. Please … please wake up."

He didn't respond. Instead, he repeated his loop; screaming, crying, rocking. Ashen's hands hovered over his image, uncertain what action to take. She longed to comfort him. To save him. To make things right.

She spun to Max and threw her arms around him, burying her face into his shoulder. He embraced her, holding her close, stroking her unruly hair as she cried.

"I promise we'll figure this out," he whispered. "We'll help him. I promise."

A voice from the darkness echoed in the night. "Ya got more problems than yer Drifter friend thar."

Max released Ashen, pushed her behind him, and rolled up his sleeves. Tattoo whips exposed, his energy, once a vibrant blue, had turned weak. Perplexed, Max regarded the barbed wire along his forearms before he balled his hands into fists.

From the evening gloom that concealed him, the tall Unseen, Eli, appeared. "I ain't here ta fight ya. I'm here ta warn ya."

The creature's appearance had altered. The aubergine hue Ashen had seen at the train and the Divide was still present, but it had grown brighter, radiating from his smoky black exterior. It highlighted the creases of his felt hat and the ridged hollows of his cheeks. Even his distinctive long fangs had shortened, now barely reaching his jawline.

"Where's your boss, Eli?" Max asked. "Gone to throw someone else to the Divide?"

"I do reckon Mister Glick would toss me in next if'n he knew I were in yer company."

Ashen moved next to Max. The soldier examined Eli, taking mental notes as if he had also noticed the differences.

Max dropped his fists to his sides. "Why are you here? What do you want?"

"Thar be a reason why yer light thar ain't workin'."

"Mine's fine—" Ashen paused and looked down at her silver blaze. It, too, had dwindled to a washed-out tinge.

The Unseen gave a throaty grunt. "Ain't workin' right, see?"

As soon as Eli spoke, two orbs of light burst from the

direction of Windsor Lake and immediately materialized into the forms of Angry Fox and John. Grateful to see them again, Ashen fought the urge to run to them and embrace them, but her relief soon turned to anxiety. Upon seeing Eli, Angry Fox drew her weapons, but her tomahawks' familiar glow had become subdued. John's cuffs were also dim. Timid green sparks of electricity crawled over them, but he readied them all the same.

Eying Eli, John asked, "What are you doing here?"

"He said he's here to warn us," Max said. "Something about our energy."

"And you believe him?" Angry Fox said between gritted teeth. Her tomahawks throbbed with a dull intensity. "He might be part of why this is happening!"

"If'n I help you'uns, I reckon I'll get ta repay Thaddeus for what he done."

"You seek revenge for your miscreant of a brother?" Angry Fox asked.

The Unseen nodded. "Maybe he deserved ta be throwed in. I'm awares that he weren't a' agreeable sorta feller, but he were my one and only kin."

Angry Fox lowered her weapons. "Your desire for vengeance is strangely humanizing." She raised her tomahawks again. "However, if you attempt anything, I give you my word that I will strike you down where you stand."

"On my honor, ma'am. I ain't wantin' trouble."

The girl's dark eyes narrowed. "Is that what you told Vana's people that day on the plains?"

Eli's features shifted. "Not a day goes by where I ain't feelin' regret fer what I done."

"I was unaware your kind could identify an emotion like regret," Angry Fox spat back.

"Fox," John said. "We don't have time—"

"I ain't one of them no more."

Angry Fox seemed caught off guard. "What do you mean?" she asked, a brief moment of confusion on her face.

"I ain't Unseen. Not altogether." Eli lifted his hand. Purple light danced around his elongated fingers, shimmering in the velvet night. "I'm a-changin'."

Ashen leaned toward Max and whispered, "That even possible?"

"Not sure," Max said. "I know spirits can become Unseen, but I've never heard of one returning once they've made that choice."

"It's rare, I reckon," Eli said. "But I ain't cravin' ta walk that path. Not no more."

"Vana's not going to be enthusiastic," John said, speaking as if choosing his words carefully, his expression quizzical. "But we can't waste more time. We have to head back to the station." After a couple of steps toward Windsor Lake, he stopped, scanned the Unseen, and added, "We better bring Eli along, too."

"John? Why?" asked Max. "What's happened, anyway?"

John's gaze broke from Eli. "We're not exactly certain, but something's wrong with the Divide."

17

No Dang Sense

"Hurry, Unseen," Angry Fox said as they exited the Union Station mirror.

"Yes, ma'am," Eli said. His black boot had lodged in the surface of the glass, so he pulled with more force to break free. Head hung, he regained his balance and stood in the hallway to await further instruction.

During their walk from the site of the bus crash to the lake, Angry Fox had kept her hands on the hilts of her tomahawks and a suspicious eye on Eli. Ashen couldn't blame her. Though new to all of this herself, she agreed with Fox—doubtful of the new leaf Eli was trying to turn.

John and Max, however, remained optimistic, suspecting the Unseen might know more than he was aware. No matter how hard Ashen tried to convince herself that the Unseen would bring trouble, she found a part of herself hoping that Eli would prove to be an asset in piecing together Thaddeus' plans.

Once the rest were through the mirror, Fox motioned for Eli to follow. Together, the posse headed down the hall while the Unseen straggled behind, staring at his own feet.

The group exited the corridor. In the center of the lobby, Macajah and Vana spoke in hushed, frantic tones.

"Sakes alive, Vana! Where the heck are they?" Macajah asked, taking his Stetson off and running his fingers through his thick white hair. "They can't have disappeared! People die all the time!"

"Yes, Hollow Iron, but new souls have been diminishing for many years now. You know this. You have seen it."

"This makes no dang sense. More folks are being born now, aren't they? The city's population is increasing on the daily. How can their numbers be decreasing?"

Max jogged up to them. "John filled us in on the way. Did you find the cause?"

Before Macajah answered, he noticed Eli, head lowered and lurking behind the rest of the posse. Mustache puckered in disgust, the cowboy slammed his Stetson back on his head. "What in the ever-lovin' blazes! Which of you derned idjiots determined it was a fine idea to invite an Unseen along?"

"Apparently, he wants to … help?" Max answered.

Vana's face hardened, her normally soft age lines deepening like fissures in stone. "Men like him do not help. Only destroy."

"I reckon…" The Unseen's voice was quiet. "I reckon I ain't agreein' with Thaddeus no more. Haven't fer many a year."

"Then why continue to serve him?" she asked.

"Ta watch over my brother, but Thaddeus done tuck 'im from me." He looked at the older woman with a peculiar plea in his inky dark eyes. "I know me and my kin done ya wrong. I ain't expecting ya ta put yer trust in me, nor forgive me my trespasses. Ya could even turn me, if'n ya want. Make me a Drifter. I surely wouldn't blame ya none."

With cold intensity, Vana stared at the Unseen. An orange smolder, not as weak as the rest of the Warders', pulsed from her; at first, it emerged as a low, faint mist that wove its tendrils between the fringe hanging from the hem of her buckskin dress. The mist swirled, thickening, growing larger until tall stalks shot up to form delicate aspen trunks. The trees matured—their branches and leaves expanded, reaching skyward until they loomed over the older woman, her small build hunched in the midst of the lingering fog as if she were before the throne of Mother Nature.

Spectral stones rose into the air. They orbited her body, flickering in and out of sight, and the largest—a strange, glowing, peach-toned rock the size and shape of a toddler's skull—settled in her outstretched palm.

"You chose darkness. I did not."

Once Vana spoke, her orange light dimmed, the stones dropped and disappeared, and the aspens faded to nothing.

"I'm awares. Right about now, that dark of mine's itchin' ta make Mister Glick pay fer what he done." Eli stepped forward with conviction. "You'uns should be wary. He's got plans fer that yonder tunnel."

"Time to fess up and acknowledge the corn," Macajah demanded. "What's your role in this plumb crazy performance?"

"I ain't done much and I weren't told much. He keeps things purdy quiet, but fer the past long while, he's been assignin' us what he called 'mudsill work.'"

"Assignments?" A creeping nervousness clawed up Ashen's throat. "What did he make you do?"

"Youngins," he said. "We was made to spook youngins."

"Why?"

"I ain't knowin' but we made them afeared, over and over, till they gone a-changin'. Till we made 'em dark."

Made them dark. The first day of Ashen's dead existence flooded back. Even though over a week had passed, it felt like ages since her encounter with Silas. Ages since Max's whip had disfigured his face. Ages since she'd read the magazine headlines that continued to plague her.

Ages since Thaddeus said it was unfortunate that Ashen hadn't turned dark.

"'Dark Forces,'" she muttered. Quickly, she asked, "How? How did you scare them?"

"Did as we was told, ma'am. Pick out some poor lonesome youngin that was more easy ta forget. Go ta their bedroom, spook 'em near ta death, do it anew later. Sometimes the comin' night. By and by, they broke—lash out at carin' folks, get theyselves in a bad fix, hear voices. Start seein' things the rest of the livin' said weren't thar." The Unseen shrugged. "Think Mister Glick's got a hankerin' fer spookin' youngins. He's powerful fond of it."

Ashen remembered how Thaddeus had hovered over her when she was little, breathing in more deeply the more terrified she became. He was an addict, no different from her own mother. Instead of booze, he fed on emotions. Fear.

"What the heck does that have to do with our current predicament?" Macajah asked.

"I ain't sure, but we was made ta do mudsill work on the regular. Our numbers was a-growin' while we was out, huntin' all through the shadow hours."

"I still don't know what we're dealing with," Max said, addressing Macajah. "What, exactly, is happening with the Divide?"

The cowboy gestured toward the courtyard. "Best you

folks go see for yourselves."

The posse walked out of the lobby doors. From a distance, Ashen could see that the internal spiral of the Welcome Arch, just recently a coil of multiple colors, had paled—the tunnel extending from the courtyard into 17th Street scarcely visible. The once steady stream of spirits that had been traveling through the archway had reduced to a mere trickle. In front of the Divide, the few remaining newly-deads crossed paths with the living, mingling for a brief moment with the oblivious people going about their day.

"I don't understand where the new souls have gone so suddenly." John squinted, removed his glasses, and began to clean the lenses with the tail of his shirt. "The Divide has gotten worse in the short time it took to get you. It's become frail."

"Without the dead ones passing through," Vana said, lifting her hand to observe the muted sunset orange filter from the tips of her fingers before it vanished into the night, "the Divide will die."

"Die?" Max repeated with alarm. He looked to Vana's diminished light, then down to his own dulled tattoos. "And we're somehow connected to it, aren't we? Warders, I mean."

"I believe this is true," said Vana.

"And that's why our energies are unstable?"

"Yes," she said. "That is how it appears."

"What occurs if its strength wanes further?" Angry Fox asked. "Does it become an empty husk? Or does it seal so the dead cannot move on?"

"If that happens, we're in a big ol' world of hurt," Macajah said. From beneath his Stetson, his eyes met Eli's dark orbs. "Tibbits, what do you know of that hustler Thaddeus' intentions?"

The Unseen shifted his feet. "I ain't knowin' nothin' of note, Mister Sloan."

"You certain?" Macajah asked.

"I reckon...," Eli hesitated, staring into the arch before saying, "Ya know as well as me, Mister Glick's a powerful braggart. In recent years, he were boastin' that if this here tunnel were gone, Unseen kind would be stronger then you'uns."

"Than Warders?"

"Yessir," Eli said. "Said we'd get ta go where we want. Do as we please. Figured it were only words. I swears I ain't knowin' he'd do somethin' like this. Denyin' the dead their rightful rest."

While the posse continued their discussion, comparing abilities and testing their current limitations, Ashen, half-listening, gazed off. Posted on a billboard near the train station was an advertisement for the Denver Art Museum's exhibition featuring various paintings by American war veterans.

She looked at Max. The soldier. The ex-Drifter. He had once been a lost soul, but four years after his death, the first thing he remembered was his mother saying she was proud of him and he was home. What was the trigger that woke him? Could anyone have woken him? A neighbor? A friend?

What if she couldn't figure it out? Time to wake Jacob and move on was running out even without this new, real possibility that the Divide might be closing to the newly-dead. Perhaps forever.

A snide voice projected through the courtyard, disrupting her thoughts.

"This is obviously your people's fault. At least I was able to witness that fat Unseen receive a just end, no thanks to your posse."

A blinding white light approached. The soul within took shape as long robes rustled and thick heels clipped on the concrete sidewalk. Constance emerged, arms folded, a large judge's gavel in her grasp.

"That Unseen were my kin," Eli snarled. "Weren't aware we had a' audience."

The woman ignored him, turning her attention to Macajah. "Another Unseen to question, Mr. Sloan?"

"Why're you here, Miss Callahan?" Macajah asked. "We police you—not the other way 'round."

"Oh, I'm here to offer my services." The gavel Constance held glowed a steady, brilliant white. "If your way doesn't produce results with the Unseen, I can assist."

Without missing a beat, the cowboy said, "Rest assured, Miss Callahan. We plan on bein' thorough with this no-good ruffian, but we'll be hollering if'n there's difficulties."

"At least you're proceeding with some form of action. Why, by the way, did it take an Unseen to execute proper punishment, and against one of his own?" She pointed her mallet at Eli. "Wasn't the offender this one's brother? Isn't it your responsibility, Vana, to discipline the corrupt?"

Vana glared at Eli. With a sturdy, articulate tone, she said, "We maintain the balance, *Mo'óhtávóéstá'e*. You know that kind of discipline is not our way."

"Your way is ludicrous," Constance hissed. "The very fact that you and your Warders are still in charge astounds me. The Light are expected not to meddle. We're required to abide by your rules, yet the Unseen are unsupervised and left to do as they please, creating havoc. Mischief. We should have been handed the reins years ago."

"Why?" Angry Fox asked, her fists clenched. "So you can impose your own judgment on others?"

"That's rich coming from a Warder," Constance said.

"The Light only desire to help believers—those who have faith in a higher power—and snuff out," her eyes flicked to Eli, "darkness."

"Through deception," said John. "You perform illusions and sleight of hand to convince people that they're witnessing miracles."

"We provide hope!"

"Ma'am," Macajah said. "You ain't providing nothin' but a sack of lies."

"I've no time for this!" Constance said.

As she spun and marched off, Macajah called out after her. "All you got is time! Same as the rest of us dead remnants!"

She whirled. "I wouldn't be so certain of that, Mr. Sloan. Best of luck with the Divide collapsing under your watch."

For a brief moment, the judge's severe, thin lips broke into an unnatural smile, and she walked away, the sound of her heels tapering as she disappeared into a curl of white mist.

"Collapsing?" The word filled Ashen with dread. "Why is she talking as if this is all normal?"

"I'm none too certain," Macajah said. "But I'm itching with the distinct impression that woman knows more than she's letting on."

"That woman," Eli said. "Always 'round when Mister Glick were present. Stickin' ta dark places. Tryin' ta stay hid, I reckon."

Macajah smoothed his mustache. "As of late, she's been everywhere, it seems."

"Spying, you think?" John asked.

"Suppose so." The Unseen frowned. "I minded her whenever she were 'round. I ain't the trustin' sorta feller, but Mister Glick ain't never seemed bothered. Always said if'n the Light tuck youngins we ain't recruited, he'd prove we was stronger. Better then them Light folk."

"That's not suspicious at all," Max said.

"That ain't the half of it." Eli's dark eyes settled on Ashen. "He were mighty keen on yer whereabouts—both when ya was livin' and when ya was dead."

"Me?" Ashen suppressed a shiver. "Why?"

"Ain't certain. When ya ain't joined us, he were upset, but reckon he were more upset when ya ain't joined the Light, neither. Hell, he were madder then a rattler when Macajah tuck ya in. Always says ya was his first failure—that he aimed ta rectify his error."

Failure? Ashen felt ill. Did Thaddeus fail when he didn't kill her as a child? Was Toad's orchestrated bus accident part of his plan to somehow "rectify the error"?

"Land sakes, not a derned bit of this smells right," Macajah said. He looked to each posse member, his hands on his hips. "Welp, we best pony up and prepare. Get word out to the others that something big is coming. We're gonna need every spare fella and lady we can get."

18

DEATH OF A PEOPLE

Ashen sat on the curb and tapped the toes of her sneakers against each other.

"Jacob, do you remember your mom's special lasagna?" she asked, staring at her white shoelaces as they bounced with each tap. "I loved going to your house whenever she made it. Ate myself sick so many times, more than I can count, but it was worth it."

She glanced up to check if Jacob's repetitious movements had altered at all, but he stayed the same. "Couldn't believe she made it from scratch." She smiled a little. "Later, I found out that, all along, she'd been sprinkling extra herbs and cheese on top of some store-bought frozen kind. I could hardly believe anything anymore. Was like the whole world was a lie."

Her eyes lingered on him. He remained on the ground, curled in the fetal position, unresponsive. Her smile turned to a frown.

Beyond where Jacob lay, a beetle crawled over some pebbles. As the daylight glittered off its wing casing, Ashen went through her mental list. Another week had passed. She felt like she was repeating herself each session.

All the while, the Divide's call to her—that strange pull—had become more faint. She was almost out of time. Either that, or the death of the Divide was near.

"Hello, Ashen Deming."

From behind her, Vana's orange orb floated into the street. She materialized, taking deliberate steps until she stood at Ashen's side.

Ashen's attention returned to Jacob. "Hi, Vana."

"Is there progress with your friend?"

Ashen sighed. "Not yet. I've talked to him about everything. Everything I can come up with, anyway. Nothing works."

"I see. I am sorry."

"Good thing I'm determined, right?"

"Yes. He is very lucky."

Vana's words stung. Ashen didn't think Jacob was lucky. If anything, she felt she wasn't doing enough to help him.

"So, what are you doing here? I haven't seen you leave the train station much."

"I have come for you," Vana said. "The others gather now. We are having what Hollow Iron calls a meeting."

The thought of going back to the station wasn't appealing. It was already bad enough being the new girl among Macajah and the posse. Now that a big crowd of veteran Warders were joining them, she had nothing to add. Nothing of value, anyway. She was clueless.

"I doubt I'll be a lot of help with the whole Divide collapsing thing, you know?"

"All people have a strength."

"What strength do I have?" Ashen said, looking to the woman. A tight lump lodged in her throat that she couldn't swallow away. "I can't even help my friend."

Vana simply placed her hand on the top of Ashen's head. Ashen fought back tears as the older woman stroked her unruly hair; it was not unlike something a caring mother would do, and Ashen found herself leaning against the woman's leg.

When Ashen calmed, she asked, "Vana, you're kind of like, the main leader, right? Or one of them?"

"Yes."

"Then why didn't one of the others come get me? I mean, why aren't you doing leadership stuff with Cage?"

Unease flickered across Vana's features. "I did not wish to see the Unseen any longer."

Pieces of a once ambiguous puzzle fell into place. Even though Ashen hadn't been spending much time at the train station, it dawned on her that Vana had become curiously absent whenever Eli was around. The Unseen had been keeping to himself, wandering the lobby like a misplaced puddle of oil, slinking from shadow to shadow to escape the uncomfortable sunlight.

"Vana, can I ask you something?"

"Yes, child."

"Why is it that you don't like Eli? I mean, yeah, I get that he's a bad guy and he's definitely done some questionable things, but everyone else seems to think that he's telling the truth."

"I do not trust him. I have good reason."

"I guess I get that, too," Ashen said. "I'm sure he has his own reasons for helping us."

The small woman grunted. Carefully, she lowered herself to the curb's edge, a faraway look in her eyes as she studied

Jacob writhing about on the concrete.

"It is not good to watch your friend all the time," she said.

"Sounds like you're trying to change the subject."

Vana grunted again. "I am older. Wiser. And I am stubborn like an elk."

"I owe it to him." Ashen flashed a weak smile. "To stay. To, at least, try. I know he'd do the same for me."

"I understand. But it is bad to dwell with the lost."

The lost. There was comfort in assuming Jacob was only lost, not dead like Ashen. Dead sounded too final.

"Have you ever lost anyone?"

The woman didn't answer. Instead, she pressed her palms to her knees for support and stood. "We should go. Max would like to see you."

Odd flutters started again when Vana mentioned Max's name. Ashen scowled, bit the inside of her cheek, and followed Vana. Halfway there, as they walked side by side on the Windsor Lake trail, Ashen couldn't hold back her thoughts any longer.

"Why is he so … so … well, him?"

"Ashen Deming, who are you talking about?"

"Max."

The woman chuckled. "He finds you interesting. What is wrong with this?"

"It's almost like he's always around. Trying to shelter me or protect me like I'm something fragile."

"Is this bad?"

"Not bad," she admitted and swiped at some tall, yellowed grass as they passed. That satisfied sensation returned when it swished at her touch. "Annoying, though."

"He is only worried for you," Vana said.

"Well, he shouldn't be. I've managed to take care of myself fine for most of my life." She paused, catching herself, and added, "Took care of myself. When I was alive."

"Why does it trouble you that he cares?"

"Uh..." Ashen looked down at the trail, getting mad at herself. Why did it bother her? She considered saying she didn't like the hyper butterflies zooming around in her gut whenever he was near, or how she didn't like hoping he would turn up. And if she told herself the truth, she wasn't sure if what she was feeling was dislike.

Vana stopped and turned to the girl. "It is nice to be cared about."

"I guess. I mean, Jacob cares. Cared. But he's like family."

"And your mother and father?"

"Dad left a long time ago. Almost before I can remember. Mom, well ... she was never the same after that. We didn't have a great relationship through high school."

Vana seemed to ponder Ashen's words. "This is sad. Family is sacred. Do you know if your mother grieved your death?"

"She died. Last year. And since I've not seen her here, I guess she moved on. She's not really the type to stick around." Ashen huffed out a tense laugh. "The day I died, Jacob had come to get me from the Children's Home so we could finish out our senior year together. He was more my family than..." She paused. "Anyway, he shouldn't have even been on that bus."

"I am sorry."

They walked in silence the rest of the way. When they stepped out on the surface of the lake to travel back to the train station, Vana said, "Ashen Deming, before we join the rest, I would like to show you something."

"Okay, sure. Where are we going?"

"We call it, *Pónoeo'hé'e*. Dry Creek." The old woman grasped Ashen's hand. "I believe others call it Sand Creek."

"I've never been there. Where is it?"

"Far from here."

Ashen let her mind latch onto Vana's words and thought of Sand Creek. As they sank together, the water crept up their ankles, their legs, thighs, past their chests up to their necks. The liquid's jaws opened wide as it rose, swallowing them whole like a gluttonous monster from a fairy tale. Even though Ashen had traveled this way several times now, when the pain of the mirror hit her, she couldn't stop from instinctively holding her breath. The pair traveled through starlight and galaxies, exiting through to the other side almost as soon as they entered.

The afternoon sun blared in the pale blue desert sky. Ashen winced even though it didn't blind her like when she had been alive. Next to her, a barren tree, twisted by the wind of the plains, had been stripped of its leaves. The warm spring weather had not yet replaced the shoots. Orange baling twine dangled from one of its naked branches, and tied to its dull threads, a single shard of mirror swung in the breeze. Clusters of prairie grass and stubby sagebrush grew all around them. No water could be seen.

"This is Sand Creek? I guess I know why they call it sandy. Not much of a creek, though. Or very big."

"There are many things existing that cannot be seen." Vana began walking toward a rolling hill several hundred yards away. "You should know this, child. Remember, winter has ended. The creek exists. It will show itself again soon."

The soft ground beneath Ashen's feet made her steps silent as she trailed behind. Ahead, the fringe detailing on the hem of Vana's dress swayed back and forth. Every cut in the buckskin was precise, the pieces grouped in knotted sections and decorated with a pattern of dark blue and red beads. A mesmerized Ashen didn't realize they had reached the slope's apex until a movement, brilliant and bright, caught her attention.

A herd of buffalo grazed at the top of the mound, their humpbacked shapes fluctuating between electric greens, blues, and purples. As the two women approached, a young bull raised his head to regard them, his ears flicking. When he had determined that the ghosts posed no threat, he snorted and continued to chomp on the phantom prairie grasses, tugging fiercely to loosen it from non-existent soil.

"They're massive!" Ashen said, slack-jawed as they navigated their way through the thickly packed herd. She reached out and brushed the back of a small calf. His coat rippled in vivid pigments. "I never realized how tame they are. When they're not trying to trample new dead people, anyway."

"They are beautiful, sacred beasts," Vana said.

"Do they know they're here? I mean, are they like us? Aware? Or more like … Drifters?"

"They are similar to us," Vana said. "They know they are of Nature. Their spirits endure. But like my people, they were slaughtered. Murdered. Made into trophies. Their bones heaped high and left to rot. So they remain; mists on the prairie. Safe. Free. Always there, even if you cannot see them."

The calf turned to Ashen and gave her a curious sniff. With a broad grin, she bent down low, her face close to his, and stroked the fine fur above his muzzle.

"He's so cute!"

In reply, the calf's long tongue darted from between his lips, licked across the front of his entire nose before reaching into one of his own nostrils.

"Cute in a disgusting sorta way," Ashen finished with a

grimace.

The old woman smiled. "You cannot change a buffalo's spirit."

A gust of wind rustled the prairie grass. The herd tensed—their chewing ceased as they looked around. Alarmed, they moved as one in a swift motion, churning up spectral dust as they flowed down the side of the shallow bluff and vanished into the high desert plains.

The departing stampede revealed the expanse of the stark prairie. As motes of colorful dust settled, Ashen could see the flat landscape dotted with an occasional ridge, not unlike the hill they stood upon. Along the distant horizon, a glistening curtain of iridescent light draped from the sky, billowing in and out as if made of a fine fabric with no apparent beginning or end, oscillating between the hues of the Northern Lights before disappearing altogether, only to reappear as Ashen turned to Vana.

"What is that?" Ashen asked. "Part of the Divide?"

"That is the edge. The boundary. Before the mountains formed, it was there. We spirits cannot cross it."

"Is it against the rules or something?"

"No. Many have tried. All stay on this side." The old woman started her descent. "It is for the best. Things lurk beyond."

Eyebrows furrowed, Ashen caught up to Vana and picked her way down the slope. "It's just us, the Unseen, and the Light, isn't it?"

Vana only grunted. Situated at the bottom, a heavy mist coiled around structures of varying size. The conical outlines became more defined as the women approached. Nestled near the curve of the stagnant creek, a shimmering village of phantom tipis were huddled close, each one unique and decorated with vibrant scenes painted using geometric patterns.

"Vana, where are we?"

"This was my home. These were my people." Tears flowed down the deep wrinkles of the old woman's face. "We were told by white men to move here. That we would be safe. We believed this to be true."

Not understanding, Ashen scanned the spaces between the tipis and lodges. Within the mist, wispy forms of people emerged. Her breath caught.

Drifters. Two hundred, maybe more. All dressed in the same style as Vana. All in different states of being. Old men, women, children. Tiny infants. Some mutilated. Horribly mutilated. Some running and screaming, only to reset and repeat. Others on their knees, their hands raised to the skies, wailing in absolute silence.

"This is what men like the Unseen did," Vana said. Her gaze traced the movements of a specific Drifter. A little girl, no older than six, hid behind the trunk of an oak tree before throwing her arms up and being struck by an invisible force. Like a paused film, the girl shuddered, stopped, and replayed her death again, over and over.

"But Eli didn't do this," Ashen said. She looked at Vana, meeting her eyes. "Did he?"

"Now you see. Now you understand. There is a reason I do not trust him."

"How many of your people did he—"

"Many," Vana interrupted. "We have lost many."

19

VANA: MANIFEST DESTINY

Vana
Born: January 13, 1792
Died: November 29, 1864

November 29, 1864

A glass bead, blue and beautiful, twinkled in the dawn. Vana admired it in the dim light, rolling it between her fingers before sewing it to the buckskin garment.

"Grandma! Grandma!"

Little Yellow burst through the tough leather hide flap that hung over the entrance—a heavy fur wrapped around her tiny frame, her breaths rapid from running.

"Quiet, child," Vana scolded in a hushed tone. "You will awaken everyone with your noise."

The girl grinned. As soon as she saw that Vana had prepared herself for their normal greeting, Little Yellow sprinted and tumbled into her outstretched arms. They embraced for a moment before the girl saw the buckskin lying in the old woman's lap.

She ran her small finger over the detailing. "I wanted. To see. If it was. Done," Little Yellow said, pronouncing each broken phrase with stiff precision as she tried to whisper, but her voice came out loud and raspy despite her efforts.

"Your idea of quiet is different, Little Yellow. Your parents should have named you 'Has Big Voice' instead."

"No, Grandma!" the girl blurted before quickly throwing both hands over her mouth, her eyes wide and shining.

"Come. Keep your grandmother company while she adds the last bead," the woman said, chuckling. "You must be patient. Everything of beauty takes time."

Little Yellow hopped up and flung herself onto the pile of buffalo pelts and blankets. She lay on her back, braiding a lock of her hair as she giggled to herself, gazing up at the crown of the tipi where the poles met and stuck out of the smoke flap into the lightening night sky.

Vana smiled at her granddaughter. These early morning visits were something she cherished. The old woman both dreaded and yearned for the day when Little Yellow grew older. When she would be too busy being an adult. But perhaps she would have a little one of her own, just as spirited as she was.

"Child," she said, securing the last knot, "it is finished."

The girl rushed to her feet. "Can I put it on now?"

Vana handed it over. "Yes, ye-"

Little Yellow snatched the garment and held it up, letting the skin wrapped around her fall to the ground. "It's so pretty! Thank you!" she said, beaming as she put the new dress on over the one she already wore.

"Child, that old one is too small for you. You should remove it."

"But it's cold! And I want to show what you made to my friend."

"Your friends and the sun are not yet awake," Vana said, winding excess sinew thread. "It is too dark for playing."

"That's okay," Little Yellow said. "My new friend's made of light!"

Vana put the coiled sinew down. "What do you mean, Little Yellow?"

The girl shrugged. "She's got lots of rainbows on her skin."

The old woman's bones objected as she leaned forward. "Child," she said, trying to conceal the alarm in her voice. "May I meet your friend?"

The girl nodded with enthusiasm. "Yes! She's very pretty! You'll like her!" She grabbed her fur, slung it around her shoulders, and vanished through the door flap. As Vana struggled to stand, Little Yellow's head popped out from behind the leather hide.

"Hurry, Grandma!"

Vana stooped, her knees complaining, and picked up a thick pelt to bundle herself in before stepping outside into the cold morning. Above the distant snowcapped peaks, the dark purple sky was awakening with streaks from the east of blue, pink, and gold. The land glistened with fresh, glittering frost, making it look new.

Troubled lines gathered on her forehead as she scanned the large village. A young warrior named Ridgewalker spoke with Chief Left Hand of the Cloud People. The tribes had recently joined camps after Left Hand, Black Kettle, and the other chiefs negotiated a treaty of peace and the promise of protection. A white man walked between the tipis. He interpreted for the Tsitsistas and had taught Vana some words and phrases in his language. Two younger boys trailed after him, laughing and pointing at the man's strange soldier coat and hat.

By the edge of the encampment, Little Yellow waved her hand at Vana before skipping off, disappearing behind a prairie tree's crooked trunk. Vana took a labored breath and shuffled over, carefully stepping down the short embankment to where her granddaughter waited on the mud of Dry Creek.

"This is my friend!" Little Yellow said, grinning at empty air.

The old woman scanned the area with clouded eyes. "Child, is your friend hiding?"

"No! She's right next to you! See?"

Vana looked to where her granddaughter indicated. Nothing was there. She reached out to a breeze far colder than the crisp morning surrounding them, as if she had plunged her wrinkled hand in the ice coated streams of the big mountains. Was this an omen? Panic festered in Vana's breast. Something was not right.

"Come." She grasped Little Yellow's hand. "We must return to your mother."

The girl protested as Vana hauled her back to the village. "But my friend!"

"I will meet your friend another time, child."

As they made their way past the tree, Vana saw Chief Black Kettle outside his tipi. He and a few other Tsitsistas were looking out toward the sunrise in the plains. Through the mist veiling the horizon came the sound of an approaching herd.

"Grandma?" Little Yellow asked, tugging on her sleeve. "Did the buffalo come back?"

The white interpreter stepped forward. "That's not buffalo," he said, his face draining of color.

More Tsitsistas and Cloud People came out of their homes, murmuring to each other with worried expressions. The white interpreter went to Chief Black Kettle and spoke with urgency. Black Kettle nodded. He retreated into his tipi, coming out moments later with lengths of fabric.

"Do not be frightened," he said with a strained smile. His face reflected an odd combination of confusion, fear, and hope. "The camp is under protection. There is no danger."

While Black Kettle attached the material to a pole, the white interpreter and Ridgewalker got on their horses and rode out toward the advancing group. Others followed them. Within the haze, Vana could make out glints of metal, and the wind carried the sound of galloping horses. She held Little Yellow's hand and made her way back toward her tipi. As she passed, Black Kettle raised the pole with a flag made of red, white, and blue. The flag of the white people. A plain cloth flew beneath it, a signal to any strangers that they were unarmed and peaceful.

As Chief Black Kettle instructed villagers to stay near the flag, Little Yellow asked, "Grandma, what's going on? Why aren't we staying here?"

"It is best to be hidden," she said, her eyes fixed on her hide flap door.

That was when Vana noticed something dark fly overhead. She staggered to a stop. Heaviness filled her mind. A lone owl perched on the apex of her tipi, his yellow eyes scrutinizing the pair from under horned tufts. His white feathered chest billowed and swelled as he let out a low cry, a moan of voices lost long ago.

Wherever an owl flew, Vana knew death followed.

The sharp noise of a hollow iron came from the plains. She whirled to see the dark outlines of the men galloping back to camp. More shots fired, striking a retreating rider.

His body slumped before he fell from his horse and tumbled through the prairie weeds below.

There were wails from those huddled by Black Kettle's lodge. Little Yellow whimpered.

"Grandma?"

"It is the soldiers," Vana said. "They are coming."

The girl's eyes reflected concern, but there was a fierceness layered beneath. She was a Tsitsistas—a child of the plains. Strong, like her people. And no matter the dangers she faced, she would survive, just as she had when her father had passed, two winters prior. She had to. She must.

"Be silent like a rabbit," Vana said. "We need to find your mother and get to the clearing."

Some people stayed while the rest gathered in chaotic clusters, searching for loved ones to cling to and protect as they moved to the opposite side of the village. Vana held tight to Little Yellow's hand, gritting her teeth through her aged aches, weaving around structures and people, keeping out of sight.

When they made their way to the border of the camp, Little Yellow broke free from Vana's grip. Before the old woman could react, the girl dashed into her family's nearby tipi. Vana muttered under her breath. As she pushed herself to catch up, she peered back through the open spaces between the lodges.

The strange, drab film now covered the village. Light from the cold autumn sun splintered, piercing the mist and highlighting several hunched shapes. Her eyes settled on Chief Left Hand. Arms crossed and shoulders back, he stood waiting with a group beneath Black Kettle's flags. If peace was what he desired, Vana doubted these troops would listen. Peaceful men do not shoot unarmed riders.

A fat silhouette emerged from beyond the gray murk. He wore a small, round hat and strolled with an easy calm as if it were an average day. The man's meaty fist clenched a hollow iron. Upon seeing Chief Left Hand, the man raised his firearm without hesitation, took aim, and pulled the trigger. Vana clamped her hand over her mouth. She could not allow her own cry to escape and join the screams of those witnessing their chief crumple to the ground.

The fat man lumbered over, fanning his face with his hat. He kicked Left Hand's body. When Left Hand did not move, the man grinned, placed his hat back on his head, and reloaded as women and children clung to him, pleading for their lives.

Behind him, hundreds of troops appeared from the gloom. A few remained on horseback while the rest walked nonchalantly into the village. Some Tsitsistas got up to run away while the others stayed and begged for mercy. The white men hollered out angry, hateful words Vana did not fully understand, and as they began to shoot people at random, she turned from the carnage and hurried to her daughter's tipi. When she reached for the heavy hide flap, Little Yellow rushed out.

"Grandma, why are they shooting?"

"Like a rabbit," Vana hissed. "Where is your mother?"

"She's not here!"

Vana glanced toward the advancing men. "We will find her, child, but we must move. Now."

They ran alongside others, dodging behind tall brush and ragged trees. Women carried toddlers. Young men sprinted ahead, stopping briefly to shoot at their pursuers with arrows and the occasional firearm. Children around Little Yellow's age tried to keep up as their people scattered in all directions. Most split off, dashing down the embankment of

Dry Creek, while Vana and Little Yellow continued east with the rest.

Before they reached the clearing, Vana could tell that the horses weren't there. Her steps slowed as she frantically scanned the flat landscape. She spotted the ponies trotting off into the distance.

"They are gone," someone said. "White men ran them off."

Vana spun. Eagle Leggings, her friend since childhood, knelt near an oak.

"None are left?" she asked, but the woman did not seem to hear her.

"They attacked knowing there would be no warriors to protect us." Eagle Leggings folded her arms and rocked back and forth. Her deep-set eyes met Vana's. "They planned this."

Vana took an uncertain step toward her friend. A shot rang out. Eagle Leggings fell, her face bloodied and unrecognizable. Little Yellow gasped. She began to pivot toward the shooter, but Vana jerked the girl's arm.

"Do not look," she said. "Run."

The chaos of the slaughter followed them, muffled only by the sound of the old woman's beating heart. She led Little Yellow to the far bank of Dry Creek. The screams and hollow iron blasts grew louder. Closer.

She forced her stiff legs to slide down the rocky slope of the trickling creek, her feet catching on snarled desert roots. Once she regained her footing, she helped Little Yellow down and together they searched for cover. In the bend, they found where the swollen spring waters had eaten away at the soil walls, leaving an overhanging of earth and grass behind when the river receded in winter. Vana used her hands and dug in the frozen mud while her granddaughter kept watch. The skin of the old woman's palms broke open and she bled on the bronze-colored muck, but she kept digging, carving a crevice until there was a large enough space.

"Climb up, Little Yellow."

"But there's no room for you!"

"I will be safe, child," she said, hoisting the girl into the hole. "I am good at hiding."

"What about Mother?"

"I will find her," Vana said. "No matter what you hear or what you see, do not come out. Do you understand?"

The girl's lower lip trembled. "Please don't leave like Father."

The old woman clasped her granddaughter's hands with her own battered, red-stained ones. "I will be back. I promise."

Yelling sounded from down the riverbed. Vana quickly concealed Little Yellow with the long prairie grass hanging over the ledge before crawling on her throbbing knees up the steep bank. As she nestled behind a bush, a man stomped into view, splashing through the stagnant water puddles with the grace of a delirious, furious bull.

She held her breath and peered between the branches. The man's nostrils were flaring, his eyes bulging. His hands and the sleeves of his shirt were caked with blood. He swung at the bushes and prodded the earth with his hollow iron, hunting for her people, drawing closer to where Little Yellow hid. Vana readied herself. If she could get him further down the river, it might give her granddaughter a chance.

She got into position. A call sounded. Behind her, Ridgewalker aimed his firearm. When the cavalry man turned, the Tsitsistas warrior fired over Vana's head. The shot hit the man in the shoulder, spinning him off-balance. He fell in the mud, clamping onto his wound with his bloody hand, shrieking and writhing as Ridgewalker took another measured shot. The man lay on the ground, silenced.

Ridgewalker gave her a curt, quick nod and disappeared into the shrubs that grew along the river. She glanced to where Little Yellow hid. After reassuring herself that the girl would be safe, she headed back toward the encampment.

Icy grass crunched beneath her as Vana hobbled from tree to tree. Weapons cracked in the distance. It appeared most of the attackers had left the camp, pursuing the Tsitsistas and Cloud People across the plains, but she remained cautious, crouching within tall weeds circling the clearing to peek between the divided clumps toward the village.

Mere feet away, a woman's lifeless eyes stared. In her arms, she held an infant swaddled in a pelt. Neither moved. Beyond where she lay, bodies and dark red covered the frost. Women, elders, children. A young girl, still alive, staggered blindly. The top of her scalp was gone, cut off by a sharp blade, and she held the skin of her face up with her hands.

The sight of the massacre devoured Vana. She choked out a sob, her pain erupting into a fierce agony. She stabbed her fingernails into the wounds of her hands in order to concentrate. Regaining her composure, a thin line of hope lingered. Perhaps her daughter wasn't among the dead? She scanned the clothing of her butchered people, blinking back desperate tears. By the border of the camp, she could make out a familiar pattern, and her breath caught in her throat.

Without a second thought, Vana charged out from the grass. She ignored the murky shapes within the village as she drew nearer, concentrating on her daughter, Bear Claws.

When she had reached her side, she saw that she still breathed.

"Thank the Great One," Vana whispered.

"Little Yellow," her daughter groaned.

"She is safe. She is hidden. We must move before they..."

A low chuckle came from behind her. The fat man, his bulbous hands filled with long, black hair, approached. Vana's eyes flitted to bodies lying in the mud at his feet. They had been scalped like the young girl she'd seen before, the crowns of their heads bright with red and white.

The fat man's bloated bullfrog face sneered from beneath his hat. He said something, but she only recognized the words 'injun' and 'kill'. Stuffing the scalps into a sack attached to his belt, the fat man laughed. He drew a small firearm while calling out to another in the camp, and took a heavy step toward Vana and her daughter.

In response, a tall man wearing a crumpled and discolored felt hat exited one of the lodges. His angular face stern, he seemed to listen impassively to the fat man's blathering. Vana could only catch a couple of words as the fat man waved his weapon at her. She glared at him without flinching. He ceased speaking and smiled, pointing the barrel at Bear Claws.

"No!" the old woman said. She threw herself onto her daughter, clutching her, shielding her.

The fat man laughed again. The two men talked, the tall one nodding, a hint of pity in his eyes. He let out a sigh and squatted next to Vana, pulling her away by her shoulders. She jabbed her elbows and kicked at his shins, but he held her with a firm grip and didn't let go.

The rest was like a dream, a nightmare from which Vana could not wake. Powerless, she watched as the fat man raised his hollow iron at Bear Claws. A shot fired, and Vana wailed with a voice she did not know. A distant, high-pitched scream blended with her cries. The scream of a little girl.

In front of an old oak by the camp stood Little Yellow, her breaths rapid beneath her mud-smeared dress. She stared at her mother, motionless on the ground. The fat man shouted and jogged toward her. Little Yellow froze. Her dark eyes flashed to her grandmother.

"Run!" Vana moaned.

When he had almost reached her, Little Yellow sped around the trunk of the tree. Vana dropped to her knees and turned to the tall man, grasping at his legs.

"Please!" she begged, using whatever white man words she could remember. "Please, no!"

The tall man's face reflected doubt. He glanced at the fat man. "Toad!" he yelled, but the fat one's weapon went off. It struck Little Yellow in the calf and she fell behind the tree. Vana shrieked. Her granddaughter cried. Throwing his hollow iron down, the fat man picked up a large stone. He swung it downward. Little Yellow no longer wept.

Panting, the fat man rose from his stooped position, rock in one hand, wiping blood on his trousers with the other. Vana sobbed as she looked out at the destruction the troops had left in their wake. The countless bodies of people she knew and loved. Her daughter. Her innocent little granddaughter. There was no hope. There was no coming back from this.

The fat man pushed the stone into the tall man's hands. "Eli, kill the injun," he said.

The tall man winced, but Vana no longer cared. Nothing lives long, she thought, only the earth and the mountains. She gazed up at the deceitful clear blue skies. Her tears ceased. There was no one left to cry for.

As the tall man prepared, hoisting the rock high above her head, Vana said one phrase in the language her murderer would understand.

"Do not forget us."

20

DECISIONS

Ashen was numb. For the first time, traveling through the mirror hadn't affected her like it had in the past. In fact, she hardly remembered the journey. Visions of the tortured souls of Vana's people played over and over again in her mind. A broken record of broken records.

As they exited the baggage claim hallway, Vana said, "I must go. The meeting will start soon."

The old woman had shown her something close to her heart. Something intimate. Private. Ashen wanted to thank her for trusting her, for believing in her, but she didn't know what to say or how to say it. At the same time, she wanted to hug Vana, but the thought of doing so was awkward. How do you console the inconsolable?

Ashen cleared her throat and muttered, "Is there anything I can help with?"

"No, child," the old woman said. Her clouded eyes twinkled. "You have much to consider. When it begins, we will come for you."

"Vana?" Ashen asked, wringing her hands together as she tried to find her words. "If you can make spirits into Drifters, can you, I dunno ... reverse it?"

"No, Ashen Deming. I cannot. For many years, I tried to bring my people back, but I did not find a way. It became too much, too painful, to watch the lost dead and remain helpless. I do not want you to suffer the same."

Vana reached up and stroked Ashen's cheek. The old woman smiled, morphed into an orb of sunset orange, and floated through the vacant lobby, vanishing into one of the outer walls.

"Alone again," Ashen sighed.

All of what Ashen had witnessed since she had died felt as if it was taking up too much space in her brain, crowding out the memories of her own life. Frustrated, she shook her head hard, determined to knock some of those images from existence, but the new memories clung to her, refusing to release their sharp claws from the deepest, darkest corners of her mind.

She sighed again and wondered if any of the Warders were around. As she headed toward the telegraph room near the rear exit, she caught a glimpse of glistening silver light. She stopped. From behind one of the tall benches, her pet turtle, Langhorne, peeked out. She frowned. He was so close to her this time. Why did he never get close enough?

Not wanting to scare him, she took a few quiet steps toward the bench he hid beneath. The turtle regarded her with a sideways glance. A sly smile curled the corners of his mouth as if he had heard a somewhat amusing joke. The bizarre expression made Ashen stop dead in her tracks, her forehead creased while she watched him waddle from the bench and out of the front doors. Once he was out of sight, she raised her eyebrows, shrugged, and followed, passing through the thick wood and into the blazing daylight.

She squinted to scan the immediate area. Across the courtyard, a trickle of newly-dead were crossing over, one at a time, under the signs reading 'Mizpah' and 'Welcome' and through the arch. There were fewer souls—even fewer than before—and after Ashen observed some fade into the churning hues of the Divide, she caught sight of a small silhouette. Her turtle sat at the entrance, waiting, unfazed by his instant teleportation.

"How the...?" she said to herself in awe. "Do dead turtles get speed powers or jet packs or something?"

The strange, familiar pull of the Divide festered in her gut, and she found herself walking until she stood before the threshold. At her feet, Langhorne poked his snout inside the arches, disturbing the swirling colors so that they resembled ripples on water. He turned to her and blinked.

"You want me to go in there?"

Langhorne blinked again.

"But what about Jacob? I can't leave him."

Blink.

"You're being less than helpful, Langhorne," she said with a huff. Taking a step back, she sat cross-legged in front of the tunnel. Langhorne shuffled over, and she stroked the top of his head with her thumb as he settled next to her, his eyelids drooping on the verge of sleep like they used to when he had been alive.

At this reminder, she wept, a flood of emotion coursing through her. "I'm so sorry I didn't save you, little guy. I'm so, so sorry."

Ashen buried her face in her hands. After a moment, her turtle climbed up her shins. When she peeked between her fingers, Langhorne had taken up residence on her thigh to gaze up at her.

Blink.

She spent the balance of the day petting Langhorne while a scarce amount of souls entered the Divide to turn into prisms of color and light. To those who chose to stay behind, where the tunnel led was an unknown. Ashen didn't like unknowns. Still, it was obvious that some force was telling her she needed to go there, and although she was surprised that she wasn't afraid, she couldn't abandon Jacob to a fate worse than death.

And it wasn't only Jacob now. She tried to make sense of it all, but it was too hard to accept. Now she knew that Vana's people, those poor souls forever stuck as Drifters in a nightmarish limbo, were the result of other people's actions. Others' rushed decisions. Others' bad intentions. People like Eli. Perhaps even people like herself.

Maybe, she thought, there was something she could do. Maybe she had a purpose beyond simply moving on.

Once twilight fell, Ashen put Langhorne on the ground, got to her feet, and approached the Divide. She caressed it, making vibrant waves on its surface. The weird pulsing energy surged through her fingertips. The strong draw would make it easy to walk inside.

"You weren't thinking of leaving without saying goodbye," Max said behind her, "were you?"

She whirled to find a trace of sadness in his eyes.

"No, I wouldn't do that," she said. "Langhorne's being pushy, is all."

The soldier let out a relieved breath. "Good. I'd at least want another hug before you went AWOL."

She felt her cheeks prickle with warmth. In order to avoid eye contact, she bent down to pick up Langhorne and said, "Well, it's possible you won't be getting a second one."

Max frowned. "You know you can't use the excuse that I stink or something. Ghosts don't smell."

"I'm sure you had, uh, a very nice scent when, umm ... when you were alive. And stuff." The blush now felt like it had crawled across her entire face and neck. "But that's not why. I think I've decided to stay."

"Really?" Max grinned before his features abruptly hardened. "Are you certain? I mean, Macajah did make it clear that you won't get a second chance to move on, right?"

"Yeah, he told me." She held Langhorne to her chest as she stared into the depths of the tunnel. The whirlpool within coiled with bright greens, pinks, and purples. A promise of something new. "I want to stay. I can't imagine moving on without even trying to help Jacob. Or the other people like him."

The urge to enter the Divide receded as soon as she spoke. Her turtle peered up at her, blinked a final time, and disappeared.

She sobbed at her empty hands. "Langhorne..."

"It's okay, it's okay." Max said and wrapped his arms around her. "You'll see him again. I still see mine every once in a while."

"You had a turtle?" Ashen asked, sniffling.

"No, everyone's is different. Macajah has Agnes, his old horse. Mine, for whatever reason, is a giant bird."

She wiped at her face, her thoughts traveling to her favorite childhood book. "You had a pet bird? Like a falcon or something?"

"A golden eagle. And no—never had any animal like her when I was alive," he said, chuckling. "I'm pretty certain she thinks of me as her pet rather than the other way around. I guess I always assumed she chose me. Had no idea what she was when I first saw her. A huge raptor tailing you is more than a little unnerving."

"But I don't understand." She pulled from his embrace. "What are they? If some are our old pets and some are wild, why are they even here?"

Max shrugged. "I think they're a type of spirit guardian. Something similar to what Vana's people, the Cheyenne, believe. They help you when you need it."

When everything surrounding Ashen was so foreign, the realization that someone, or something, else was watching out for her brought her comfort. For the first time in a long while, she let herself smile.

"I like seeing you smile." The soldier's eyes sparkled. "Didn't take you too long to cave on that hug, either." He winked, and she felt the creeping heat again. "Anyway, I've been sent to collect you. Care to accompany me to the meeting?"

As they walked side by side toward Union Station, Ashen asked, "Since your eagle decided to follow you around, did you ever end up giving her a name?"

"Yeah," Max said with a smirk. "I named her Cuddles."

21

A DARK CLOUD RISES

The lobby of Union Station was packed with ghosts. Absorbed in deep discussions, they gathered in small, broken-off clusters, all dressed in clothing from different eras. More recent fashions blended in with a mix of western and rancher attire, but certain distinct styles—psychedelic sixties flowers, seventies bell-bottoms, eighties mullets—stuck out amid the mundane earth tones.

As Ashen and Max weaved between the groups and made their way to the baggage claim hallway, a man with a red face and well-groomed, impressive beard waved his felling axe above his head.

"Look at mine!" he bellowed, and he lowered his weapon, pressing the flat edge of the blade against the navy blue and maroon flannel of his shirt. It's faint evergreen glow barely cast upon the fabric.

One of his companions agreed. "All ours are getting worse, Blake."

"Met up with a lower-ranked Unseen on my way here," the man named Blake said while he examined his axe. "Fought that demon off, but I had to work harder than usual."

A queasiness washed over Ashen as she glanced from group to group, from faded weapon to faded weapon. One look at Max told her that the soldier shared her unease.

"Max. Little Missy," Macajah's voice drawled from the hall as they approached. "Good to see you."

"Hey, Cage," Max said. His eyes flicked around the crowd while Macajah sauntered over. "Is this everyone?"

"Dang near, I reckon. Katie and John should be returning directly. Set off to fetch a few fellas north of Fort Collins."

Worried, Ashen scanned the hall and lobby. "Where's Vana?"

"That woman's ornery as a mule," Macajah grumbled. "Criminy sakes, she endeavored to set off unaccompanied to Estes Park. Took a lot of bellyaching on my part to get her to acquire some volunteers."

Ashen smiled. "She's a tough one."

"Reckon so." The corners of his mustache curved up. "She does possess a heap of grit."

The gilded hall mirror behind Macajah shuddered. John appeared, then Angry Fox and a few others.

"Gathered anyone we could locate, Cage," John said. "But I doubt they know anything more than we do."

The cowboy eyed the dim weapons of the Warders in the lobby. "Folks on the perimeters lost their life currents as well?"

"Yeah. Every Warder within the barrier."

Leaning toward Max, Ashen whispered, "Is that the weird shiny see-through thing hanging from the sky? The one we can't cross?"

She felt him move nearer. "Didn't know you'd seen that yet."

"Uh, yeah, Vana showed me. She called it the edge." His voice in her ear caused a shiver along her spine. She leaned in more. "Is it true that people have tried to go through it but can't?"

"Not entirely."

She turned to him. Their eyes locked. The few occasions they had hugged hadn't felt as intimate, as close, as this. She'd never noticed that the shape of a burst star, hazel in color, haloed the pupils of his gray eyes. Or how each of the star's multiple points led to ice-blue tips. Or how impossibly blond his eyelashes were. Delicate, fine, like feathers.

With a dry voice, she managed to squeak, "It's not?"

"I died in France, not Colorado. Somehow I managed to get through as a Drifter. I guess I stayed with my body when the Army shipped me home." He smiled. "You have lovely eyes."

"You, umm, yeah, you too." She broke eye contact. Her cheeks burned. "Uh, you haven't been able to cross back since?"

"I tried. Twice or so over the years, but whenever I went in, everything became murky. Unclear. I lost sense of myself, who I was, and when I woke, I had returned to the Divide and Union Station without remembering how."

"So, I'm guessing since none of us can leave, other Warders can't enter, either? No out-of-state help?"

"That's right. We're on our own."

"Fantastic."

The mirror shimmered and Vana stepped out from its rainbow ripples, the souls she had amassed trailing behind her. She gave a slight nod to Macajah.

"Are we ready to begin?" she asked.

Macajah grunted. "Reckon now's as good a time as any."

Together, the posse walked to the center of the lobby. Ashen tagged along, navigating between the unknown Warders, until she found herself waiting between Max and Angry Fox. As Macajah helped Vana up onto one of the phantom benches, the soldier whispered to her.

"I meant to ask you before, how is your friend? Jacob?"

Ashen looked down. "No change."

"Well, like I said before, I have faith in you. If anyone can figure it out, you can."

A warmth flooded through her. Her entire life, she had only heard doubt from her mother and Jacob. Doubt about what she had witnessed, doubt about how she had coped, doubt about anything she decided to do. It took meeting dead people, complete strangers, to find anyone who believed in her. She couldn't help but smile.

"Thanks."

Vana raised her hands. The Warders' murmurs decreased to a respectful silence. Once satisfied, the hunched woman stood above the crowd, looking more regal in her elevated position. From the top of the bench, she gazed at the various faces as if memorizing every single one.

"Hello. I am Vana of the Tsitsistas. I, and those who fight with me, protect the Divide. The balance has been disturbed. The Divide has become frail. We do not know how—or why—it has happened. We need your help."

The crowd of Warders peered around, one to the other, as if searching for any sign or answer. When no one said anything, someone shouted, "It's those Unseen! We all know they're up to something!"

"It is possible they are responsible," Vana said. "But we do not know for certain."

"Why do you downtown Warders have an Unseen in

your employ?" another yelled, gesturing to Eli standing alone. The crowd's rumbling escalated. Eli shifted from foot to foot and backed away.

"The Unseen has his reasons for being here. We do not..." Vana paused as though she were choosing her next words with care. "He is willing to help. We will not hold judgment against him."

The first man spoke again. "What if he's a spy?"

"We must believe he is not. If we do not trust, we are no different than the Unseen. Or the Light."

The Warders mumbled, some frowning or shaking their heads, the rest nodding in agreement.

"If we do not work as one," she continued. "If we do not find why we are losing our power, we cannot maintain the balance. If we fail—if the balance is broken—those with dark souls will threaten, control, and defeat those who live."

Outside, a low, hollow whistle blew. Any existing pigments at the front of Union Station diminished as if the hues of the world were being sucked dry. The window panes darkened to ebony as whispers spread within the crowd, and the unmistakable clamor of a locomotive grew louder. Two Warders barged through the front doors, lusterless weapons drawn, faces grim.

"Unseen!"

Vana frowned. "Let them speak. Let us listen to what they say."

"Listen to them? Why?" It was Blake, the man with the axe. "They're cruel! Greedy! They only want control of everyone, living and dead!"

"All are allowed their opinions," Vana said. "Even the Unseen know that the dead have had their chance. Life always has priority."

A voice boomed through the lobby. "Them living fellers

squandered their chances, injun."

At the back of the room the iron teeth of a cowcatcher pierced the physical wall of the station. Both wall and locomotive remained unscathed while the phantom machine passed through, its giant chimney belching thick, black soot.

Engine 191's brakes screeched to a halt. Several dark orbs took shape. Smoke spiraled around the lead sphere, expanding until it loomed over the Warders. Thaddeus emerged from its swollen gloom. Behind him, an informal line of shadow men and women materialized—their eyes gleaming beneath diverse hats—and created a plasmic barricade of troops.

In a smooth, practiced reaction, the Warders unsheathed their weapons simultaneously, but the dramatic effect was cheapened—their unstable armament looked more like simple toys. As the events unfolded, Ashen stood stock-still, eyes wide, unable to make herself move, hoping what she saw before her was some other horrid vision or dream.

To her right, Macajah rushed ahead, aimed Agnes at the horde of Unseen, and pulled the trigger. The Winchester misfired. Its golden light blinked out.

Max grabbed Ashen's elbow. He jerked her back and raised his clenched fists in defense, but his tattoos did not manifest. They only glistened. To their left, Angry Fox and John had their arms drawn, but their unique powers also throbbed dim. Dull.

"Yer guard dogs here are mighty keen, Vana," Thaddeus said, his weasel's sneer flashing through curled lips. "They've not yet realized they're but helpless pups."

The Unseen leader threw his shoulders back. His jaws unfastened, the black gap between widening in rapid, quaking spurts, like a rusty bear trap that hasn't been oiled. At the sight, most of the Warders' nerves shattered. Some of their stares shifted, their focus dropping to their weapons to watch them fizzle and weaken with every convulsion of the Unseen's mouth.

A laugh echoed from the back of the creature's open throat. A tornado of smog swirled in the palm of his hand until, from the midst of the miniature twister, a giant miner's pickaxe formed. To look at it made Ashen uncomfortable. The simple hand tool ate any light that neared it.

"Enough!" Blake stepped out from the crowd, the wooden handle of his felling axe clutched in his paw-like hand. "Just you and me, Unseen. For old times' sake."

"Ain't time fer ya," Thaddeus said. He snapped his elongated fingers. "Lizzy!"

A petite figure came forward from the jumble of creatures. She wore a bell-shaped hat, and her huge, inky eyes peered from under its slight rim. She held a baseball bat as long as she was tall, the barrel slung over one shoulder and balanced near the base of her neck. Walking closer, she gripped the handle with both hands and swung through vacant air.

"Sending one of your thugs to fight is cowardly," Blake said. "Even for you, Thaddeus."

The one called Lizzy took another practice swing. "You're givin' me the heebie-jeebies, baby," she said with a wink. "Shouldn't be too difficult for big ol' you to get through lil' ol' me."

The burley Warder glowered. "I don't want to injure you."

"You slay me!" Lizzy laughed. She beckoned him with a clawed finger. "Come on, now. Don't be shy."

Expression serious, Blake clutched his evergreen axe. He lowered his stance, rolled his massive shoulders forward, and lumbered toward her, his heavier build gaining speed until he reached a full run. Casually, Lizzy raised her bat behind her head, knees bent, as if waiting for a pitch. Once Blake was a few strides from her, she swung, her aim high.

The bat connected with the Warder's skull. A sickening crack followed. Ashen's stomach lurched. Like a mountain timber, Blake fell, his ghost body sprawled on the tile of the lobby. Gasps and sobs and yells traveled through the crowd of outraged Warders.

"Blake's dead? He's dead-dead?"

"Their weapons! They shouldn't be able to touch us!"

"She killed him!"

In the commotion, Ashen could make out a peculiar sound. A bleating. From the dense group, a large ram appeared. After trotting to Blake's side, the bighorn sniffed the man, nuzzled his cheek, and let out a final, long cry. Ashen's eyes welled as the images of the ram and Blake crumbled into spectral dust.

With a smug smile, Lizzy returned her bat to her shoulder. When she turned on her heel and strolled toward the cheering Unseen army, a pulsing orange light shone from the heart of the group of Warders. Lizzy spun back, eyebrows knitted with concern.

"That is your third offense, Lizzy," Vana said, her clear voice strong but full of wrath. It made Ashen shiver.

"Go chase yourself! I never had a single mark against me!"

"To murder in death," Vana said, lifting her palms toward the sky, "counts as three."

Orange tree roots, their light muted but far brighter than the other Warders' energies, spread from below the old woman's moccasins and throughout the lobby. A peach-colored mist hung low. Stalks shot upward, the forming trunks twining around each other, constructing long legs, a body, and a neck that led to a proud head capped with towering antlers. When the roots ceased growing, an elk, raking his hoof at the floor, stood behind Vana.

"Says you...," Lizzy muttered. A snide smirk twisted around her fangs. "Better lay off, old lady. You and the rest of your goons are done."

Vana did not respond. Instead, she began a quiet chant. The elk cocked his head as if he were listening. His eyes burned orange. Nostrils flared from violent snorts, he shook his shaggy mane and lowered his antlers at the Unseen girl. Under Lizzy's feet, more tangled roots tore through the ceramic tile, the vines coiling up her shadow legs, wrapping around her waist up to her chest. They crawled along her arm, squeezing until she dropped her bat with a thud.

Lizzy threw a frantic look at Thaddeus. "You said they'd be powerless! Do something!"

Thaddeus studied the sunset glow radiating from Vana while using his elongated finger to trace the sharp point of his pickaxe. "I will refrain from interferin'."

"What! Why?"

"Curiosity."

Gritting her fangs, Lizzy yanked at the roots but they held solid, secure, as the elk charged. The shadow creature screamed. The animal collided with her and disappeared into vapor.

All emotion fell from Lizzy's face. Her features remained impassive as she stared at nothing while the darkness melted from her body, dripping, collecting into a black puddle, leaving behind the image of a young woman in her mid-twenties, mascara smudged. She wore a straight-cut flapper dress of red velvet adorned with rhinestones and fine embroidery. Beneath her bell-shaped hat, beads of sweat clung to her brow. As if a switch had been flipped, she became animated—rushing about in a frenzy, rifling through papers or documents that Ashen couldn't see.

The girl Lizzy stopped. Eyes wide and frightened, she mouthed indiscernible words to an unknown presence. Ashen struggled to understand until Lizzy threw her hands up to protect herself. Through the blubbering, the Drifter was begging 'please' and 'no.'

Ashen jumped when holes blasted into her pretty gown. The girl tumbled, fluttering from sight, and reappeared again, repeating her endless search for whatever she'd lost or misplaced. When she stopped again to plead with her invisible murderer, her image flitted away, slowly, peacefully, as if dispersed by a soft breeze.

Macajah removed his hat. "Darn shame. Back to her bones she'll go."

"Don't bother feigning concern, Sloan," Thaddeus snarled. Behind him, the rest of the Unseen erupted with angry screams and shouts. Goaded by their reaction, he added with a raised voice, "Admit it. You'uns desire nothin' more than Unseen kind ta suffer the same fate."

"Horse feathers! We want harmony!" Macajah slammed his Stetson back on. "You keep a'pushin' and a'pushin'— and at the expense of your own." The cowboy glared at the shapes behind Thaddeus. "You folks bore witness to what he did to Lizzy. Don't lie to yourselves. He'd feed any of you to the wolves if it meant savin' his own hide."

"Ya all high and mighty," Thaddeus said. His eyes darted to Vana looking on from the bench. "Particularly when ya have that heathen doin' yer bidding."

"I answer to no man, Thaddeus Glick." Vana said, her expression solemn, yet sad. "I do not like imprisoning anyone's spirit. You know this. There is no joy in it. Lizzy was a wayward child. Corrupted."

Fangs exposed, the Unseen leader growled, his voice a series of rumbling echoes. "Ya punishin' those ya think done wrong. Ya possess no right."

"It is true. I may not be worthy, but neither are small men," she said. "Men like you."

Pure rage altered the shadow's face. As his fury inflated, so did his stature until he gained twice his normal size, the wide brim of his hat threatening to scrape the high ceiling. He wrapped his hand around the handle of his pickaxe and squeezed, over and over, each flex of his fist making his knuckles jut out like obsidian shivs.

"Squaw, ya ain't knowin' a thing about men like me."

Thaddeus launched at Vana, his pickaxe raised high. Specter adrenaline pumped through Ashen. Even though she had no idea what she could do to stop him, fear didn't strangle her—not like it used to—and without hesitation she leapt between the approaching Unseen and Vana.

And she wasn't alone. At her side, Max and the rest of the posse held their ground, their feeble weapons brandished as the smoky figure of Thaddeus drew closer. A simmering heat swelled in Ashen. Lackluster sterling flames ignited over her body. She swallowed hard. Together, she hoped their efforts would be enough.

Bright red and pink streaked past. Low to the ground, the tiny blaze bolted for Thaddeus, becoming clear as it chomped down on the Unseen's ankle. A fox. A fox made of light.

The Unseen leader hissed. His attack on Vana halted, Thaddeus kicked his leg in an attempt to fling the animal away, but the fox's sharp teeth clamped deep in the shadow creature's plasma. Thaddeus swung his pickaxe. He missed the animal, but before he could try again, another red bolt zoomed into the shadow's torso.

A deafening shriek filled the room. Ashen winced, clasping her hands over her ears. Near the creature's collarbone, the head of a crimson tomahawk stuck out from his tarry flesh. The hatchet faded away, leaving an ugly, shallow gash behind. Angry Fox sprinted past Ashen and the posse toward Thaddeus. She wielded only one of her weapons, but as the warrior girl dodged another wild kick from Thaddeus, the particles of her missing tomahawk twirled back into existence within her grip.

The Unseen leader ignored the small canine at his feet, scowled at Angry Fox, and chucked his pickaxe. Angry Fox ducked. The weapon narrowly missed the top of her skull, sailing over her as she skidded to a crouch.

"Fox!" John yelled. He sprang forward, but before he could reach her, his path became blocked by a sudden electric brilliance blasting from the other side of the room. A floor-to-ceiling dome appeared in the middle of the lobby and surrounded the Warders, separating them from Angry Fox and the Unseen. The dome's walls bled violet.

Thaddeus' features scrunched up in rage. The tip of his thrown pickaxe, stuck in the purple veil, hung in the air. He tore the canine from his leg, hurled the animal to the side, and stomped to the new barrier, passing Angry Fox as she rose to her feet.

"No!" he screamed. He ripped the pickaxe free and struck the wall over and over. He stopped, breath rapid, shaking with fury. Although his violent outburst visibly weakened the obstacle, it held, and he staggered back a couple of paces, livid.

"Now, now," Eli said, stepping from the group of gathered Warders, tendrils of luminous deep purple spiraling around the tips of his fingers. "Ain't that thar a pickle?"

"How?" Thaddeus said through gnashing fangs. "Ya ain't Unseen no more!"

"Reckon that's my decidin'." Eli observed the light filtering from his own hand. "I'm Unseen enough ta siphon some a that mighty fine life current ya done cooked up."

"Ya yellow-bellied traitor!" Thaddeus turned to his Unseen army. "I came fer that old squaw's head! Break through! Now!"

On command, the shadows marched, their claws and teeth displayed. But between them and the barrier, Angry Fox waited; her weapons, barely lit and useless, ready—her chest rising and falling with calm, certain breaths.

"Ya ain't gonna do nothing thar," Thaddeus said, circling until he faced her. "Are ya Katie?"

Her eyes narrowed. She bent her knees as if in preparation. "I protect those who cannot protect themselves."

"Is she crazy?" Ashen asked aloud.

"No. She's amazing," Max said, "but there's no way she can take on all of them alone," Max said. "We're too weak individually."

John, tense and distressed, yelled at Eli. "We have to help! Drop the wall!"

"Apologies." The creature frowned, a sheen of plum-toned sweat on his forehead, his purple tint quivering amid the blackness. "I ain't got enough power ta do this again. You'uns won't be protected."

"I don't care!" John yelled.

Angry Fox glanced over her shoulder. "Keep Vana safe, John."

The barrier seared John's flesh as he pressed his palms against the dome. "Please, Eli!"

His pleas became lost as the battle began. Thaddeus

lunged with his pickaxe. Angry Fox sidestepped it, avoiding the strike, and pivoted to crash a tomahawk into the creature's back. He growled, punching back, but she tumbled with grace out of the way, as if she were performing a choreographed dance, before battering him on all sides with one dramatic blow after another.

Though her red hatchets hardly scratched Thaddeus, Angry Fox was the superior fighter. An ember of hope formed in Ashen's core as she watched the creature flounder to land a single blow. After every missed attempt, the Unseen groaned, the Warders exclaimed with nervous loyalty, and Ashen let a shaky breath she had been holding escape. With the power between the factions unbalanced, it would only take one bash from Thaddeus. One solid hit to incapacitate Angry Fox.

Or worse.

A strange light caught Ashen's attention. For a brief moment, behind the roaring Unseen army, something twinkled. Certain it had been there, she tore her eyes from the fight, scanning the mob of shadow figures to search for the source.

A pulsing ray shot over the heads of the dark creatures. The spectating Warders gasped, the Unseen army cackled, as the light—a white light—flew at Angry Fox.

"Fox!" Ashen screamed.

The warrior girl whirled, but not fast enough. The beam struck. Thrown to the ground, Angry Fox recovered quickly and jumped to her feet, but the distraction had given Thaddeus the edge he needed. With the handle of his pickaxe, he clubbed her under the chin, snapping her head back and knocking her to the tile, her tomahawks flying from her strong grasp.

The shadow creature's sunken eyes glinted. His

blackened tongue licked over his cruel smile. "Getting yerself killed by the same soul twice. Mighty unfortunate luck, Katie."

Glare steady, unwavering, the girl said, "My name is not Katie. It's Angry Fox."

Thaddeus tsked, and the pickaxe bore down on the warrior girl, sinking into her. She no longer moved.

John beat his fists against the dome wall, blisters on his knuckles, tears streaming down his cheeks, bellowing, but Ashen couldn't understand the words over the screams of the other Warders. One person's wails were so loud, so startling, Ashen wasn't sure if she'd ever stop hearing them. She was terrified to discover that the awful sounds were coming from her.

Orange reflected within the dome, the color blossoming and diluting the purple and black tones of the wall around the Warders. Ashen spun to Vana. The old woman's palms were facing upward; her elk guardian beginning to take shape from root to hoof to leg. Though Thaddeus's weasel sneer contorted with amusement, even contempt, Ashen noticed a new emotion surface. Fear.

"The Divide'll collapse," Thaddeus spat, scrutinizing each of them through the purple veil as he retreated. "Ain't no matter what Vana or the rest tells ya. And when it does, the Warders will be no more. Ya will be forced ta choose—dark or light—soon enough."

He motioned to his army. The Unseen troops transformed back into their orbs and hovered next to Engine 191 while it backed through the front of the building and vanished. More sniffles and crying could be heard as the locomotive rumbled away.

From the edge of the room where he had been thrown, the red and pink fox limped into view. As Blake's ram had done, the animal padded over to where Angry Fox lay motionless on the Union Station tile. He sniffed her face and hairline, gently licked the tip of her nose, and curled up next to her.

The two ghosts dissolved until they no longer existed.

PART FIVE:
ACCEPTANCE

22

BACK IN THE MINES

An earthy fragrance lingered in the dank air. She opened her eyes. Nothingness stared back. Beneath her, uncomfortable bits of stone and chunks of wood jabbed into her spine, forming a primitive cradle she sensed was meant to toughen her. Meant to make her stronger.

Faint multicolored rays shone from the far end of the stretched mine shaft. The beams turned to warped spirals, growing more powerful, devouring the surrounding darkness. As they illuminated the silver ore veins laced through the bedrock wall, she saw what looked like the Divide within the light's depths. Bright pink, purple, blue, green. Glistening. Enticing.

She rose from the diminished gloom and made her way toward the beacon. As she approached the first set of support beams, a pair of lanterns that hung from the timber abruptly lit, blazing with a silvery gleam. She paused at one. Confined in glass and brass, the flame served as a flickering reminder of her own blazing energy.

Every other stride, a new lantern came to life. The harsh characteristics of the mine shaft stone softened until the initial menace she'd felt ebbed away. Her path became clearer, and soon, her walk turned into a jog, then a run. She tried to reach the tunnel's end, but no matter how far she ran, the distance remained the same, never closing—never getting nearer.

She rested against the wall, feeling helpless. Useless. Head lowered, she bit at her lip and glanced toward the light. In the earth floor ahead was a shadowed depression. A gaping hole.

Instinctively, she stumbled back. But as she retreated from the opening, each lantern's fire fluttered and began to die. She stopped. She took a deep breath and walked forward. Their silvery shine returned, becoming more vivid with each step.

When she approached, she touched the once jagged cart rails sticking out from the mouth of the pit. The metal was smooth. It left no trace of rust on her hand. She inched closer to the cavity's edge and peered into the void. A blurred memory of things gone wrong echoed in her mind. Panic swelled, curdling like spoiled milk in her gut, and in the deep, deep dark, a faint, wispy glow emerged. It fractured, breaking off replicas before those copies shattered and produced more of the same.

The individual motes sharpened, becoming more defined as they multiplied. The Drifters from Sand Creek floated in vacant space, suspended in the air, wailing and crying and screaming without making a single sound. They repeated their actions, muted and blanched like sun-bleached gauze.

Determined to avoid whatever else dwelled in the hole, she circled it to continue. But as she passed, a nearby Drifter who was more familiar to her than the rest stuck out. She squinted, studying the person's smudged face. In midair, lying on his side, was Jacob.

She dropped to her knees and clawed her way to the ledge, stretching her hand out as far as she could, struggling not to fall, but he did not notice her. He did not respond. She tried again, and this time, her fingers brushed the side of his image. Something that had been obscured within his center shivered. A sliver of brightness, not unlike an aurora. Not unlike the Divide. Her eyes flicked to the people in the pit. They each contained the same kaleidoscopic radiance. The broken fragments were small, but they were there. They existed.

Voices spoke to her. They were the same whispers as before—not above her, but under the dirt, stones, and wood. They called from below where the Drifters lingered. The voices wanted her to go with them. To accept her fate. To give in.

But they didn't want her to come alone. They wanted her to bring them more.

She pleaded to Jacob with frantic, soundless words, taking a desperate swipe to catch hold of him. She moved too far out and slipped, tumbling into the hole...

But she didn't fall.

Instead, she hovered among the lost ones, watching their repetitious shudders smear their features. Next to her, a girl appeared. Long black hair flowed down her back, wafting about her shoulders and coiling around the collar of her blue dress. A silver pendant dangled from her neck. A fox.

As Angry Fox came into focus, her face melted, oozed, and burned away.

"*My mother,*" the warrior girl said with Max's voice. "*She kept saying how she was proud of me. How she was glad I was finally home."*

Down in the pit, something darker than the darkness materialized. A total absence of color filled hundreds of hollow eye sockets. Frightened, Ashen reached out for Jacob's hand, but rather than passing through his form, her fingers clasped his. She recoiled in shock. His ghostly mist faded and he opened his eyes, cloudy and confused as if he had woken from a fathomless sleep—a hint of recognition in his baffled gaze.

"Ash?"

Ashen's eyes flew open to the daylight. As usual, she sat on the curb at the side of the road with Jacob huddled on the ground next to her. She studied him, hoping maybe something in her dream had become reality, but his motions replayed the same as always. Nothing had changed.

Perplexed, she stared at her hands, contemplating the mine shaft. Was that a dream? Not a dream, perhaps. More like a nightmare. The dead can't dream, can they? There's no brain, no cells, no firing neurons. Maybe a vision? A weird knee-jerk reaction to missing her old life?

She crawled to Jacob's side. After she let her phantom lungs take in air, she reached out, but like every other attempt her hand sank through him, her fingers meeting the tarred asphalt. Pulling away, she sat cross-legged on the ground next to her friend, sad, yet relieved. At least her friend existed in some way. At least he wasn't like Angry Fox.

A lump formed in her throat. She'd left after what happened at Union Station and wandered, not knowing where she was headed, until she found herself here—the

262

spot where she had died. The only place she felt connected to. The idea of looking at any of the posse, especially John and Vana, proved too much. With Angry Fox ceasing to be, what they had lost as a team was unimaginable and she, a newly-dead, couldn't help them.

But maybe ... maybe she could help Jacob.

Something in the back of her mind gnawed at her. The words that Angry Fox had said using Max's voice played over and over. The first thing the soldier recalled after he awoke was his mother telling him that he was home and she was proud of him. Why did that make Max wake? Why did those same words fail with Jacob? She cringed. Would she have to wait until Jacob's mother died to wake him?

Within the folds of Jacob's image, Ashen scrutinized where she had seen the sliver of light in her dream, but no color lay buried inside him. Her friend remained the same. Translucent. Vague. Nothing of substance.

Silently, she yelled at herself for the last thought. Of course there was substance—worth—curled up on the road. This was her best friend, and even if she could not feel him, he was there. He was once a living being like she used to be. How could she be so callous? His soul was just as important as her own.

At that thought, something clicked into place. Jacob was valuable, yes, but not only as a person or because he was another human spirit. Even though he couldn't perceive her, Ashen leaned over him, her wide eyes attempting to peer into his.

"Jacob? You're important." She swallowed. "You're important to me. Did you know that?"

Nearly undetectable, his blurred face shifted, like a sheet unveiling an item of value underneath only to be dropped before the reveal.

"Jacob! Jacob, can you hear me?"

She stretched to touch his arm, but as usual, she didn't make contact. The tiny shift she'd seen in his features reverted back to his same repeating actions. But it had been there. He had heard her.

"Jacob—listen. You gotta listen. I need you to wake up." She sighed, her eyes fluttering upward, and hoped. "Please. I miss you. I miss you so, so much."

Pigments leeched from the ground around him. His pale, shrouded appearance faded away. A blush returned to his flesh. His writhing ceased, each movement calm and slow as his cloudy eyes cleared. Confused, he turned his head to her.

"Ash? Umm ... why're you grinning at me all ... creepy-like?"

She grabbed his hand, yanking him upright before she threw her arms around him. He took in a sharp, surprised breath. He returned the hug, and when she pulled away he looked happy, yet utterly perplexed at the same time.

"Alright. Who are you and what have you done with Ashen Deming?" he asked in a mock serious tone.

"Dude, you have no idea how glad I am to see you."

"You must be. We both know you're not really the huggy type." He beamed, then glanced around them. His eyebrows knitted. "Uh, why are we sitting in the middle of the street? Where's the bus?" He paused and squinted at the gravestones on the other side of the chain-link fence. His bewilderment deepened. "And why are we hanging out next to the cemetery? Yeah, all of this is totally, completely normal."

She grinned and got up, running off toward the lake. "Come on, Jacob! I think we found a way to save the Warders!"

"Wait, the who?" he yelled back, trailing behind her.

"Who are the Warders? And why do they need saving?"
"I'll explain as we go! We have to hurry!"

23

AWAKE

Jacob stared at the fish in the lake. "I'm dead?"

Ashen could have kicked herself. The excitement of waking her friend had blinded her to the fact that he wasn't aware he no longer had lungs to breathe with. She hadn't thought about how he might react. Or how hard he might take the news.

"I'm so, so sorry, Jacob."

She sat down on the warped wooden park bench next to him and crossed her legs. She searched for words that didn't come. A horrible, guilty feeling settled in her gut, but her foot bounced up and down on its own, wiggling with impatience. They had to get back to the train station. If her hunch was correct, perhaps the Divide could be saved and the Warders' upper hand over the Unseen could be restored.

"It's okay," he said. "In a weird way, I'm glad you're here. Not like, glad you're dead too, just ... yeah."

"I know. It's good to have a friend."

At the word 'friend,' a quiver of rejection crossed his face. Ashen smiled and gave him a firm pat on the back. One that didn't linger and complicate things with mixed signals.

"It's not so bad," she said. "At least everything looks pretty cool here. And hey! You can even walk on water."

"Walk on water? Guess that's pretty righteous," he said, gazing at the vibrant birds flitting from tree to tree before snapping from his sad daze. "Listen, don't get me wrong, Ash. I'm glad you woke me from eternal torment and all, even if I can't remember it. I guess it's like Alzheimer's for the dead? Talk about a nightmare."

She nodded, the whole time fighting the urge to rush him through his stages of grief, then chastising herself for wanting to rush him. It had taken her several days to accept her fate. How could she expect Jacob to accept his immediately?

"To be honest," he said as if he could read her thoughts, "I'm not too freaked out."

"What?" She blinked. "You're not?"

"Nah, being dead isn't nearly as harsh as I thought it might be." He propped his arms on the back of the bench. "The part that bugs me is, you know, my parents."

Ashen frowned. "You'll see them someday. If you decide to stay."

"Stay? Is there somewhere else we go?"

Before Ashen could explain the Divide and its mysteries, a voice cooed behind them.

"Well, well, well. Macajah's newly-dead."

Out of the tall lake grasses stepped Governor Silas Lydford. The charred scar left by Max's whip spiraled up his brilliant white features. One huge protuberant eyeball hung from a socket, and it appeared he'd tried to pinch the plasma where his nose used to be into an awkward shape, making it look more sunken than it had been before.

As soon as Jacob saw Silas' face, he shot up from the bench, his anxious eyes darting to Ashen. Ashen's mouth fell open.

"Didn't your parents teach you it's not polite to stare?" Silas asked, his soft voice sounding tight.

"Sorry, Governor Lydford." She averted her eyes and got up from the bench to join Jacob. "Uh, what are you doing here?"

"I'd heard about your young friend's plight. The Drifter." He eyed Jacob with suspicion. "Thought I might be able to provide some," his face twitched and the plasma rippled, "counsel."

"Oh. Well, Mister Governor, sir, that's really very nice of you, but we're okay."

Silas took a few steps closer. "I also figured without that wretched cowboy around, you and I could finally have a little chat about you joining the Light."

"You know, can we talk about that some other time?" An uncomfortable warning crawled up her spine. She hadn't forgotten the man's initial hostility toward her or that weird, unexplained white light that had hit Angry Fox. "I uh, promised to get Jacob back to Union Station."

Jacob's brows furrowed. He glanced at Ashen and she quickly glared back. The governor looked from one to the other. He grinned. The corners of his mouth broke open and oozed a thick, clear slime.

"He's welcome to join as well. We desire additional youthful spirits among our ranks. Besides, your friend doesn't seem like he's in a hurry."

"I, I am!" Jacob stammered. "I was a Drifter, and—"

The governor's one good eye widened. "You're the Drifter friend? Awake? That's some wonderful news!" He turned his attention back to Ashen. "How is it, Miss Deming, that he's no longer a lost soul?"

"I...," she paused. Something about how the governor asked seemed predatory. "You know, I'm not sure. He just woke up. Like Max."

"That's rare. You could say almost unheard-of. And you are departing to the station to share this joyous news, I take it?"

"Yeah," she said. "I mean, the main reason I stuck around was to make certain Jacob was okay."

"Rare indeed," Silas said. He stood there without offering another word, staring at the two of them while licking at the goo on his lips as if starved.

"Uh," Ashen said. She tugged on Jacob's sleeve. "We're ... gonna go now."

As they stepped backward toward the lake's surface, a ball of white formed around one of Governor Lydford's clenched fists. He flashed his mad grin through the ragged remains of his face.

"Jacob," she whispered. "You know that whole, 'walking on water' thing I just told you about?"

"Yeah?"

"No time like the present. Get on the lake."

They spun and bolted. Before they had reached the reflective waters, a beam of light shot in front of them, blocking their escape. It was identical to the one that had struck Angry Fox before she suffered a ghost's death. Ashen whirled to seek the source, but wherever the light had come from was back behind the lakeside reeds and beyond where Governor Lydford studied them.

"You're both going to stay precisely where you stand," Silas said. "You're a loose-end, newly-dead. One meant to be tidied long ago. We're too close now. Too close. We can't afford you locating more souls to cross over, now can we?"

Jacob leaned over and whispered, "Not getting the vibe he's a good guy."

"Of course I am!" he bellowed, ectoplasm seeping from his open wounds. "I am of the Light! The very representation of purity!"

Ashen spoke low and fast. "Remember what I said about traveling through reflections?"

The governor smiled. His features dissolved further. "We can't have that. You may meddle unintentionally."

A cold shiver moved through Ashen. Silas had no intention of letting them go. That realization made her panic swell, but instead of allowing it to paralyze her, Ashen concentrated, imagining the dread she felt warp, change, construct itself into a protective shield; a barricade. Flames expanded from her core, growing, spreading over her until her weakened, silvery light danced upon her skin.

"What do you think you're doing?" the governor asked.

Ashen's eyes flickered with a sterling silver blaze. "Jacob. Run."

The explosion from Ashen hit Silas with force, knocking him off balance and into the reeds. Ashen grabbed Jacob's wrist and together, they ducked beneath the white beam obstructing their path and ran to the lake. Maybe recalling what it was like to be alive and fearful kicked in for Jacob, but whatever it was, he didn't struggle on the water's surface. Instead, he sprinted alongside Ashen to the center, water splashing with each step as balls of white light darted past.

"Think of Union Station!"

Jacob closed his eyes, but nothing happened.

"You're not going anywhere!" Governor Lydford stomped toward them, his fists raised and glowing with energy.

"Jacob!"

A bolt zoomed over their heads and Jacob squeezed his eyes tighter shut. When he started to sink, Ashen did the same, willing herself to go faster.

"That can't happen! Your power—" Silas' tantrum cut off as she and Jacob submerged into the abyss.

Every trip through a mirror had been the same. Scattered stars. Black holes. Ancient exploded supernovas and clouds of cosmic dust flew past, each nebula a distinct colorful tone or shape or size. Though the terror remained that Governor Lydford was on their heels, Ashen found herself pondering time itself. The journey always felt incredibly short, yet incredibly long, and whenever she exited a reflection, she was left uncertain. Had they been traveling for less than a second? A day? Years?

As she thought on this, Ashen noticed something she hadn't before. Beyond the rings of an unknown planet, space itself cracked open to reveal something like a mirage—a city? No ... a town. An Old West town with wood plank sidewalks where the main street stretched far into the Rocky Mountains.

The strange sighting ended almost before it began. Jacob was waiting in the hallway when Ashen popped out the other side.

"What the...! Did we go through space back there, Ash? Tell me we just went through space!"

"Priorities, Jacob!"

"Right, sorry! Sorry! Can that guy follow us?"

Remembering her bedroom all those years ago and the dark orb that had taunted her, it was clear that the Unseen had been able to use mirror travel far longer than they were letting on. If that were the case, what else were the Warders not aware of?

"He shouldn't be able to. I think. I really have no idea anymore," she sighed. "We need to find Max and Cage."

They ran down the hall into the empty lobby. No sound, no spirits, not even the living souls who normally hustled and bustled about. "Cage? Max? Are you here?"

Creeping dread fell over her. She searched, running through the inner walls into every small room, from the Pullman room, to the ticket and information booths.

"Cage! Max! Anyone!"

"Ash?" Jacob pointed to the front lobby doors. His voice shook. "What is that?"

Distant, brilliant light refracted through Union Station's present-day arched windows. Multicolored residue filtered through the clear panes of glass as if a fireworks display had exploded outside. The familiar blue, gold, and green hues were blotted out and overpowered by a grimy, polluted gloom.

Ashen's panic rose. She barreled through the closed door to the courtyard and into the midst of a raging battle. About two hundred Warders, backs to each other to form a circle around the Divide, were using their now-timid powers to deflect incoming attacks. Three times as many Unseen surrounded them, gnashing their teeth, lunging at them like wild dogs.

She scanned the Warders and saw Cage with Agnes, his Winchester, rapid-firing in different directions while he urged a few frightened newly-dead souls to continue through the arch. When one Unseen, claws raised, catapulted toward the cowboy, blue whips slung out from the crowd and curled around the neck of the creature. Max tugged hard, pulling the squirming shadow to the center of the circle near the Divide's entrance.

The Unseen sneered. He ripped Max's whip from his throat, tearing off scorched chunks of his own plasma, and leapt at the closest newly-dead, but right before his claws sliced into the defenseless spirit, two Warders barreled into the creature. Pushed off-balance, the creature teetered at the Divide's threshold until he fell into its open mouth.

The tunnel surged with energy like it had when Toad had been thrown into its depths. All of the weapons the Warders wielded brightened, their strength returning with trembling, vivid bursts. In response, the shadows hissed, cramming themselves behind one another for cover from the growing light.

Grabbing hold of Jacob, Ashen rushed toward the Warders, bobbing and weaving between the oily black Unseen. The disoriented creatures swatted at them with their long dark claws. A talon or paw connected. Ashen yelled out. Searing pain spread across her upper back.

Max looked in her direction. "Ashen?"

She gritted her teeth and wrenched Jacob forward while Max bulldozed through the throng. He seized her free hand, hauling them both into the ring of Warders and relative safety.

"What are you doing here!" he said, outraged. "You're hurt!"

"I had to find you and Cage," she answered with a voice that sounded more confident than she felt. "And I can take care of myself. Looks like you could use all the help you can get, anyway."

Macajah hustled over. "This ain't no place for newly-deads," he drawled, his features stern until his sights shifted to Jacob. The cowboy's amber eyes displayed his bewilderment.

"Well, I'll be. Ain't you full of surprises, Little Missy?"

"Jacob?" Max's cross expression softened. "Wait, how did you wake him up?"

"We have something bigger to deal with right now, guys," Ashen said. "Governor Silas Lydford. I think he's finally gone off the deep end."

Max and Macajah looked confused.

She took a deep breath. "On our way here, we ran into him at Windsor Lake. Something's not right. As soon as he found out I woke Jacob up, he started getting … aggressive. Like how he was when I first met you, Max—back in that living boy's bedroom."

"What did he do?"

"Was a general creep and chased us," Jacob said. "By the way, what is wrong with that dude's face?"

Macajah grunted and hustled from Warder to Warder. "Keep an eye out, ladies and gents. We might have some difficulties beyond our current Unseen predicament."

"How'd you do it?" Max asked. "Wake him?" A thread of awe wove through his tone. Ashen felt herself blush.

"I thought more about what you'd told me. About your mom. And, I don't know, something sorta—"

An ivory radiance interrupted her. It throbbed from the outer skirts, beyond the border of Unseen around them. Several luminous figures came forward and began pushing their way through the dark horde of shadows. Ashen sighed with relief. The Light had come to help.

The Unseen army parted. Robes billowing, the Honorable Constance Callahan headed the group, an oversized judge's gavel in her grasp. Ashen jogged forward and stopped. Her smile faded.

Next to Constance walked Silas.

"Oh, no," Ashen whispered. Her mind scrambled to think of how she could warn Constance—tell her that Silas' allegiances were compromised—when an intense white blared from the head of the judge's mallet.

It emitted a beam of white light. The same beam from the lake that had attempted to hinder her and Jacob's escape. The same beam that had distracted Angry Fox and resulted in her murder.

"You stupid girl," the judge's shrill voice called out. She pointed her gavel at Ashen. "You should have joined us or moved on. Didn't I caution that you shouldn't trust anyone?"

Peculiar pearly rays volleyed from behind Constance. The projectiles flew over the heads of the Unseen. As they descended upon the Warders, a huge dome appeared above, shielding them, the Divide, and most of the Union Station building. The structure looked similar to the one Eli had created, but when the first of the volleys struck, the colors of the barrier altered, flickering from lavenders to pinks to yellows and the various shades of each individual Warder.

The Unseen army roared, pressing closer to the shield now wedged between them.

"How long will this hold?" Ashen asked Max.

"Not long," Max said. His arms were raised, his blue glow uniting and combining with the rest. "We got a boost to our power from a few Unseen falling in, but I can already feel it diminishing. We need more souls to enter the arch."

Souls. Her thoughts returned to her latest dream of the mine shaft pit and the Drifters with the vibrant shards inside each of them. How Silas had become enraged when he discovered Ashen had awoken Jacob.

"Max, I have an idea that might help with the Divide."

"What?"

"The Drifters. We need the Drifters."

He looked at her, puzzled. "What can Drifters do?"

"They might be lost souls but they're still souls, right? If we can wake them like I woke Jacob, convince them to move on, then—"

"You could do that?"

"Maybe? I hope." She paused until her eyes found Vana and John, the sage and the scholar, in the crowd. "I might have an idea how, but I'll need some help."

24

JOHN: SIZZLIN' SALLY

John Porter
Born: November 25, 1930
Died: July 12, 1954

July 12, 1954

"'The soul that is within me no man can degrade,'" John whispered in the dark.

He sat on the gritty floor, resting his arms on the tops of his knees. He was grateful to still have his shirt, but the unrelenting July heat made it stick to his skin in uncomfortable patches. Most of his belongings had been confiscated. His saddle shoes. His hat. His glasses. They'd also forced him to remove his suspenders until it became quickly realized they were the only thing keeping his pants from falling down. So, for the sake of modesty, they'd let him keep them.

They had taken the only possessions that he cared about.

A few tattered old books and his dog, Hughes—his German Shepherd and the only family the young man knew. Every time he thought about the dog not being there with him, he'd blink the tears away, refusing to give those that held him any satisfaction, and concentrate on some other line or lyric, repeating whatever quotes he could remember. "The soul that is within me no man can degrade" was the main one to stick. His latest mantra.

John wasn't certain if it was evening yet. He looked around the now familiar space, his eyes settling on a small window with iron bars near the ceiling. A slapdash brick wall blocked off the outside world, but he assumed half the day was already spent. In the darkness, time didn't move.

Aside from the window, the cell had a solid door and mostly bare floors. An empty pail, swarming with blow flies, had been chucked into the distant corner. Other than his makeshift bathroom, he wasn't provided with anything. No meal. No water. Not even a blanket.

He heard the metal of the outer jail door shriek, followed by hard-soled footsteps. The sharp sound approached and stopped outside his cell. Brass keys rattled, and the guard swung the door open before throwing John's shoes near his feet.

"Wakey, wakey, negro."

"My name's John," he said, glaring up at the man.

"Not no more, it ain't. Get your shoes on."

The guard watched, arms crossed, as John pulled his shoes on. John frowned. "Where are we going?"

"Well, we happened to get a special visitor from out of town and wanted to introduce you."

"Is he here about me getting a trial?"

The guard chuckled. "Yeah, sure. A trial."

After securing John's ankles and wrists with shackles, the

guard escorted him out into the hall and down a short corridor past a few empty cells, each door ajar. A snoring man, clothes filthy, lay sprawled on the concrete inside the final cell. Dark stains covered his trousers and sleeves. The stink of alcohol seeped from him.

The guard banged on the door at the end of the hall. Someone on the other side slid aside a metal plate. A pair of eyes scrutinized them.

"Let us through, Harold. Got the accused here for the governor."

The eyes scanned John before disappearing behind the sliding plate. The lock turned, and the screech of the door echoed down the hall.

The guard shoved John. He stumbled over his binding chains, tumbling through the opening into the jail's small courtyard, and landed on the metal handcuffs. A searing pain flared in his wrists.

"A bit of a simpleton, isn't he?" said a low, silky voice. "Difficult to believe he committed a murder when he can't manage his own feet."

John winced and pushed himself to his knees. Standing over him, the voice's owner wore a double-breasted midnight blue suit and matching tie. He looked like most rich white men John had seen before. Clean-shaven, hair styled to perfection and peppered with a distinguished gray, shined tan Oxfords. If it hadn't been for the man's intense gaze, John would have considered him to be wholly unremarkable and forgettable.

The man unbuttoned his jacket with leather-gloved hands. He swept one side back and tugged on a chain that hung from his front vest pocket, revealing an intricate gold watch dangling from the end.

"We have just enough time to get this over with so I can

get home for a late supper." He closed the case with a snap and placed the watch back in his pocket.

"Yes, Governor Lydford," said the guard.

Experience had taught John that saying too much could make his situation far worse, so he kept quiet. The guard gripped him by the elbow, yanked him to his feet, and escorted him through the courtyard and out to a small parking lot. There, they forced John into the back seat of a brand new Cadillac Fleetwood, its black paint buffed and polished. Governor Lydford got behind the wheel. He smoothed his pants to avoid wrinkles before turning the key. The engine roared to life.

"Still has that new smell," the guard said as he climbed into the front. "She's a beauty, governor."

"Yes, she is." Governor Lydford reached over to a small silver box beneath the dash. He flipped a switch. John felt a cool breeze for the first time since arriving in Colorado.

"Golly, Governor Lydford," the guard said. "I've never been in a vehicle with air conditioning."

The governor flashed a wide grin. "All the bells and whistles. Only the best."

They pulled away, passing a few scattered homes and businesses before the governor turned onto First Street and headed toward the outskirts of town. John watched the deserted train tracks alongside the road. He sighed with relief. Maybe he would get his trial after all.

Muffled chanting could be heard as they approached the railroad depot. Cars were parked in a semicircle, their headlights illuminating the entrance to a building. John swallowed hard. The chanting became more distinct. People began to gather around the Fleetwood. Through the closed windows, faces filled with pure, unfiltered anger wailed for justice. A chain gate opened and they rolled inside, past a parked silver box truck and around the backside of the building, away from the mob.

The guard got out and led John from the car to the back door. The percussion of the chains binding John created a doomed beat. A cruel prophecy of his fate.

"'The soul that is within me no man can degrade,'" he reminded himself, but he couldn't stop his voice from shaking.

The door slammed behind them. The chaos outside dampened. Through the front windows, an orange glow from the protesters' vehicles filtered into the dim room — some kind of storage facility for the railroad. Boxes and tools were stacked along one of the walls and a few small desks were placed in a corner.

The murky shapes of several men stood around a large object in the middle of the room. One of the men noticed they had entered, and he reached up and tugged the string of an overhead bulb. The room flooded with light. The large object was a chair, its high back fashioned from a solid plank of wood with two wide, unfastened leather straps draped around it. Additional straps and buckles were attached to the legs and armrests. John had never seen anything like it before, but it was clear it was intended for some kind of torture.

A blot stained the concrete beneath. It had a similar appearance to tar, brownish-black and sticky, but along the edges, it thinned into a muted crimson. There were clumps of something stuck in it. Long threads. John squinted to focus. The threads were strands of hair.

Eyes wide, John whirled to the guard. "Is this where it happened?"

"You should know, negro. You were the one that did the deed."

John felt his mouth fill with a fear he could taste. Back in the Cadillac, he had hope that they were going to leave the small town of Limon and travel to Denver. At least in a city courtroom, he'd have a chance that the assigned judge wouldn't have premature opinions about him. But now, standing there, staring at a pool of drying blood, his optimistic determination faded away. Whatever interrogation they had planned would be conducted on the spot.

"Now, now. Don't you worry," said the governor, smiling grimly at him. "This'll all be over soon. Assuming you cooperate."

The guard wrenched John's chains to the middle of the room, unshackled him, forced him to sit, and bound him to the chair using the leather straps. When he'd finished, the guard leaned in close.

"This here is Sizzlin' Sally—that special visitor I promised."

John's eyebrows drew together in confusion. The guard chuckled. "She came all the way from Mississippi. Travels all over the country for lowlife nosebleeds like you."

The back door swung open. John glanced behind him. The silver box truck backed up to the entrance, and from within the hollows of the trailer, he could hear a hand truck's wheels squeak from a heavy load. Two men rolled a large metal contraption down a ramp, maneuvered it inside, and placed it on its sturdy legs near the front entrance. A dial, controls, and indicators were on the flat side, while the other had a mess of mechanisms.

"Lucky for you," the guard said, motioning to some of the men. "She's supposed to be more 'humane' than a hanging. I've been itching to try her out."

Reality sank in as cables were tossed from the truck. John

strained to free himself, looking frantically at the men around him, but his restraints held. One kneeled on the floor to connect the chair to the cables that snaked from the machine. The man turned and nodded, and the guard rotated the dial, firing up the generator. He fiddled with the controls. An electrical whine sounded from its bowels. The humming changed tempo and tone as he cranked the lever, winding the current up and down.

John's heart raced. "No, wait!" he pleaded. He fought with urgency against the straps. "I didn't kill that girl! You have to believe me! Please!"

A whimper John recognized came from the shadowed corner of the room.

"Hughes?" he asked.

One of the men stepped forward with the German Shepherd leashed to a rusted chain. The man's face scrunched up the way it does when someone is trying to hold back a combination of rage, torment, and hate.

"That little girl was my daughter," he said.

"I swear, sir, I didn't do anything. I wasn't even in Colorado yet-"

Pain, solid and hot, erupted in John's cheek followed quickly by another punch to his nose, and his head snapped back, hitting the wood of the chair. He blinked, trying to see through blurry tears, the fresh sting of the blow dulling to a thud.

"Shut up and don't move," the guard said. He wiped his bloodied knuckles on a dirty rag and threw it into a bucket full of foul liquid.

The man in the corner wrapped Hughes' chain around his flexing fist. He yanked hard. Air restricted, the German Shepherd let out a dry, hacking cough before limping with the man over to the machine. While the man worked on locking Hughes to a metal strut, the dog sat on his haunches and waited, peering at John with his big, questioning eyes.

"You care about this mutt?"

John nodded. Tears dripped from his quivering chin. "Please let him go. He didn't-"

"What'd I say, boy?" the guard said, rapping the back of his hand against John's temple. "Shut them thick lips."

"Richard," the governor's perfect teeth gleamed in the gloom as he addressed the man tying up Hughes. "I'm sorry for your loss. Truly. Know that I'm here to make certain the peace is kept by taking monsters like this colored off our streets."

The man named Richard ignored Governor Lydford. Instead, he stood and scowled at John. "Maybe after this, your kind will learn to keep far, far away from here. People like you, who look like you, need to learn they aren't welcome."

The governor cleared his throat. "Why don't you and your eldest come by the new mansion when all of this ugly business is over?" he said, smiling while wrapping his arm around Richard's shoulders. "Just had it built. It's beautiful! Has all the latest technology, straight out of an issue of *Popular Science*."

Richard gave a mournful look. "Sure. That sounds fine."

"Good. Good. Now, let's get on with this, shall we?"

Blood and tears mingled, running down John's face and dropping to his bone-colored shirt. "Governor Lydford, I didn't kill anyone. Please, don't do this."

"All coloreds are criminals," the guard said. "You ain't no different. You gotta pay the price."

"You're murdering an innocent man," John said, jaw clenched.

"Boy, this isn't murder. This is justice." The governor

released Richard's shoulder and turned his attention to John. "Every Sunday, the good pastor tells us we're all sinners, but I happen to believe those bearing the mark of Cain, like yourself, are less valiant—less righteous—than the rest of us. Your ancestors were sinners. They begot sinners who then begot more sinners, and so on—vermin breeding and breeding. You're just one more animal that happened to take the shape of a person."

"'No man can put a chain about the ankle of his fellow man without at last finding the other end fastened about his own neck.'"

"Oh, that sounded almost smart!" the governor exclaimed. "I'll venture a guess that you didn't come up with that on your own, did you?"

"It was written by Frederick Douglass."

The guard laughed. "Never heard of him. Must not be all that smart, then."

"He was an abolitionist."

"Don't know what that is, but like I said, must not be all that smart."

The governor made a gesture to the guard, quieting him before flicking his eyes back to John. "Do you know how to read, boy?"

"Yes."

"Then it's better we resolve this little issue now. Bad enough that this town threatened violence in Denver if we brought you to trial, but it would be even worse if they knew you were attempting to be an educated sort. That's ... rebellious."

John closed his eyes. "'The soul that is within me no man can degrade. The soul that is within me no man can degrade. The soul that is within me no man can degrade.'"

"Shut his yap, will you?"

The guard obeyed, taking the rag from the bucket of water. He shoved it into John's mouth, dunked another rag, and slapped it to the crown of John's head. The sopping cloth tasted of motor oil and kerosene, and while John gagged, tainted water dribbled from the rag on his head down to his nostrils, filling them with a vile stench.

The guard finished by jamming a leather helmet on top. He buckled it beneath John's chin, clamping his jaw shut, tightening the straps that secured John until the leather cut into his skin. Two other men pushed the chair a few yards, turning it around until it faced the front entrance of the building.

The father of the dead girl, Richard, stood next to the humming machine with Hughes while Governor Lydford checked his hair and straightened his tie in a grimy mirror near the door. Walking in front of John, he ran his glove-clad hands down the lapels of his jacket, buttoned it, squared his shoulders, and glanced at John. He grinned.

"It's showtime."

A barrage of outrage blared through the door as the governor opened it, jeers and taunts filling John's ears. There were so many voices, he couldn't distinguish between them, only catching random words here and there. Repulsive words. Hate-filled words.

"Go back to Africa!"

"See if that thing got a tail!"

"Fry 'im!"

The governor raised his hands. The headlight beams from the vehicles splintered into butterscotch-colored rays between his fingers. "Friends! Friends! Please, I must insist that you all stay calm."

The yelling subsided. The man continued, and although his back remained turned, John could tell by the way he spoke that the governor's wide grin was still plastered to his face.

"It's a pleasure to see my constituents take such an active interest in assuring that justice is served."

The crowd responded, yelling out ideas on how that justice should be inflicted. As John sat, trembling in the chair, witnessing the resentment surge through the congregation like a growing infection, a few, eerily appropriate lines from his favorite poet popped into his mind:

That Justice is a blind goddess
Is a thing to which we black are wise.
Her bandage hides two festering sores
That once perhaps were eyes.

He wasn't getting out. He wasn't going to make it to California. He was going to die here, tonight. And it wasn't going to be quick and painless.

"It is with a heavy heart that I speak to you today," the governor said. "You all know the innocent girl's father, Richard Callahan, as well as her older sister."

From the depths of the crowd, a teenage girl with long blonde hair came forward and joined them, her head hung.

"However, a righteous act will be born from this tragedy." Governor Lydford put a hand on the young girl's upper arm. "Constance, go on and tell the good people what you told me."

She lifted her head. Her eyes were red-rimmed and puffy. Bitter tears spilled out. "I'm going to be a judge. Put evil men — things — like him behind bars."

The crowd began to chant. Richard embraced the sobbing teenager, Constance, and joined in. The word "kill" rose above the vocal clutter of the mob, the heckles crashing against the walls of John's soul, eroding away any fight he had left.

After a few moments, the guard bent down to John's ear. "Now, we're gonna test this machine here. Make certain it works and all."

Though putrid water streamed from John's head, obscuring his vision, he could make out one of the men approaching Hughes.

"You better watch, boy," the guard whispered. "Watch every moment or I'll slice those eyelids off and force you."

John's dog began to whine.

The air reeked of burning flesh and fur. John had no toes left. He faded in and out of consciousness while each of his appendages was lopped off with a pair of bolt-cutters, the pieces of him distributed to a member in the mob as a sort of grisly souvenir. When they were done with his toes, they moved on to his fingers, plucking one at a time, letting his blood join the dried stain beneath his chair.

All the while, the crowd cheered, laughed, took photographs. Either of him being hacked away little by little, or of the smoking body of Hughes lying on the floor. John imagined once he finally died, there would be more pictures, more giggles, more celebration. He was their entertainment for the evening, and the final act drew near.

He had no more tears to weep. The pain was so great and so terrible, he would welcome its cessation. He hoped it would be soon. He hoped.

As his eyes rolled, he felt the presence of the guard next to him. The man slipped something into the front pocket of

John's shirt.

"Put your spectacles here so you can see the devil when he comes to fetch you." The guard leaned in close. "Sure glad you came into town when you did, boy. You see, my brother Frank … he didn't mean to harm the girl. He gets like that when he drinks and she wouldn't shut up."

John's senses awoke. His mind flitted to the drunk man with stained clothing, asleep in his open cell. He tried to scream, but all that escaped between the rancid cloth were mumbles. Richard stood with Constance near the machine. Pleading with his eyes, John tried anything to sway the grieving man, but Richard only answered by placing one hand on the switch and the other around the waist of his eldest daughter, Constance, who glared at John with unadulterated contempt.

The guard placed a full face blind over John's eyes and mouth, leaving only his nose exposed. Horrified, John exhaled air through his nostrils in forced bursts while the sound of the guard's hard-soled steps moved away, blending with the shouts of the unseen spectators. The machine's electrical current buzzed at a higher frequency. John rocked the chair back and forth, screaming muffled screams until the switch clicked.

25

MISTS ON THE PRAIRIE

At the base of the bluff, hands raised, Ashen gestured at the passing apparitions as they wandered in their private emotional torment.

"We're here to let you know people care. We don't want you to suffer." She cleared her throat and thought back to when Jacob had awoken. "We wanted to tell you … to say that you are all missed."

None responded. They continued their predestined path between shade and daylight.

Ashen dropped her hands to her sides and sat with a huff to stare out at the large camp. She had been certain—so certain—that she knew the answer, but since they had arrived at Sand Creek, everything she had attempted had failed.

"This is so frustrating!"

John slouched on a rock next to her. Mourning glazed his eyes. His cheeks were gaunt, as if he'd shed twenty pounds, and around his neck he fiddled with the bead strands where Angry Fox's medallion hung, sometimes touching the face of the fox as if memorizing every line and curve.

"These poor souls," he said. "I've never understood how humans can treat others with such inhumanity."

"There is much ugliness in the world, John Porter, but it is worth fighting for," Vana said. While she observed her cursed tribe, a single tear spilled over her lower lashes. "When my people were lost, Angry Fox helped me to grieve. She became my sister. She taught me English. She showed me beauty again."

John nodded. "Frederick Douglass said, 'A smile or a tear has not nationality; joy and sorrow speak alike to all nations.'" He looked at Ashen. "We cannot let Fox's sacrifice be for nothing, Ash. Keep trying."

"I know. I know."

"You awoke your friend, Ashen Deming. Deep within you, you know how to solve this," the old woman said, "but we must hurry." She placed her frail hand on Ashen's shoulder. Ashen winced.

"Do you have a wound, child?"

"Don't worry. It's only a scrape," she said, waving her off. "Let's go in. If we're closer, maybe what we're saying will make more of a difference."

Taking a deep breath, Ashen headed toward the heart of the village, past a herd of spectral buffalo who flicked their ears, but otherwise ignored her. Vana and John followed, picking their way across the creek that had swollen during a recent flash flood and left behind pools of stagnant water.

The three ghosts meandered between the silent, oblivious Drifters who remained on the outskirts of the camp. The first tipi, a twenty-foot-tall cone-shaped ghostly structure, was covered in buffalo hide and decorated with shimmering painted images of horses. Diamond patterns lined the bottom, and from between the long lodge poles sticking out of the open top, blue and purple phantom smoke poured out to create an eerie haze overhead.

Further in, Ashen avoided the faces of the lost, wandering souls by peering at the multiple tipis, each decorated in its own way. Some were intricate, with geometric patterns covering almost all of the visible leather, while others had large, circular ornaments, buffalo horns, or simple paintings, like feathers. Most were unadorned.

At the center stood the tallest structure. A simple black pattern ringed both the top and base. Attached to a pole next to the entrance flap, an American flag waved. It had fewer stars than those from Ashen's time, but it was unmistakably an earlier, older version. Beneath, a small, white cloth fluttered.

Ashen paced in front of the pole. "We've tried bribing, begging, telling them what we think they want to hear ... did I already say begging?"

"Logic dictates there's a solution," John said. "We need to figure out what the key is, so, start over. What woke Max?"

"His mother telling him she loved him and was proud of him."

"And Jacob?"

"That I missed him." Ashen rolled her eyes. "A bunch."

"Did you say anything else?"

"Ugh, I said a lot of things, John." Ashen rubbed her eyes with the heel of her palms. "Old memories, feelings— whatever I could think of, but he didn't really acknowledge anything until he finally snapped out of it."

"Didn't really?" John asked.

"I'm not sure. I mean, he may have reacted to one other thing I said, but I was so desperate, I could have imagined it."

Vana studied the bright buffalo grazing on the hillside. "What was it, child?"

"That he was important to me. He sorta … twinkled? I mean, I think he did, anyway."

"Max: pride and love. Jacob: needed and important." As John mused, he flipped the fox medallion from back to front to back again. "What's the common theme?"

"John, I've been wanting to ask something." Ashen pursed her lips. "How did you, well, how is it that you have Angry Fox's necklace? We're ghosts, right? How can someone's possessions be around if, you know, they aren't anymore?"

At this, John gave a slight smile. "Yet another unsolved mystery. After Fox was gone, I didn't leave the spot where," he paused, "where it happened. I ended up sitting there, hoping it was a horrible nightmare or one of those visions we spirit kind get. But when I realized it was real, I panicked. I guess I finally realized I'd never see her again."

"I can't imagine," Ashen shook her head. "I'm sorry, John."

"I was afraid—so very afraid—I'd forget her." He shrugged. "So I wished I had something to remember her by, and when I looked down, her medallion was on the tile next to me. I don't know why it's here, but it comforts me to think that maybe before her spirit scattered to the far corners of the universe, whatever was left of Fox was made into this necklace."

"Afraid," Vana's eyes flitted from Drifter to Drifter, and for a moment, she rubbed her hands together as if concentrating. "I have not forced many into being Drifters. When I have, it felt—" She stopped and closed her eyes a bit, her hands open as if she cradled something of weight. "It felt like I held a weapon, not unlike Hollow Iron's rifle. But instead of bullets, or life currents, terror shot from it."

"Vana?" John asked.

"Max Churchill is a proud man." Vana said, snapping from her daze. She motioned to Ashen. "And your Jacob, does he desire more between you? More than you may want to give?"

"Uncomfortable question, but yeah."

The old woman looked to each of them and smiled. "What is an emotion all people share?"

"Love, hate, anger," Ashen suggested. She sighed. "Regret. Felt a lot of that one in particular lately."

"Sorrow." John touched the fox necklace again.

"Good answers," Vana said. She stepped closer to one of the large, circular ornaments and ran her fingers over the design. "But not all people love. Or hate. Not all people are proud, or sad, or happy. Or full of regret. These feelings blend together, like the quills of the porcupine woven into this medallion." She stopped and cocked her head at them as if amused by their puzzled expressions. "When it is most pure, what emotion controls a person? If they allow it? An emotion they must defeat in themselves to live a full life?"

In frustration, Ashen folded her arms and sat in front of the pole. At her feet, tiny ants illuminated with color collected bits of twig and branch before heading in a uniform line toward a collective destination, and she watched them, her mind listing off whatever emotions she could think of. None fit.

She sighed again and glanced at John. He played with the silver fox around his neck, staring at nothing, his thick brows furrowed in thought. As if a gear had clicked into place, his features shifted. His lit eyes looked to Vana.

"Fear."

Vana smiled again.

"Hang on," Ashen said. "That doesn't make sense. Max is probably the most courageous person I've ever met."

"After knowing Max for as long as I have," John said, "you soon see the chinks in his seemingly impenetrable armor. He wants nothing more than to be accepted. Valued. Not be a disappointment to those he cares about."

Ashen felt like slamming her head against a brick wall. How could she have missed this? Especially when Jacob had accused her, a couple of weeks ago on the bus, of not caring about him at all.

"She kept saying how she was proud of me. How she was glad I was finally home."

Vana's eyes shone with clarity. "My people do not often speak the name of those who die. Instead, we recite their memory and their stories as remembrance. There is little we fear."

"Then what could keep them like this?" Ashen asked.

Closing her eyes, Vana spoke. "My people, my family. You are not lost. You are among the plains. You are among the buffalo. But your journey is not complete. You have yet to travel the Road of the Departed. You have yet to join our ancestors and become one with the skies." Her eyes opened. They glowed with warmth. "You have not been forgotten."

In her native tongue, Vana sang. Her tones were even, rhythmic, and as they carried on the wind, Ashen found herself lost in the chanting. The tune became more fierce and quick, and in a pleading gesture, Vana lifted her hands. They burned orange and the surrounding gloom lessened.

The Drifters ceased their repetitive movements, eyes blinking as if roused from a restless slumber. The nearest looked around, confused until they noticed others, their elation amplified when they saw a loved one. A sibling. A father. A child.

A small girl peeked from behind the trunk of a nearby oak tree. On the fateful day Ashen had first seen the tribe's plight, Vana had stood tall on the ridge, crying as she watched this same girl echo the moments before her murder. Now, the girl was alert. Awake.

Upon seeing Vana, the girl darted around the tree and collided into the old woman's legs, disrupting her speech. Vana looked down. Her eyes filled with tears.

"*Véxah?*"

"*Néške'e!*"

She swooped the girl into her arms. Holding her close, Vana whispered words into the child's ear, words that Ashen didn't understand. But she didn't mind. Even though spoken in a different language, she felt everything said.

After a few moments, Vana, happy tears streaming down her face, placed the girl back on the ground. Hands clasped, the two walked together to where Ashen and John sat, and Vana's broad, bright smile could have lit the furthest, darkest corner.

"Thank you, Ashen Deming." She regarded John. "And thank you, John Porter."

Ashen felt embarrassed. "Don't thank us. We didn't do anything."

"Your youthful optimism gave me hope that not all had been lost." She looked lovingly at her granddaughter before shame replaced it. "After so many years, I had become old and cynical. I could not make myself witness their pain and suffering. It hurt too much."

"I can imagine it was difficult."

"I do not know why I did not become a Drifter while the rest of my people did. I have thought about it. Many, many times. They did not deserve this fate."

The little girl giggled in wonderment at the strangers her grandmother spoke to. Her tiny hand tugged on the skirt of Vana's dress. Large, dark eyes flicked to Vana, then to Ashen, and back again.

"Oh. I see. I have been rude," Vana said in a matter-of-fact tone. "John Porter and Ashen Deming, this is my granddaughter, *Heóváhéso.*"

"Nice to meet you." Ashen paused and struggled on the name. "Hey-yo-fas?"

The girl laughed and said something to her grandmother.

"You may call her Little Yellow. She said you speak Tsitsistas poorly. She is a truthful child."

"Tell her that her grandmother will teach me better," Ashen said with a smile.

Little Yellow pulled Vana down so she could whisper in her ear. She gave Ashen a delighted glance.

"She likes your hair. It is like the buffalo, she says."

"Oh. Uh, tell her thank you. I like hers, too."

The girl grinned after hearing the news and scampered off toward some other ex-Drifter children who had awakened.

"I thought I would never see her return," Vana said.

"I'm glad you figured it...," Ashen's voice trailed off. The distant, glistening curtain of light that marked the edge of the Warders' territory had dimmed, and beyond the almost translucent boundary, dark things stirred.

John followed Ashen's gaze. "We have to go. If that perimeter is related to the Divide, we're running out of time."

Vana turned and spoke to her people in their native language. The Tsitsistas nodded and hurried up the ridge toward the twisted tree, several of them reaching out to each other to embrace, while the Warders trailed behind. Little Yellow ran and skipped and jumped between and around her people, halting only to squeal at the rainbow glimmers of the buffalo as they fed on spectral grasses.

Once at the top of the hill, Vana's people grouped around the broken mirror hanging from the tree to wait for instruction. Vana gestured at the shard, speaking with urgency, and the first man walked forward, an elder, and stood before it. His eyes narrowed as if he were concentrating, but when he walked toward the mirror, it did not envelope him. Perplexed, he mumbled something under his breath and looked to Vana for guidance.

A worried expression crossed Vana's features. "No..."

"Vana, what is it?"

"We can no longer pass this way."

"What do you mean?" John said in disbelief. "We used it only a few hours ago."

Vana turned her hand over, her typical orange glow now barely present. "The balance has shifted."

"You mean we can't get back?" Ashen's voice was choked and dry. "Max and Cage are there! And Jacob! I left him so the others could protect him!"

"We can return, but we must hurry. Our path will now be slower."

"What do we have to do?" Ashen asked. "Walk? Run?"

"No. We must be like ravens," Vana said. "We fly."

26

FLYING

Ashen had never enjoyed airplanes. She'd been on one or two when she had been living, but the herky-jerky nature of turbulence tended to turn her stomach. Once, on a trip to Las Vegas with Jacob's family, she'd been hooked up to a zip line. When she was released, she shot out over a large crowd of people, screaming as she imagined plummeting and breaking every bone in her body. When her feet reached the ground, she had the shakes so severely that for a few minutes she couldn't walk. That was when she realized that maybe heights were not her thing.

But flying as a dead person was altogether different. Albeit strange, it didn't alarm her. Maybe her old fear of falling was now lacking, or maybe she wasn't bothered due to the experience being more like a slow, steady glide. Or perhaps, knowing something had gone terribly, horribly wrong back at the station had her so preoccupied, she no longer cared.

Either way, she felt like a leaf on the breeze. Or more like a leaf on a roller coaster. She would linger on a gust, rise up near the clouds, and then plunge toward the ground to drift past gnarled oak trees and jack rabbits.

The jolted movements made her mind spin, but she kept mentally reciting what Vana had told her: Remember your path; your purpose. Remember to be the wind.

Other thoughts snuck in, intruding on her resolute goal. Was Max okay? As soon as she wondered about him, she'd feel guilty and worry about Macajah. Jacob, too. She had left him at Union Station, newly deceased and alone, because Max had given his word that he'd keep him safe. What if the Warders had been overrun by the Unseen and the Light? What would happen to them?

Willing herself to go faster, she darted past other misty orbs of varying colors and sizes, all headed west over open fields of tawny gold toward the Rockies. It seemed that Vana's people took to learning spirit ways without questioning them. While Ashen struggled, bumbling along even with Vana coaching her through each step, flight was natural for the Tsitsistas.

"Keep your head clear. Stay focused," she whispered, trying to soothe her insecurities. But the distance was so great. Almost two hundred miles. She sighed. Macajah had been right. Even at this speed, which was not much faster than if they had been running, it would take the balance of the day to get there.

While thick clouds heavy with moisture formed above, Ashen attempted a graceful descent toward John's emerald sphere, the whole time bobbing up and down like an intoxicated bee, then over to an orange orb floating nearby. A smaller, more energetic ball of orange and lilac bounced around Vana's larger one, resembling the illustrations of atoms from Ashen's old science books.

I ain't no idjiot either, Missy! In fact, I'm mighty fond of the subject of science.

Recalling Macajah's words only succeeded in making Ashen concerned all over again.

"Any way for us to speed up, Vana?" she asked.

"Ashen Deming, we are at the wind's mercy."

"Hopefully we can beat this storm," John said. "We can't afford to be hindered."

Ashen scanned the landscape behind them, back toward the plains that led to Kansas and the flat, unadorned belly of the United States. Angry-looking clouds hung low on the horizon. The darkening pea-green sky swirled with grays and odd golden hazes.

An adolescent tornado brewed.

"Vana," she said. "If, by chance, the breezes got stronger—and if they worked in our favor—could that help us move quicker?"

"If the desire of the wind is to gust, yes."

"What if, say, we had a tornado behind us?" Ashen asked. "Think that might cause gusts in the right direction? Or are we in some major trouble here?"

"Like John Porter said, it may work against us. We cannot risk the tornado hurting those souls who live on the plains." Vana paused as if in thought. "But perhaps," she said slowing to a stop. "We can protect the living if we call upon our ancestors. Maybe they will grant us speed and give us wings."

The tiny ball of Little Yellow bounced here and there, orbiting around Vana's orb as she called to her people. The tribe gathered, their orbs hovering in a near perfect circle, and listened to the sage woman.

When she finished, the orbs oscillated, swooping and

dancing to a silent rhythm Ashen couldn't hear. They danced in their own unique way, but each movement appeared to be choreographed. Rehearsed. Even the small orbs of the children participated.

"What are they doing?"

"Something well beyond my knowledge, Miss Deming," John said.

A song echoed on the wind. A sorrowful male voice tinged with hope. Other voices joined, repeating the words of the first, and beneath the singing came a distinct percussion. Bells or metal rattles jingled alongside loud, deep booms of drums.

A hawk burst from the core of a teal orb. The bird of prey released a high-pitched screech. From within another, a mountain lion bounded forth and let out a rumbling, growling scream. Even timid creatures like prairie dogs and porcupines and skunks traipsed about, flowing around the orbs of the dead, swelling with their song, each glowing the same as the soul they were attached to.

"Spirit guardians," Ashen whispered.

To her right, John's orb flickered. His kelly-green light had become weaker than the ex-Drifters', but as the singing intensified, so did his hue. From the center of his sphere leapt a jade-colored German Shepherd. The dog spun around to circle the green orb.

"Hey, Hughes," John said.

At the sound of John's voice, the dog cocked his head, wagged his tail, and after a soft whine and a bark, he gave the green orb tender kisses.

"Good boy, Hughes. Good boy," John said with a little laugh. As the singing surrounding them reached its peak, he added, "Please, go with the others. Help us."

Hughes barked once more and sprinted off to join the

rest. Together, all of the spirit guardians vaulted for the prairies, straight toward the maturing tornado—its funnel stretching from the darkened storm clouds to touched the grasslands. When the tip hit the earth, it gutted the saturated soil, kicking mud and desert debris up into the massive vortex.

But the guardians kept flying.

"Be prepared," Vana said.

"For what?" Ashen asked. Excitement pulsed through her.

"To soar upon the winds."

The circle of Tsitsistas rose higher. As they continued their flight toward Union Station, Ashen followed, casting nervous glances at the trailing tornado catching up to them. Mixed with the tumbleweeds and dirt clods were the vibrant streaks of the spirit guardians. Multiple corkscrews of color transformed the funnel into something supernatural. Something horrifying yet powerful. A phantom force beyond Nature's capability of creation.

The wind dipped. Everything hushed and became still. The pressure subsided. It felt as though Ashen's ears were submerged under water.

The cyclone hit the group. It lifted the orbs, spinning them, whirling them around each other along the inner walls of the vortex. The animals pranced in rapid spirals, working hard to move the ex-Drifters and Warders up through the phantom tornado. As each orb exited the opening at the top, they were hurled like pebbles from a slingshot to sail above the blackened storm clouds toward the city, while the tornado retreated to the empty plains and away from the living.

They were traveling far faster than before. Despite the height and velocity, Ashen giggled as cattle, small homes, and cars passed beneath them. Ahead, she could make out the suburbs of Denver. They might get to the battle in time.

Filled with a renewed optimism, she hoped they might actually win.

27

REIGNED OVER BY THE DEAD

The blur of phantom bricks streaked past as they flew down Sixteenth Street. At the far end ahead, the electric lights of Union Station sparkled like a beacon, its former clock tower protruding from the center of the building, ghostly and bright against the darkness.

Ashen fixed her eyes on the hands of the clock and concentrated on flying faster. They approached at a quick clip. Beneath them, a continuous ribbon of living souls—their silhouettes outlined on the concrete—lined the downtown sidewalks. From the north, south, and east, they marched in tandem toward the train station. Toward the Divide.

In the courtyard, members of the Unseen and the Light clashed against the Warders' dome, weakening the shield further as light and dark struck from all sides. Underneath the faltering barrier, the Divide remained intact. Ashen squinted, but she couldn't tell if the tunnel itself was still lit with energy.

An amber glow appeared within the chaos. The cowboy's powers had diminished to a visible whisper. Ashen's heart sank as she, John, and the Tsitsistas flew over the arch to the top of the dome. Once in position, a muted orange vine darted from Vana's sphere, and the plant snagged itself into the polychromatic shield and grew, working to crack the barrier open like an overripe gourd. Inside, Macajah's dull amber beam reached toward Vana's vine. The fissure widened.

As the orbs hovered in wait, a bolt whizzed past—near enough that Ashen could feel its phantom heat. A heavy volley of black and white beams followed. One smashed a fuchsia orb, then one of turquoise, disintegrating both into wisps of fine dust.

"Everyone!" John yelled. "Quickly!"

While projectiles of shadow and ivory light rained down, the orbs darted through the opening in swift succession. Once all were safe inside, a group of Warders defended the fresh aperture, wielding whatever power they had remaining while their allies worked together on repairs, their progress hindered by the missiles assailing the barrier. Frantically, Ashen scanned the crowd of Warders for Max and Jacob as the ex-Drifters materialized.

A crash sounded above. An Unseen clawed wildly at the dome. He shoved his slender, angled skull into the breach he created and gnashed his teeth. To avoid the creature's lengthy fangs, Ashen ducked and fell to the ground, turning to stare up at the shadow.

A drab blue whip cut through the night. The wire sliced the Unseen's chin. The creature hissed. From the midst of the pandemonium, Max trotted forward with Jacob close behind. When the soldier struck the shadow again, Jacob raised his fists. Glass shards radiating lemon yellow protruded from his knuckles, the sunny color contrasting with his serious expression—more serious than Ashen had ever seen him—as he helped to mend the hole.

Unfazed by Max's weapon, the lanky Unseen squirmed further in, his mass breaking through, his jaws snapping mere inches from Ashen's nose. The reek of decay wafted at each clack of his fangs. A scent that matched the Unseen's decomposed soul.

A surge of ferocity overtook Ashen. Eyes narrowed, palms outstretched, she shot a silvery bolt of faint fire. It hit the creature. He shrieked, reeling back and out of the tear. Together, all three worked to close it again.

A huffy, stressed Macajah stomped forward.

"Why in the blazes didn't you come by mirror?" he yelled. "We've been guarding that dang thing inside the station, holdin' off no-good Unseen makin' their way through, so you could return safe!"

"Mirror travel doesn't work for us anymore, Cage," John said.

The cowboy's bronze skin paled. He whirled to the Divide. The innards of the once-vibrant void looked aged and ill, and Macajah's face steeled.

"Sorry we were a bit slow." Ashen stood. Out of habit, she dusted her backside. "We had to travel by air."

"By air, as in flying?" Jacob asked. "But you hate heights!"

"Yeah, well, we were also sucked into a tornado and spat back out. There were a lot of firsts for me today."

Max's gaze shifted past Ashen to the watching Tsitsistas. He grinned. "You guys did it! You woke them!"

"It was all Vana. John and I were only support." Ashen could feel the blood rising in her cheeks. In her periphery, she could see Jacob. He had noticed. He studied her and

Max—a dawning realization reflected in his eyes.

The tunnel quavered, then dimmed. "Best we get started," Macajah said, firing his rifle at encroaching shadows. "Ain't got much time."

As the others located more tears and defended them, Ashen ran back to Vana, who was speaking to her people, her native tongue a series of echoes in the dome. The man Ashen thought had led the singing back on the plains had moved to the front of the tribe and begun for the entrance to the Divide. Vana signaled to the others to follow.

A loud shriek caused Ashen to clasp her ears as if a thousand voices were screaming in her head, and at once both the Unseen and the Light ceased their attacks and retreated from the barrier.

A quiet fell like fresh snow over the courtyard as the ghosts cleared. Behind their dwindling numbers, living souls waited, their numbers well over a thousand. They were the same silhouettes Ashen and the ex-Drifters had flown over earlier, and to Ashen's surprise, all were teenagers no older than herself. Split into two groups, they stood in rows on either side of the barrier to face the opposing side, their individual insides shimmering similarly to the Drifters from Ashen's dream. But instead of the multicolored churning hues of other living souls she'd seen, their cores were almost colorless. To the south, their essences had darkened with little or no luster left. To the north, they were verging on white, again, lacking pigmentation.

"What in tarnation are they doing?" Macajah said.

All along the crystalline wall of the barricade, the Warders lined the edge to watch, ignoring the newer chinks that had appeared across the protective shell. The teenagers stared past the Warders like granite statues. None moved. None blinked. It felt as though the whole world had stopped. Even living souls walking by paused to watch the gathering, curious as to their intentions.

From the east, Thaddeus barked a command.

"Ya may commence!"

In unison, the teenage shapes revealed different objects from pockets and bags. Many were large kitchen knives. A few were pistols. Any observing living souls around them cried out, hollering for police as each group of teenagers advanced toward the dome that sat between them, their weapons held in front of them.

"Oh, no." Ashen flicked her eyes to Macajah. "They're gonna kill each other."

Upon their approach, the rival sides of the living raised their weapons.

"Cage, do something!" she shrieked.

The cowboy squinted down his rifle sights, ready, but his expression told Ashen that he had no idea how to stop them. Behind her, John yelled at Max and Jacob as they worked to wrench one of the fractures in the dome open in order to get to the living. Vana's voice rang out over the Warders, a warning to them and to her people, but by then, it was too late.

Abruptly, the living stopped mere inches from the barrier. Eyes glazed, not focused on anything in particular, they extended their weapons in front of them. But rather than run through the ghost dome at each other, they pointed their weapons at themselves. At the same time, they thrust or shot, and their bodies dropped to the concrete. Blood merged into huge pools as the teenagers gasped their final breaths.

Many Warders cried out, horrified, reaching out to help in a sad attempt to rewind time itself. When death finally smothered the teens, the Warders and ex-Drifters were left gaping, trying to make sense of the senselessness lying before them as ambulance sirens wailed in the distance.

All the while, the Unseen and the Light waited at the courtyard border. Watching. Waiting.

One by one, the pools of blood to the south stirred. From the ripples, dark shades poured up into the air, almost as though they were one with the liquid. As the new Unseen rose, they clicked their jaws open and closed in quick snaps like starved animals.

Stunned, Ashen pivoted to the northern group. Forms rose up and out of their own dead blood, becoming white shapes that beamed with a willful self-righteousness, their figures blinding to look upon.

As the new members of the Light rose, the Divide quivered, becoming more and more translucent, its internal swirls winking out. The aurora shimmer of the tunnel weakened and its walls began to bow, crumbling in on itself, imploding in slow motion like a star reborn.

"We have to hurry!" Ashen yelled to Vana. "Go now!"

Vana nodded and urged the older man from her tribe to the Divide entrance. At the threshold, he glanced back at Vana and his people, smiled and stepped through, dissipating into colorful prisms that twirled and danced down the length of the collapsing tunnel.

With his passing soul, the interior rebounded. A pulse of energy throbbed along the constricted throat of the Divide and every weapon the Warders held became more luminous. More powerful.

While the Tsitsistas entered one by one, outside the barrier, the new Unseen and Light completed their materializations. The strays that had finished their forms now scaled the barricade, slashing into the dome with their crooked, long nails and teeth. Behind them, their veteran counterparts lobbed missiles of dark and light energy. Several smashed into the dome. The shield above made an odd, creaking groan—its light fluttered.

As the Warders fired their strengthening energies into the barrier to stabilize it, the largest eagle Ashen had ever seen soared over the dome. Once the raptor had a target, she descended, knocking once unsuspecting Light to the ground where she sliced at the creature with her electric-blue talons.

"Cuddles," Ashen whispered.

The other Warder's spirit guardians joined in. A whinny preceded Macajah's mare, Agnes. She flew through the air, her legs at a gallop, tossing her mane as she kicked the newly hatched Unseen and Light from the dome. Near the base of the barricade, John's green German Shepherd, Hughes, shook a limp Unseen in his jaws. Vana's massive elk slammed into the invading crowd, his head low, and flung several ghosts through the air. Cats, wolves, even a marmot scurried about to assist in the fight.

"Vamoose, Vana!" Macajah yelled between rifle blasts. "It's working!"

The remaining Tsitsistas filed through, leaving only a sprinkling of Vana's people. Standing at the threshold, one frail hand resting on her granddaughter's shoulder, her other arm around her daughter, Bear Claws, Vana peered into the healing Divide. She turned to her daughter, whispered a few words, and embraced her. Bear Claws blinked hard, a sorrowful smile on her face, and nodded back to the old woman.

Little Yellow's expression was quizzical. She jerked on Vana's dress. The older woman carefully crouched and nuzzled her granddaughter's forehead with the tip of her nose. Tears filled her eyes.

"I hope to see you again, Little Yellow. I must stay."

Even though she didn't understand Vana's English words, the innocent girl smiled and gave her grandma a quick hug. She grabbed her mother's hand, her eyes lit with excitement, and both walked straight into the Divide without a second thought or glance.

Ashen put her arm around Vana. "Now that they're in the Divide, does that mean they'll find the Road of the Departed?"

"That is our belief," she sniffed. "We hunger for where it leads. Few of my people wander this plane."

"I'm sure it leads somewhere good."

"Yes, Ashen Deming. My people have found their way."

Vana gave Ashen a reassuring squeeze, took a deep breath, and turned her attention back to defending. When Ashen went to join her, a warm hand seized her elbow.

"I'm going too."

"Jacob?" Dismay engulfed her. "What do you mean, you're going too?"

"I'm supposed to. I think, anyway." His gaze deviated to the tunnel, and Ashen recalled that intense, urging pull she had experienced before her decision to become earthbound. Jacob's eyes returned to meet hers. "The question is ... are you coming with me?"

"Jacob, I can't—"

"Yeah, I know." Lips tight, he glanced at Max fighting in the background.

"It's not that simple." She raised her voice over the clash of the battle around them. "I already made the decision to stay. If I go in there—" She bit her lip.

He gave her a single, heartbroken nod. "I gotta take a chance, Ash," he said as he watched the last Tsitsistas walk through the Divide. "And my chance to go is running out. I can feel it. There's no place for me here. Not anymore."

"But I can't go." Hot tears stung her eyes. "I've been here for too long. It's too late for me."

He placed his hands on her shoulders and stared directly into her eyes. "You should stay. This battle? This wanting to change things for the better? This is you. You're a stubborn do-gooder, I'll admit, but I think this is where you belong."

"You're my only family."

"I was." He sighed. "I've seen the way you look at Max. You've never looked at me like that. I know you never will."

She felt her cheeks flush. Jacob smiled.

"That's why I should go," he said. "I've been slowly coming to grips with this. If I stay, I'll be forced to watch you fall for someone else for eternity. I also don't want to turn into a Drifter again, and honestly, watching the girl I've been in love with since I was a kid fall for someone else might be the thing to put me over the edge."

Her bottom lip trembled. She felt numb. All she could manage was to stare back at him, feeling that she should say something, that she should protest more, but she knew that he was right. She couldn't lie to him and tell him she felt something more for him when she didn't. That would be unfair. It would be cruel.

"Are you sure you want to do this?" she said. "I mean, no one knows what's on the other side."

"Ash, you and I know I'm not really the adventurous type. Not a fighter like you. But, in the pit of my stomach, I know this is what I'm meant to do. That feeling is ... strangely comforting."

The tears fell harder. She wrapped her arms around Jacob's neck and hugged him close.

"I'll miss you."

"I'll miss you, too," he whispered. "Thank you for not giving up on me. You gave me a second chance."

He let her go and smiled. "Oh, and one other thing. If you see my parents come through, can you let them know I'm okay and where I went?"

She smiled back. "Of course."

He sighed. "Good. `Cause I know once they found me, I wouldn't hear the end of how I didn't have the decency to leave them a note."

A bold purpose in his stride, he walked away, past the struggling Warders and to the Divide. At the brink, he paused and reached out. The surface enlivened at his touch, vibrating, its colors coiling along the tunnel walls in timid spurts. He grinned over his shoulder at Ashen, stepped through the gate, and disappeared into brilliant curls of pigment that dispersed down the tube to whatever destination lay ahead.

Using the back of her sleeve, Ashen wiped at her tears. She brimmed not only with incredible sadness, but relief, and also a little bit of pride. For once, she thought, she'd done what she'd set out to do. No matter what, her best friend would be safe, even if that meant she'd never see him again.

"He decided not to stay?" Max asked behind her.

Startled, she spun. With the shield more stabilized and a chunk of the other Warders' powers rejuvenated, the posse had gathered together at a slight distance. Enough to give Ashen and Jacob some privacy during their farewells.

"Yeah."

"I'm sorry, Ashen."

She let a small smile play on her lips. "It's okay. This time, he wanted to be the brave one."

The posse approached, concern painted upon their faces. But Ashen soon realized they weren't looking at her, but beyond her, each fixated on where Jacob had gone. Though the added Drifter souls and Jacob had invigorated the guts of the Divide, she saw that the damage to the tunnel had not recovered, making Ashen think of an overdone hollow noodle. The structure gave way in parts, opening to the evening skies above, while the ceiling draped here and there like shabby, torn rags.

"We're still short on power," Max said.

Ashen perked up. "If we've gotten some of it back, we should be able to mirror travel, right? So, we can send out teams to Fairmount Cemetery and any others. Wake more Drifters to-"

But Macajah was already shaking his head. "Ain't got time for that, Little Missy. You did good, though." Beneath his thick mustache, the corners of his lips curled up a little, but he seemed worn out. He ran a calloused hand over the barrel of Agnes in thought. "I reckon we might need to resort to somethin' more drastic."

She studied the combat around them. The Unseen and the Light swarmed the dome. Endless projectiles continued their assault. Although the Warders' weapons had become more potent and reliable, they hadn't strengthened enough to give them the upper hand. Soon, it would get bad. The ex-Drifters had only been a temporary remedy.

From the outskirts of the battle came loud howling. A black orb glided from the enemy horde toward them, followed by two smaller ivory orbs which weaved around the tendrils of dark smoke trailing from their leader.

Thaddeus. Constance. Silas.

When the three drew near, the swarm of Unseen and Light parted. Right outside the dome, they materialized, weapons in hand.

"Reinforce!" Max yelled.

The posse responded, pouring whatever powers they had

left into the shield, but Thaddeus only smirked. While Constance and Silas shot their beams into the barricade, Thaddeus raised his giant pickaxe and swung down hard, aiming for the spot where the two Light were focusing their energies.

From the hole left by Thaddeus' pickaxe, the dome shattered. The breach moved quickly over them like a virus, disintegrating the shield, leaving the Warders and the Divide vulnerable.

"That's enough a' that now," Thaddeus said, striding into the circle of Warders. A couple of Warders swung at him, but their weapons fizzled on contact. Taking his axe, he swung in response, backhanding them, sending them flying to the edges of their circle.

"You best stay clear of the Divide, Glick." Macajah cocked his rifle. The rest of the posse and Warders readied their own weapons.

The Unseen tsked. "Ya've already lost. Mere moments 'til it's collapsed. We've only come to partake in the festivities. Obtain a nice, front-row seat."

As he spoke, Constance and Silas flanked either side of the creature.

"I thought the Light was supposed to be fair-minded and just." The green glow from John's wrist cuffs emphasizing his scowl and the fox medallion around his neck. "How could you unite with the Unseen? With him?"

Gavel tight within her grasp, the displeased Honorable Callahan folded her arms. "I'm in no need of an ethics lesson from an uppity murderer."

"What's the point?" Max asked. "Is being more powerful really that important?"

"There's a saying." The governor's melted lips broke into a sneer. "Goes something like, 'The enemy of my enemy is my friend.' While it's no secret that we don't like the Unseen, at least we understand one another."

"Our current goals align," Constance added. "To be rid of Warders once and for all. Then, both sides continue collecting souls, harvesting the living and dead, without the nuisance of your so-called rules and balance." Her smile was cold. "When it's time, we will stop the Unseen for good. After all, the only way to abolish darkness is with light."

It felt like a rug had been ripped from beneath Ashen. Judging from the rest of the posse's obvious confusion, she knew she wasn't the only one.

Constance laughed. Silas joined in, but Thaddeus' ebony glare lingered on the posse, and his slight, knowing grin crept to the surface.

"Perplexed? Or am I required to speak plainly for ya supposed learned types?" the shadow asked, studying each of them. "Ya see, took near all of us to prevent newly-deads from crossing over and feeding yer energies. Our cooperation is a means to an end. Once you'uns are gone and the Divide is shut, our sides will finally have our war." He looked with menace at Constance and Silas. "May the best deceased men, and women, influence the earth."

Everything moved in slow motion for Ashen. She felt ill. It wasn't only the Warders in trouble, or the newly deceased. All of Colorado was in danger. Maybe the entire world. Since the dawn of time, humankind had been plagued with nightmares of creatures and monsters and dark entities, never knowing how accurate their bleak fantasies were. With no one to stop Thaddeus and the rest, the dead would forever reign over the living.

Ashen refused to let that happen.

She whirled to Macajah. "We have to do something!"

"Without a steady stream of newly-deads, Little Missy,

we're running out of options." With grim acceptance, the cowboy scrutinized the enemies blocking the path to the Divide and the tunnel. He took a solid step forward. "I reckon all we really need is one big soul."

Macajah didn't have to say another word. She knew what he meant. Their choices were dismal. Either they let the Divide fall, or they sacrifice an earthbound soul to regenerate the Divide, repair the balance, and save everyone. Everyone except the friend who would cease to exist in the process.

Ashen felt like she had been punched. She bent at the waist to catch her fictional breath, struggling not to panic.

"All's well, Clementine. All's well." Thaddeus' long, bony arm yanked Ashen to him. As he trailed a knobby finger down her cheek, he said, "Ya know, I tasted power the night ya and me became acquainted. I weren't aware we shadowkind could travel by mirror, but when I slipped on through, I knew we could shift the balance with some tenacity. Grit. And I reckon I possess a great deal of grit. Though, I must admit, ya did vex me all those years ago. I didn't intend to kill ya—just change ya. My first and only failure." The Unseen stabbed his grubby nail into her flesh and wrenched her chin up. "Now, ya've little time to decide. Join us, light or dark. Or perish."

"Let her go!" Max yelled.

Ashen winced, but didn't break eye contact. She could perceive flashes of blue and amber and green and orange as the posse fought to get to her. She stared back at the Unseen, and the commotion of her friends became muffled until it turned into a flat hum. Her eyes watered. She choked on nothing. The creature holding her laughed.

As her vision clouded, she caught sight of a movement. Inside the shallows of the gleaming Divide, beyond the cackling Unseen, Langhorne appeared. The turtle nosed the entrance. Timid ripples disrupted the surface like rain drops on water.

Blink.

If one powerful soul was enough to save them, what about two?

Blink.

"Okay, Thaddeus," she rasped. "I've decided."

The Unseen flashed his weasel sneer. He released Ashen and she turned to the Warders, rubbing at the small gash his claw had left.

"I have a few things to say first," she said with a frown. She walked forward a few paces, paused, and looked back at Thaddeus. "If that's okay?"

The grin he wore widened. "Why, of course."

"Macajah, Vana?" She sighed and approached the posse. "Thanks for being like parents to me. John, well, thanks for being my older, smarter, better brother."

Shocked, Vana and John studied her as she spoke while the cowboy's face turned a deep crimson of rage and utter disappointment.

"You ain't seriously considering aligning with that no-good—"

"And Max," she interjected before Macajah could say anything more. "I don't need to be protected, and I don't need to be saved. Oh, also, so you know, I like you and think you're cute."

She smiled at Max's baffled expression. That simple gesture had never come so easily, even as a child. It had always felt forced—like she was donning a mask. She let the feeling of that smile build, and with it, the blaze within her burned.

Silvery light radiated from her whole body as she turned

back to Thaddeus and the Divide. Behind him, Constance and Silas, suspicious, retreated a little, but the Unseen stayed stock-still, watching her with a frozen grin.

Head held high, she raised an eyebrow in return. "Like Fox said, I'm no damsel."

The rest became a blur. Protests could be heard behind her as she ran full-force, focusing on the Unseen creature. While his eerie grin began to falter, she thought of everything that had happened. How her life had been taken. About the people she cared for and those she would never know. Of those who still lived who were unaware of the threat ready and waiting on their doorsteps. How the lives of those souls would be controlled—manipulated—until they had no choice but to become slaves to the dead.

And how the world was worth dying for.

She concentrated. From somewhere Ashen couldn't explain—and didn't expect—her light flared, far brighter than ever before. Silvers and greens and blues and pinks surged from within her. The hues made Thaddeus grimace, and when he threw his arms up to block the brilliance, Ashen collided with him. Knocked off his feet, the creature tumbled backward into the mouth of the Divide. The tunnel throbbed with strength as the Unseen lay, screaming, ripping at his own obsidian features while he crumbled to ash, his dusty fragments vanishing down the tunnel.

At the edge, an outraged Constance and Silas quickly peered into the Divide, then both morphed into white orbs and darted off. The remaining Unseen and Light scattered. While they retreated, the Warders and the posse disregarded them, their attention never straying from the tunnel where Ashen stood inside the threshold. Her brown eyes flicked to the posse. Each of their horrified faces stared back.

Max sprinted to the gate. His gray eyes glistened as he

shook his head in disbelief and placed his palm on the entrance's surface, ignoring how the Divide burned his skin. In response, Ashen placed her hand on his, and the walls of the tunnel flexed with power.

As pieces of her peeled off to drift away, she smiled and mouthed, 'It's okay.' Then Ashen closed her eyes.

28

A Ghost's Death

The mountain wind moaned through the creaky ponderosa pines of Colorado's Black Forest. A moon sliver hung in the dark. It cast no light on the blanket of branches and decaying pine needles that carpeted the forest floor. Within the sheltering limbs of the trees—no sound of night birds or nocturnal animals. All was silent.

From behind a curtain of tree trunks, a small orb of light appeared. It could easily have been mistaken for a lightning bug if such insects had been prevalent in the foothills of the mountains. It dipped and bobbed here and there, following an indirect path as it bounced, brightened, and stopped to settle on the soft ground.

There it transformed from a tiny ball of light into something not much larger. As it changed, it sank into the earth, its silvery glow refracting from beneath the cover of dried foliage and scattered clumps of prairie junegrass.

The light dissipated. The debris rustled. A tiny snout

appeared from between some twigs and the head of a silvery box turtle emerged. He crawled out from the soil and shuffled between the pines, his image flickering until it disappeared, returning the forest to the velvety blackness once more.

Printed in Poland
by Amazon Fulfillment
Poland Sp. z o.o., Wrocław